W9-BLW-235

Eye of the Red Tsar

EYE OF THE RED TSAR

A NOVEL OF SUSPENSE

SAM EASTLAND

BANTAM BOOKS
NEW YORK

Eye of the Red Tsar is a work of fiction. Names, characters, places, and incidents either are the product of the author's imagination or are used fictitiously. Any resemblance to actual persons, living or dead, events, or locales is entirely coincidental.

Published in the United States by Bantam Books, an imprint of The Random House Publishing Group, a division of Random House, Inc., New York.

BANTAM BOOKS and the rooster colophon are registered trademarks of Random House, Inc.

Originally published in hardcover in Great Britain by Faber & Faber, Ltd., London

Library of Congress Cataloging-in-Publication Data
Eastland, Sam.
Eye of the Red Tsar : a novel of suspense / Sam Eastland.
p. cm.
ISBN 978-0-553-80781-3
1. Political prisoners—Fiction. 2. Romanov, House of—Fiction. 3. Murder—Investigation—Fiction. 4. Russia—History—20th century—Fiction. 5. Kings and rulers—Succession—Fiction. 6. Russia (Federation)—Fiction. I. Title.
PS3605.A85E94 2010
813'.6—dc22
2009052898

Printed in the United States of America on acid-free paper

www.bantamdell.com

2 4 6 8 9 7 5 3 1

First Edition

Book design by Susan Turner

This book is for P.R.

Eye of the Red Tsar

PROLOGUE

Through blood-dimmed eyes, the Tsar watched the man reload his gun. Empty cartridges, trailing hazy parachutes of smoke, tumbled from the revolver's cylinder. Clattering and ringing, they landed on the floor where he was lying. The Tsar dragged in a breath, feeling the flutter of bubbles as they escaped his punctured lungs.

Now the killer knelt down beside him. "Do you see this?" The man seized the Tsar's jaw and turned his head from one side to the other. "Do you see what you have brought upon yourself?"

The Tsar glimpsed nothing, blinded by the veil which filmed his sight, but he knew that all around him lay his family. His wife. His children.

"Go ahead," he told the man. "Finish me."

The Tsar felt a hand gently slapping his face, the fingers slick with his own blood.

"You are already finished," said the killer. After that came the faint click *as he loaded new cartridges into the cylinder.*

Then the Tsar heard more explosions, deafening in the cramped space of the room. "My family!" he tried to shout, but only coughed and retched. He could do nothing to help them. He could not even raise an arm to shield himself.

Now the Tsar was being dragged across the floor. The killer grunted as he heaved the body up a flight of stairs, cursing as the Tsar's boot heels caught on every step.

Outside, it was dark.

The Tsar felt rain against his face. Soon afterwards, he heard the sound of bodies dumped beside him. Their lifeless heads cracked against the stony ground.

An engine started up. A vehicle. A squeak of brakes and then the slam of a tailgate coming down. One after the other, the bodies were lifted into the back of a truck. And then the Tsar himself, heaved onto the pile of corpses. The tailgate slammed shut.

As the truck began to move, the pain in the Tsar's chest grew worse. Each jolt over the potholed road became a fresh wound, his agony flashing like lightning in the darkness which swirled thickly around him.

Suddenly, his pain began to fade away. The blackness seemed to pour in like a liquid through his eyes. It snuffed out all his fears, ambitions, memories until nothing remained but a shuddering emptiness, in which he knew nothing at all.

Siberia

1929

THE MAN SAT UP WITH A GASP.

He was alone in the forest.

The dream had woken him again.

He pulled aside the old horse blanket. Its cloth was wet with dew.

Climbing stiffly to his feet, he squinted through the morning mist and beams of sunlight angling between the trees. He rolled the blanket and tied the ends together with a piece of rawhide. Then he slipped the roll over his head so that it draped across his chest and back. From his pocket he removed a withered shred of smoked deer meat and ate it slowly, pausing to take in sounds of mice scuffling under the carpet of dead leaves, of birds scolding from the branches above him, and of wind rustling through the tops of the pines.

The man was tall and broad-shouldered, with a straight nose and strong white teeth. His eyes were greenish brown, the irises marked by a strange silvery quality, which people noticed only when he was looking directly at them. Streaks of premature gray ran through his long, dark hair, and his beard grew thickly over windburned cheeks.

The man no longer had a name. Now he was known only as Prisoner 4745-P of the Borodok Labor Camp.

Soon he was moving again, passing through a grove of pine trees on gently sloping ground which led down to a stream. He walked with the help of a large stick, whose gnarled root head bristled with square-topped horseshoe nails. The only other thing he carried was a bucket of red paint. With this, he marked trees to be cut by inmates of the camp, whose function was the harvesting of timber from the forest of Krasnagolyana. Instead of using a brush, the man stirred his fingers in the scarlet paint and daubed his print upon the trunks. These marks were, for most of the other convicts, the only trace of him they ever saw.

The average life of a tree-marker in the forest of Krasnagolyana was six months. Working alone, with no chance of escape and far from any human contact, these men died from exposure, starvation, and loneliness. Those who became lost, or who fell and broke a leg, were usually eaten by wolves. Tree marking was the only assignment at Borodok said to be worse than a death sentence.

Now in his ninth year of a thirty-year sentence for Crimes Against the State, Prisoner 4745-P had lasted longer than any other marker in the entire Gulag system. Soon after he arrived at Borodok, the director of the camp had sent him into the woods, fearing that other inmates might learn his true identity.

Provisions were left for him three times a year at the end of a logging road. Kerosene. Cans of meat. Nails. For the rest, he had to fend for himself. Only rarely was he seen by those logging crews who came to cut the timber. What they observed was a creature barely recognizable as a man. With the crust of red paint that covered his prison clothes and the long hair maned about his face, he resembled a beast stripped of its flesh and left to die which had somehow managed to survive. Wild rumors surrounded him—that he was an eater of human flesh, that he wore a breastplate made from the bones of those who had vanished in the forest, that he wore scalps laced together as a cap.

They called him the man with bloody hands. No one except the commandant of Borodok knew where this prisoner had come from or who he had been before he arrived.

Those same men who feared to cross his path had no idea this was Pekkala, whose name they'd once invoked just as their ancestors had called upon the gods.

He waded across the stream, climbing from the cold and waist-deep water, and disappeared into a stand of white birch trees which grew upon the other bank. Hidden among these, half buried in the ground, stood a cabin of the type known as a Zemlyanka. Pekkala had built it with his own hands. Inside it he endured the Siberian winters, the worst of which was not cold but a silence so complete it seemed to have a sound of its own—a hissing, rushing noise—like that of the planet hurtling through space.

Now, as Pekkala approached the cabin, he paused and sniffed the air. Something in his instincts trembled. He stood very still, like a heron poised above the water, bare feet sinking in the mossy ground.

The breath caught in his throat.

A man was sitting on a tree stump at the corner of the clearing. The man had his back to Pekkala. He wore an olive brown military uniform, tall black boots reaching to his knee. This was no ordinary soldier. The cloth of his tunic had the smooth luster of gabardine, not the rough blanket material worn by men from the local garrison who sometimes ventured as far as the trailhead on patrol but never came this deep into the woods.

He did not appear to be lost. Nor was he armed with any weapon Pekkala could see. The only thing he had brought with him was a briefcase. It was of good quality, with polished brass fittings which looked insanely out of place here in the forest. The man seemed to be waiting.

For the next few hours, while the sun climbed above the trees and the smell of heated pine sap drifted on the air, Pekkala studied the stranger, taking note of the angle at which he held his head, how he crossed and uncrossed his legs, the way he cleared the pollen dust from his throat. Once, the stranger launched himself to his feet and walked around the clearing, swatting frantically at swarming mosquitoes. As he turned, Pekkala saw the rosy cheeks of a young man barely out of his teens. He was slightly built, with thin calves and delicate hands.

Pekkala could not help comparing them to his own callused palms, the skin on his knuckles crusted and cracked, and to his legs, which bulged with muscles, as if snakes had coiled around his bones.

Pekkala could make out a red star sewn onto each forearm of the man's *gymnastyrka* tunic, which draped in peasant fashion like an untucked shirt halfway down the man's thighs. From those red stars, Pekkala knew the man had reached the rank of Commissar, a political officer of the Red Army.

All day, the Commissar waited in that clearing, tormented by insects, until the last faint light of day was gone. In the twilight, the man brought out a long-stemmed pipe and stuffed it with tobacco from a pouch which he kept around his neck. He lit it with a brass lighter and puffed away contentedly, keeping the mosquitoes at bay.

Slowly, Pekkala breathed in. The musky odor of tobacco flooded his senses. He observed how the young man often removed the pipe from his mouth and studied it, and the way he clamped the stem between his teeth—which made a tiny clicking sound, like a key turned in a lock.

He has not owned the pipe for long, Pekkala told himself. He has chosen a pipe over cigarettes because he thinks it makes him look older.

Now and then, the Commissar glanced at the red stars on his forearms, as if their presence caught him by surprise, and Pekkala knew this young man had only just received his commission.

But the more he learned about the man, the less he could fathom what the Commissar was doing here in the forest. He could not help a grudging admiration for this man, who did not trespass inside the cabin, choosing instead to remain on that hard seat of the tree stump.

When night fell, Pekkala brought his hands to his mouth and breathed warm air into the hollows of his palms. He drifted off, leaning against a tree, then woke with a start to find that the mist was all around him, smelling of dead leaves and earth, circling like a curious and predatory animal.

Glancing towards the cabin, he saw the Commissar had not moved. He sat with his arms folded, chin resting on his chest. The quiet snuffle of his snoring echoed around the clearing.

He'll be gone in the morning, thought Pekkala. Pulling up the frayed collar of his coat, he closed his eyes again.

But when morning came, Pekkala was amazed to find the Commissar still there. He had fallen off his tree stump seat and lay on his back, one leg still resting on the stump, like some statue set in a victorious pose which had toppled from its pedestal.

Eventually, the Commissar snorted and sat up, looking around as if he could not remember where he was.

Now, thought Pekkala, this man will come to his senses and leave me alone.

The Commissar stood, set his hands on the small of his back, and winced. A groan escaped his lips. Then suddenly he turned and looked straight at the place where Pekkala was hiding. "Are you ever going to come out from there?" he demanded.

The words stung Pekkala like sand thrown in his face. Now, reluctantly, he stepped out from the shelter of the tree, leaning on the nail-topped stick. "What do you want?" He spoke so rarely that his own voice sounded strange to him.

The Commissar's face showed red welts where the mosquitoes had feasted on him. "You are to come with me," he said.

"Why?" asked Pekkala.

"Because, when you have listened to what I have to say, you will want to."

"You are optimistic, Commissar."

"The people who sent me to fetch you—"

"Who sent you?"

"You will know them soon enough."

"And did they tell you who I am, these people?"

The young Commissar shrugged. "All I know is that your name is Pekkala and that your skills, whatever they might be, are now required elsewhere." He looked around the gloomy clearing. "I would have thought you'd jump at a chance to leave this god-forsaken place."

"You are the ones who have forsaken God."

The Commissar smiled. "They said you were a difficult man."

"They seem to know me," replied Pekkala, "whoever they are."

"They also told me," continued the Commissar, "that if I came into these woods armed with a gun, you would probably kill me before I even set eyes on you." The Commissar raised his empty hands. "As you see, I took their advice."

Pekkala stepped into the clearing. In the patched rags of his clothes, he loomed like a prehistoric giant above the tidy Commissar. He became aware, for the first time in years, of the rank smell of his own unwashed body. "What is your name?" asked Pekkala.

"Kirov." The young man straightened his back. "Lieutenant Kirov."

"And how long have you been a Lieutenant?"

"One month and two days." Then he added in a quieter voice, "Including today."

"And how old are you?" asked Pekkala.

"Almost twenty."

"You must have annoyed someone very much, Lieutenant Kirov, to have been given the job of coming to find me."

The Commissar scratched at his bug bites. "I imagine you've annoyed a few yourself to have ended up in Siberia."

"All right, Lieutenant Kirov," said Pekkala. "You have delivered your message. Now you can go back where you came from and leave me alone."

"I was told to give you this." Kirov lifted up the briefcase from beside the tree stump.

"What's in it?"

"I have no idea."

Pekkala took hold of the leather-wrapped handle. It was heavier than he expected. Holding the briefcase, he resembled a cross between a scarecrow and a businessman waiting for a train.

The young Commissar turned to leave. "You have until the sun goes down tomorrow. A car will be waiting for you at the trailhead."

Pekkala watched as Kirov went back the way he had come. For a long time, the snapping of small branches marked his passage through the forest. At last the sound faded away and Pekkala found himself alone again.

Carrying the briefcase, he walked into his cabin. He sat down on the pine-needle-filled sacks which served as his bed and placed the briefcase on his knees. The contents slumped heavily inside. With the edges of his thumbs, Pekkala released the brass latches at each end.

When he lifted the lid, a musty smell wafted up into his face.

Inside the case lay a thick leather belt, wrapped around a dark brown holster which contained a revolver. Unwrapping the belt from around the holster, he lifted out the gun—an English-made Webley revolver. It was a standard military issue except for the fact that its handle was made of brass instead of wood.

Pekkala held the gun at arm's length, staring down the sights. Its blued metal glowed in the dim light of the cabin.

In one corner of the case lay a cardboard box of bullets with English writing on it. He tore open the frayed paper packaging and loaded the Webley, breaking the gun so that its barrel folded forward on a hinge, exposing the six bullet chambers. The bullets were old, like the gun itself, and Pekkala wiped off the ammunition before he placed it in the cylinders.

He also found a tattered book. On its crumpled spine was a single word—*Kalevala.*

Setting these items aside, Pekkala spotted one more thing inside the briefcase. It was a small cotton bag held shut by a leather drawstring. He loosened the top and emptied out the bag.

He breathed out sharply when he saw what was inside.

Lying before him was a heavy gold disk, as wide across as the length of his little finger. Across the center was a stripe of white enamel inlay, which began at a point, widened until it took up half the disk, and narrowed again to a point on the other side. Embedded in the middle of the white enamel was a large round emerald. Together, the white enamel, the gold, and the emerald formed the unmistakable shape of an eye. Pekkala traced a fingertip over the disk, feeling the smooth bump of the jewel, like a blind man reading braille.

Now Pekkala knew who had sent for him and that it was a summons he could not refuse. He had never expected to see these things again. Until that moment, he had thought they belonged to a world which no longer existed.

He was born in Finland, in a time when that country was still a colony of Russia. He grew up surrounded by deep woods and countless lakes near the town of Lappeenranta.

His father was an undertaker, the only one in that region. From miles around, people brought their dead to him. They jostled down forest paths, carrying the bodies in rickety carts, or hauling them in sleds across the frozen lakes in winter, so that the corpses were as hard as stone when they arrived.

In his father's closet hung three identical black coats, and three pairs of black trousers to match. Even his handkerchiefs were black. He would allow no glint of metal on his person. The brass buttons which came with the coats had been replaced by buttons of ebony. He seldom smiled, and when he did, he covered his mouth like a person ashamed of his teeth. Somberness was a thing he cultivated with the utmost care, knowing his job demanded it.

His mother was a Laplander from Rovaniemi. She carried with her a restlessness that never went away. She seemed to be haunted by some strange vibration of the earth which she had left behind in the arctic where she spent her childhood.

He had one older brother, named Anton. On the wishes of their father, when Anton turned eighteen he departed for St. Petersburg to enlist in the Tsar's Finnish Regiment. For Pekkala's father, no greater honor could be won than to serve in that elite company, which formed the personal cadre of the Tsar.

When Anton boarded the train, his father wept with pride, dabbing his eyes with his black handkerchief. His mother just looked stunned, unable to comprehend that her child was being sent away.

Anton leaned out of the window of his railway carriage, hair neatly combed. On his face was the confusion of wanting to stay but knowing that he had to go.

Pekkala, then only sixteen years old and standing by his parents on the platform, felt his brother's absence as if the train had long since departed.

When the train had passed out of sight, Pekkala's father put his arms around his wife and son. "This is a great day," he said, his eyes red with tears. "A great day for our family." In the time that followed, as the father ran his errands around town, he never forgot to mention that Anton would soon be a member of the regiment.

As the younger son, Pekkala had always known he would remain at home, serving as an apprentice to his father. Eventually, he would be expected to take over the family business. His father's quiet reserve became a part of Pekkala as he assisted in the work. The draining of fluids from the bodies and replacing them with preservatives, the dressing and the managing of hair, the insertion of pins in the face to achieve a relaxed and peaceful expression—all this became natural to Pekkala as he learned his father's occupation.

It was with their expressions that his father took the greatest care. An air of calm needed to surround the dead, as if they welcomed this next stage of their existence. The expression of a poorly prepared body might appear anxious or afraid, or—worse—might not look like the same person at all.

It fascinated him to read, in the hands and faces of the departed, the way they'd spent their lives. Their bodies, like a set of clothes, betrayed their secrets of care or neglect. As Pekkala held the hand of a teacher, he could feel the bump on the second finger where a fountain pen had rested, wearing a groove into the bone. The hands of a fisherman were stacked with calluses and old knife cuts which creased the skin like a crumpled piece of paper. Grooves around eyes and mouths told whether a person's days had been governed by optimism or pessimism. There was no horror for Pekkala in the dead, only a great and unsolvable mystery.

The task of undertaking was not pleasant, not the kind of job a man could say he loved. But he could love the fact that it mattered. Not everyone could do this, and yet it needed to be done. It was necessary, not for the dead but for the memories of the living.

His mother thought otherwise. She would not go down to the basement, where the dead were prepared. Instead, she stopped halfway down the basement stairs, to deliver a message or to summon her husband and son for dinner. Pekkala grew used to the sight of her legs on those steps, the round softness of her knees, the rest of her body remaining out of view. He memorized the sound of her voice, muffled beneath a lavender-oil-scented cloth she held against her face whenever she stood on the stairs.

She seemed to fear the presence of formaldehyde, as if it might seep into her lungs and snatch away her soul.

His mother believed in things like that. Her childhood on the barren tundra had taught her to find meaning even in the smoke rising from a fire. Pekkala never forgot her descriptions of the camouflage of a ptarmigan hiding among lichen-spattered rocks, or the blackened stones of a fire whose embers had burned out a thousand years before, or the faint depression in the ground, visible only when evening shadows fell across it, which marked the location of a grave.

From his mother, Pekkala learned to spot the tiniest details—even those he could not see but which registered beyond the boundary of his senses—and to remember them. From his father, he learned patience and the ability to feel at ease among the dead.

This was the world Pekkala believed he would always inhabit, its boundaries marked by the names of familiar streets, by tea-brown lakes reflecting pale blue sky and a sawtoothed horizon of pine trees rising from the forest beyond.

But things did not turn out that way.

The morning after the Commissar's visit, Pekkala set fire to his cabin.

He stood in the clearing while the black smoke uncoiled into the sky. The snap and wheeze of burning filled his ears. The heat leaned into him. Sparks settled on his clothes and, with a flick of his fingers, he brushed them away. Paint buckets stacked by the side of the cabin sprouted dirty yellow tongues of fire as the chemicals inside them ignited. He watched the roof collapse onto the carefully made bed and chair and table which had been his companions for so long now that the outside world seemed more dreamlike than real.

The only thing he saved from the fire was a satchel made from brain-tanned elk hide and closed with a button made of antler bone. Inside lay the gun in its holster and the book and the unblinking emerald eye.

When nothing remained but a heap of smoking beams, Pekkala turned and started walking for the trailhead. In another moment he was gone, drifting like a ghost among the trees.

Hours later, he emerged from the pathless forest onto a logging road. Cut trees were stacked ten deep, ready for transport to the Gulag mill. Strips of bark carpeted the ground and the sour reek of fresh lumber filled the air.

Pekkala found the car just as the Commissar had promised. It was a type he had not seen before. With rounded cowlings, a small windshield and a radiator grille that arched like an eyebrow, the machine had an almost haughty expression. A blue and white shield on the radiator grille gave the car's make as EMKA.

The car doors were open. Lieutenant Kirov lay asleep in the backseat, his legs sticking out into the air.

Pekkala took hold of Kirov's foot and shook it.

Kirov gave a shout and clambered into the road. At first, he recoiled from the bearded ragman who stood before him. "You scared the hell out of me!"

"Are you taking me back to the camp?" asked Pekkala.

"No. Not to the camp. Your days as a prisoner are over." Kirov gestured for Pekkala to get in the back of the car. "At least, they are for now."

In a series of jerky turns, Kirov reversed the Emka and began the long drive to the settlement of Oreshek. After an hour of slipping and bumping over washer-board road, they emerged from the forest into cleared countryside whose openness filled Pekkala with a nameless anxiety.

For much of the drive, Kirov did not speak but kept an eye on Pekkala in the rearview mirror, like a taxi driver worried about whether his rider could pay the fare.

They passed through the ruins of a village. The thatched roofs of *izhba* huts sagged like the backs of broken horses. Bare earth showed through the coating of old whitewash on the walls. Shutters hung loose on their hinges, and the tracks of foraging animals studded the ground. Beyond, the fields lay fallow. Stray sunflowers towered over the weed-choked ground.

"What happened to this place?" asked Pekkala.

"It is the work of counterrevolutionaries and profiteers of the so-called American Relief Administration who infiltrated from the West to pursue their economic sabotage of the New Economic Policy." The words spewed out of Kirov's mouth as if he'd never heard of punctuation.

"But what happened?" repeated Pekkala.

"They all live in Oreshek now."

When they finally reached Oreshek, Pekkala looked out at the hastily built barracks which lined the road. Although the structures appeared new, the tar-paper roofs were already peeling. Most of these buildings were empty, and yet it seemed as if the only work being done was the construction of even more barracks. Workers, men and women, stopped to watch the car go past. Masks of dirt plated their hands and faces. Some pushed wheelbarrows. Others carried what looked like oversized shovels piled with bricks.

Wheat and barley grew in the fields, but they must have been planted too late in the season. Plants that should have been knee high barely reached past a man's ankle.

The car pulled up outside a small police station. It was the only building made from stone, with small barred windows, like the beady eyes of pigs, and a heavy wooden door reinforced with metal strapping.

Kirov cut the engine. "We're here," he said.

As Pekkala stepped out of the car, a few people glanced at him and hastily looked away, as if by knowing him they might incriminate themselves.

He walked up the three wooden steps to the main door, then jumped to one side as a man in a black uniform, wearing the insignia of Internal Security Police, came barreling out of the station. He was hauling an old man by the scruff of his neck. The old man's feet were wrapped in the birch-bark sandals known as *lapti*. The policeman pitched him off the steps and the old man landed spread-eagled in the dirt, sending up a cloud of saffron-colored dust. A handful of corn kernels spilled from his clenched fist. As the old man scrabbled to gather them up, Pekkala realized that they were, in fact, his broken teeth.

The old man struggled to his feet and stared back at the officer, speechless with anger and fear.

Kirov set his hand on Pekkala's back and gave him a gentle nudge towards the stairs.

"Another?" boomed the policeman. He gripped Pekkala's arm, fingers digging into his bicep. "Where did they dig this one up?"

Six months after Pekkala's brother left to join the Finnish Regiment, a telegram arrived from Petrograd. It was addressed to Pekkala's father and signed by the Commanding Officer of the Finnish Garrison. The telegram contained only five words—Pekkala Anton Rusticated Cadre Cadets.

Pekkala's father read the fragile yellow slip. His face showed no emotion. Then he handed the paper to his wife.

"But what does that mean?" she asked. "Rusticated? I've never heard that word before." The telegram trembled in her hand.

"It means he has been kicked out of the regiment," said his father. "Now he will be coming home."

The following day, Pekkala hitched up one of the family's horses to a small two-person cariole, drove out to the station, and waited for the train to come in. He did the same thing the next day and the day after that. Pekkala spent a whole week going back and forth to the train station, watching passengers descend from carriages, searching the crowd, and then, when the train had departed, finding himself alone again on the platform.

In those days of waiting, Pekkala became aware of a permanent change in his father. The man was like a clock whose mechanism had suddenly broken. On the outside, little had altered, but inside he was wrecked. It did not matter why Anton was returning. It was the fact of the return which had changed the neatly plotted course Pekkala's father had laid out for his family.

After two weeks without word from Anton, Pekkala no longer went to the station to wait for his brother.

When a month had gone by, it was clear that Anton would not be returning.

Pekkala's father cabled the Finnish Garrison to inquire about his son.

They replied, this time in a letter, that on such and such a day Anton had been escorted to the gates of the barracks, that he had been given a train ticket home and money for food, and that he had not been seen since.

Another cable, requesting the reason for Anton's dismissal, received no reply at all.

By this time, Pekkala's father had withdrawn so far inside himself that he seemed only the shell of a man. Meanwhile, his mother calmly insisted that Anton would return when he was ready, but the strain of holding on to this conviction was wearing her away, like a piece of sea glass tumbled into nothing by the motion of the waves against the sand.

One day, when Anton had been gone almost three months, Pekkala and his father were putting the finishing touches on a body scheduled for viewing. His father was bent over the dead woman, carefully brushing the eyelashes of the deceased with the tips of his fingers. Pekkala heard his father breathe in suddenly. He watched the man's back straighten, as if his muscles were spasming. "You are leaving," he said.

"Leaving where?" asked Pekkala.

"For St. Petersburg. To join the Finnish Regiment. I have already filled out your induction papers. In ten days, you will report to the garrison. You will take his place." He could no longer even call Anton by name.

"What about my apprenticeship? What about the business?"

"It's done, boy. There is nothing to discuss."

Ten days later, Pekkala leaned from the window of an eastbound train, waving to his parents until their faces were only pink cat licks in the distance and the ranks of pine closed up around the little station house.

PEKKALA LOOKED THE POLICE OFFICER IN THE EYE.

For a moment, the man hesitated, wondering why a prisoner would dare to match his gaze. His jaw muscles clenched. "Time you learned to show respect," he whispered.

"He is under the protection of the Bureau of Special Operations," said Kirov.

"Protection?" laughed the policeman. "For this tramp? What's his name?"

"Pekkala," replied Kirov.

"Pekkala?" The policeman let go of him as if his hand had clamped down on hot metal. "What do you mean? *The* Pekkala?"

The old man was still on his knees in the dirt, watching the argument taking place on the steps of the police station.

"Go!" yelled the policeman.

The old man did not move. "Pekkala," he muttered, and as he spoke blood trickled from the corners of his mouth.

"I said get out of here, damn you!" shouted the policeman, his face turning red.

Now the old man rose to his feet and started walking down the road. Every few paces, he turned his head and looked back at Pekkala.

Kirov and Pekkala pushed past the policeman and made their

way down a corridor lit only by the gloomy filtering of daylight through the barred and glassless windows.

As they walked, Kirov turned to Pekkala. "Who the hell *are* you?" he asked.

Pekkala did not reply. He followed the young Commissar towards a door at the end of the corridor. The door was half open.

The young man stepped aside.

Pekkala walked into the room.

A man sat at a desk in the corner. Other than the chair in which he sat, this was the only piece of furniture. On his tunic, he wore the rank of a Commander in the Red Army. His dark hair was combed and slicked back on his head with a severe parting which ran like a knife cut across his scalp. The man kept his hands neatly folded on the desk, poised as if he were waiting for someone to take his photograph.

"Anton!" gasped Pekkala.

"Welcome back," he replied.

Pekkala gaped at the man, who patiently returned the stare. Finally satisfied that his eyes were not playing tricks on him, Pekkala turned on his heel and walked out of the room.

"Where are you going?" asked Kirov, running to catch up with him.

"Any place but here," replied Pekkala. "You could have had the decency to let me know."

"Let you know what?" The Commissar's voice rose in frustration.

The policeman was still standing in the doorway, looking nervously up and down the street.

Kirov placed a hand on Pekkala's shoulder. "You have not even spoken to Commander Starek."

"Is that what he calls himself now?"

"Now?" The Commissar's face twisted in confusion.

Pekkala turned on him. "Starek is not his real name. He has

invented it. Like Lenin did! And Stalin! Not because it changes anything, but only because it sounds better than Ulyanov or Dzhugashvili."

"You realize," blurted the Commissar, "that I could have you shot for saying that?"

"Find something you *couldn't* shoot me for," replied Pekkala. "That would be more impressive. Or, better still, let my brother do it for you."

"Your brother?" Kirov's mouth hung open. "Commander Starek is your brother?"

Now Anton emerged from the doorway.

"You didn't tell me," protested Kirov. "Surely, I should have been informed—"

"I am informing you now." Anton turned back to Pekkala.

"That's not really him, is it?" asked the policeman. "You're just kidding me, right?" He tried to smile, but failed. "This man is not the Emerald Eye. He's been dead for years. I've heard people say he never even existed, that he's just a legend."

Anton leaned across and whispered in the policeman's ear.

The policeman coughed. "But what have I done?" He looked at Pekkala. "What have I done?" he asked again.

"We could ask that man you threw into the street," replied Pekkala.

The policeman stepped into the doorway. "But this is my station," he whispered. "I am in command here." He looked to Anton silently appealing for help.

But Anton's face remained stony. "I suggest you get out of our way while you still can," he said quietly.

The officer drifted aside, as if he were no more than the shadow of a man.

Now, with his eyes fixed on Pekkala, Anton gave a nod towards the office down the corridor. "Brother," he said, "it is time for us to talk."

It had been ten years since they'd last seen each other, on a desolate and frozen railway platform designated for the transport of prisoners to Siberia.

With his head shaved and still wearing the flimsy beige cotton pajamas which had been issued to him in jail, Pekkala huddled with other convicts waiting for convoy ETAP-61 to arrive. Nobody spoke. As more prisoners arrived, they took their places on the platform, adhering themselves to the mass of frozen men like the layers of an onion.

The sun had already set. Icicles as long as a man's leg hung from the station house roof. Wind blew down the tracks, stirring up whirlwinds of snow. At each end of the platform, guards with rifles on their backs stood around oil barrels in which fires had been lit. Sparks flitted into the air, illuminating their faces.

Late in the night the train finally arrived. Two guards stood beside each open wagon door. As Pekkala climbed aboard, he happened to glance back at the station house. There, in the light of an oil drum fire, a soldier held his rosy-tinted hands over the flames.

Their eyes met.

Pekkala had only an instant to recognize that it was Anton before one of the guards shoved him into the darkness of the frost-encrusted wagon.

Pekkala held the cut-throat razor poised beside his beard-covered cheek, wondering how to begin.

It used to be that he shaved once a month, but the old razor he had nursed finally snapped in half one day as he stropped it against the inside of his belt. And that was years ago.

Since then he'd sometimes taken a knife to his hair, sawing it off in clumps while he sat naked in the freezing water of the stream below his cabin. But now, as he stood in the dirty bathroom of the police station, a pair of scissors in one hand and the razor blade in the other, the task before him seemed impossible.

For almost an hour, he hacked and scraped, gritting his teeth with the pain and rubbing his face with a gritty bar of laundry soap he had been loaned along with the razor. He tried not to breathe in the sharp stench of poorly aimed urine, the smoke of old tobacco sunk into the grout between the pale blue tiles, and the medicinal reek of government-issue toilet paper.

Slowly, a face Pekkala barely recognized began to appear in the mirror. When at last the beard had all been cut away, blood was streaming from his chin and upper lip and just beneath his ears. He pulled some cobwebs from a dusty corner of the room and packed them into the wounds to stanch the bleeding.

Emerging from the bathroom, he saw that his old paint-spattered gear had been removed. In its place he found a different set of clothes and was amazed to see that they were the same garments he'd been wearing when he was first arrested. Even these things had been saved. He dressed in the gray collarless shirt, the heavy black moleskin trousers, and a black wool four-pocket vest. Underneath the chair were his heavy ankle-high boots with *portyanki* foot wrappings neatly rolled inside each one.

Lifting the gun belt over his shoulder, he buckled the strap around his middle. He adjusted it until the butt of the gun rested just beneath the left side of his rib cage so that he could draw the Webley and fire it without breaking the fluidity of motion—a method which had saved his life more than once.

The last piece of clothing was a close-fitting coat made of the same black wool as the vest. Its flap extended to the left side of his chest, in the manner of a double-breasted jacket, except that it fastened with concealed buttons, so that none showed on the coat when it was worn. The coat extended one hand's length below his knees and its collar was short, unlike the sprawling lapel of a standard Russian army greatcoat. Finally, Pekkala attached the emerald eye under the collar of his jacket.

Again he looked at his face in the mirror. Carefully, he

touched the rough pads of his fingertips against the windburned skin beneath his eyes, as if unsure of who was looking back at him.

Then he made his way back to the office. The door was closed. He knocked.

"Enter!" came the sharp reply.

With his heels up on the desk, Anton was smoking a cigarette. The ashtray was almost full. Several of the butts were still smoldering. A cloud of blue smoke hung in the room.

There was no chair except the one in which his brother sat, so Pekkala remained standing.

"Better," said Anton, settling his feet back on the floor. "But not much." He folded his hands and laid them on the desk. "You know who has sent for you."

"Comrade Stalin," said Pekkala.

Anton nodded.

"Is it true," asked Pekkala, "that people call him the Red Tsar?"

"Not to his face," Anton answered, "if they want to go on living."

"If he is the reason I'm here," persisted Pekkala, "then let me speak to him."

Anton laughed. "You do not ask to speak to Comrade Stalin! You wait until he asks to speak to you, and if that ever happens, you will have your conversation. In the meantime, there is work to be done."

"You know what happened to me, back in the Butyrka prison."

"Yes."

"Stalin is responsible for that. Personally responsible."

"Since then he has done great things for this country."

"You," Pekkala replied, "are also responsible."

Anton's folded hands clenched into a knot of flesh and bone. "There are different ways of seeing this."

"You mean the difference between who is tortured and who is doing the torturing."

Anton cleared his throat as he attempted to remain calm. "What I mean is that we have been on different paths, you and I. Mine has brought me to this side of the desk." He rapped the wood for emphasis. "And yours has led you to be standing there. I am now an officer in the Bureau of Special Operations."

"What do you people want from me?"

Anton got up and closed the door. "We want you to investigate a crime."

"Has the country run out of detectives?"

"You are the one we need for this."

"Is it a murder?" Pekkala asked. "A missing person?"

"Possibly," replied Anton, still facing the door, his voice lowered. "Possibly not."

"Do I have to solve your riddles before I solve your case?"

Now Anton turned to face him. "I am talking about the Romanovs. The Tsar. His wife. His children. All of them."

At the mention of their names, old nightmares reared up in Pekkala's head. "But they were executed," he said. "That case was closed years ago. The Revolutionary Government even took credit for killing them!"

Anton returned to the desk. "It is true that we claimed to have carried out the executions. But, as you are perhaps aware, no corpses were produced as evidence."

A breeze blew in through the open window, carrying the musty smell of approaching rain.

"You mean you don't know where the bodies are?"

Anton nodded. "That is correct."

"So it is a missing persons case?" asked Pekkala. "Are you telling me the Tsar might still be alive?" The guilt of having abandoned the Romanovs to their fate had lodged like a bullet in his chest. In spite of what he'd heard about the executions, Pekkala's doubts had never completely gone away. But to hear it now, from the mouth of a Red Army soldier, was something he'd never expected.

Anton looked nervously around the room, as if to see some listener materialize out of the smoke-tinted air. He got up and walked to the window, peering out into the alley which ran by the side of the building. Then he closed the shutters. A purpling darkness descended like twilight upon the room. "The Tsar and his family had been moved to the town of Ekaterinburg—which is now known as Sverdlovsk."

"That is only a few days' drive from here."

"Yes. Sverdlovsk was chosen because of its remoteness. There'd be no chance of anyone trying to rescue them. At least, that's what we thought. When the family arrived, they were quartered at the house of a local merchant named Ipatiev."

"What did you plan to do with them?"

"It wasn't clear what should be done with them. From the moment the Romanov family were arrested in Petrograd, they became a liability. As long as the Tsar lived, he provided a focus for those who were fighting against the Revolution. On the other hand, if we simply got rid of him, world opinion might have turned against us. It was decided that the Romanovs should be kept alive until the new government was firmly established. Then the Tsar was to be put on trial. Judges would be brought in from Moscow. The whole thing would be as public as possible. Newspapers would cover the proceedings. In every rural area, district Commissars would be on hand to explain the legal process."

"And the Tsar would be found guilty."

Anton flipped his hand in the air, brushing aside the idea. "Of course, but a trial would give legitimacy to the proceedings."

"Then what were you planning to do with the Tsar?"

"Shoot him, probably. Or we could have hanged him. The details hadn't been decided."

"And his wife? His four daughters? His son? Would you have hanged them, too?"

"No! If we had wanted to kill them, we would never have gone to the trouble of bringing the Romanovs all the way to Sverdlovsk. The last thing we wanted to do was make martyrs of children. The whole point was to prove that the Revolution was not being run by barbarians."

"So what were you planning to do with the rest of the family?"

"They were to be handed over to the British, in exchange for their official support of the new government."

To Lenin, it must have seemed a simple plan. But those are always the ones that go wrong, thought Pekkala. "What happened instead?"

Anton let his breath trail out. "We aren't sure exactly. An entire division of soldiers known as the Czechoslovakian Legion had mutinied back in May of 1918, when the new government ordered them to lay down their arms. Many of these Czechs and Slovaks had deserted from the Austro-Hungarian army in the early stages of the war. For years, these soldiers had been fighting for the Tsar. They weren't about to throw away their guns and join the Red Army. Instead, they formed a separate force."

"The Whites," said Pekkala. In the years after the Revolution, thousands of former White Army officers had flooded into the Gulag camps. They were always singled out for the worst treatment. Few of them survived their first winter.

"Since these men were deserters," continued Anton, "they couldn't go back to their own countries. Instead they decided to follow the Trans-Siberian Railroad across the entire length of Russia. They were heavily armed. Their military discipline had stayed intact. There was nothing we could do to stop them. In every town they came to as they headed east along the railroad, the Red Army garrisons either melted away or were torn to shreds."

"The railroad passes just south of Sverdlovsk," said Pekkala. Now he began to see where the plan had gone wrong.

"Yes," replied Anton. "The Whites were bound to capture the town. The Romanovs would have been freed."

"So Lenin ordered them to be killed?"

"He could have, but he didn't." Anton looked overwhelmed by the events he was describing. Even to know such secrets put a person's life at risk. To speak them out loud was suicidal. "There were so many false alarms—Red Army units mistaken for Whites, herds of cows mistaken for cavalry, thunder mistaken for cannon fire. Lenin was afraid that if an execution order was in place, the men guarding the Romanovs would panic. They'd shoot the Tsar and his family whether the Czechs tried to rescue them or not." Anton pressed his fingertips into his closed eyelids. "In the end, it didn't matter."

"What happened?" asked Pekkala.

It was raining now, droplets tapping on the shutters.

"A call came in to the house where the Romanovs were staying. A man identifying himself as a Red Army officer said that the Whites were approaching the outskirts of the town. He gave orders for the guards to set up a roadblock and to leave behind two armed men to guard the house. They had no reason to question the orders. Everyone knew the Whites were close by. So they set up a roadblock on the outskirts of the town, just as they'd been ordered. But the Whites didn't show up. The call had been a fake. When the Red Army soldiers returned to the Ipatiev house, they discovered that the Romanovs were gone. The two guards who had remained behind were found in the basement, shot to death."

"How do you know all this?" demanded Pekkala. "How do you know that this is not just another fantasy to throw the world off the track?"

"Because I was *there*!" replied Anton, his voice exasperated, as if this was one secret he had hoped to keep. "I had joined the Internal Police two years before."

The Cheka, thought Pekkala. Formed at the outset of the Revolution under the command of a Polish assassin named Felix Dzerzhinsky, the Cheka quickly became known as a death squad, responsible for murders, torture, and disappearances. Since then, like Lenin and Stalin themselves, the Cheka had changed its name, first to the GPU, then OGPU, but its bloody purpose had remained the same. Many of the Cheka's original members had themselves been swallowed up in the subterranean chambers where the torturers did their work.

"Two months before the Romanovs vanished," continued Anton, "I received orders to accompany an officer named Yurovsky to Sverdlovsk. There, a group of us took over from the local militia unit who had been guarding the Romanovs. From then on, we were in charge of the Tsar and his family. The night they disappeared, I was off duty. I was at the tavern when I heard that the call had come in. I went straight to where the roadblock had been set up. By the time we returned to the Ipatiev house, the Romanovs were already gone and the two guards who stayed behind had been killed."

"Did you conduct an investigation?"

"There was no time. The Whites were advancing on the town. We had to get out. When the White Army marched in two days later, they conducted their own inquiry. But they never found the Romanovs, alive or dead. When the Whites had moved on and we finally regained control of Sverdlovsk, the trail had gone cold. The Tsar's whole family had simply vanished."

"So rather than admit that the Romanovs had escaped, Lenin chose to report that they had been killed."

Anton nodded wearily. "But then the rumors began—sightings were reported all over the world, particularly of the children. Every time a story surfaced, no matter how incredible it seemed, we sent an agent to investigate. Do you realize we even sent a man to Tahiti because a sea captain swore he saw someone there who looked exactly like Princess Maria? But all of those rumors turned out to be false. So we waited. Every day, we expected news that the Romanovs had surfaced in China, or Paris, or London. It seemed only a matter of time. But then years went by. There were fewer sightings. No new rumors. We began to think that maybe we had heard the last of the Romanovs. Then, two weeks ago, I was summoned by the Bureau of Special Operations. They informed me that a man had recently come forward, claiming that the bodies of the Romanovs had been thrown down an abandoned mine shaft not far from Sverdlovsk. He said that he witnessed it himself."

"And where is this man?"

It was raining harder now, the storm a constant roar upon the roof, like a train riding through the air above their heads.

"In a place called Vodovenko. It's an institution for the criminally insane."

"Criminally insane?" Pekkala grunted. "Does this mine shaft even exist?"

"Yes. It has been located."

"And the bodies? Have they been found?" A shudder passed through Pekkala as he thought of the skeletons lying jumbled at the bottom of the mine shaft. Many times he had dreamed of the killings, but those nightmares always ended in the moment of their deaths. Until now, he had never been tormented by the image of their unburied bones.

"The mine shaft was sealed off as soon as news reached the Bureau. As far as we know, the crime scene has not been touched."

"I still don't understand why they need me for this," said Pekkala.

"You are the only person left alive who knew the Romanovs personally and who is also trained in detective work. You can positively identify those bodies. There is no margin for error."

Pekkala hesitated before he spoke. "That explains why Stalin sent for me, but not what you are doing here."

Anton opened his hands and brought them softly together again. "The Bureau thought it might help if a familiar face passed on their offer to you."

"Offer?" asked Pekkala. "What offer?"

"On successful completion of this investigation, your sentence at the Gulag will be commuted. You will be granted your freedom. You can leave the country. You can go anywhere you want."

Pekkala's first instinct was not to believe it. He had been told too many lies in the past to take the offer seriously. "What do you get out of this?"

"This promotion is my reward," replied Anton. "Ever since the Romanovs disappeared, no matter how hard I worked, how loyal I showed myself to be, I was passed over. Until last week I was a Corporal in some windowless office in Moscow. My job was to steam open letters and copy down anything which sounded critical of the government. It looked as if that was all I'd ever be. Then the Bureau called." He sat back in his chair. "If the investigation succeeds, we'll both have a second chance."

"And if we don't succeed?" asked Pekkala.

"You will be returned to Borodok," replied Anton, "and I'll go back to steaming open letters."

"What about that Commissar? What's he doing here?"

"Kirov? He's just a kid. He was training as a cook until they closed down his school and transferred him to the political academy instead. This is his first assignment. Officially, Kirov is our political liaison, but as of now, he doesn't even know what the investigation is about."

"When were you planning on telling him?"

"As soon as you agree to help."

"Political liaison," said Pekkala. "Apparently your Bureau does not trust either of us."

"Get used to it," said Anton. "No one is trusted anymore."

Pekkala slowly shook his head in disbelief. "Congratulations."

"On what?"

"On the mess you have made of this country."

Anton stood up. His chair scudded back across the floor. "The Tsar got what he deserved. And so did you."

They stood face-to-face, the desk like a barricade between them.

"Father would have been proud of you," Pekkala said, unable to hide his disgust.

At the mention of their father, something snapped inside Anton. He lunged across the desk, lashing out with his fist and striking Pekkala on the side of the head.

Pekkala saw a flash behind his eye. He rocked back, then regained his balance.

Anton came out from behind the desk and swung again, hitting his brother in the chest.

Pekkala staggered. Then, with a roar, he grabbed Anton around the shoulders, pinning his arms to his sides.

The two men tumbled backwards, plowing through the office door, which gave way with a splintering of flimsy wood. They fell into the narrow corridor. Anton struck the ground first.

Pekkala crashed down on top of him.

For a moment both of them were stunned.

Then Anton grabbed Pekkala by the throat.

The two men stared at each other, their eyes filled with hate.

"You told me things were different now," said Pekkala, "but you were wrong. Nothing has changed between us."

Unable to contain his rage, Anton wrenched the pistol from his belt and jammed the end of the barrel against his brother's temple.

The same day he arrived in St. Petersburg, Pekkala enlisted as a cadet in the Finnish Regiment of Guards.

He soon learned the reason why Anton had been thrown out of the corps.

Anton had been accused of stealing money from the footlocker of another cadet. At first, he had denied it. No evidence could be brought against him other than the coincidence that he suddenly had money to spend, at the precise moment when the other cadet's funds went missing. But that same evening, as the cadet recounted his loss to the recruit in the neighboring bunk, he noticed something on his bedside locker. He was sitting on the edge of his bed and leaning over so as not to have to raise his voice. As he spoke, his warm breath passed over the polished surface of the locker and a ghostly handprint shimmered into view. The print was not his own, nor did it belong to any of the other six cadets who bunked in that room. The sergeant was called and he ordered a comparison of Anton's handprint and the one upon the locker.

When the handprints were seen to match, Anton confessed, but he also protested that it was only a small amount of money.

The amount did not matter. By the codes of the Finnish Guards, within whose barrack walls no doors were locked and no keys were kept, any theft was punished by demotion from the ranks. When Anton returned from his hearing with the Commander of the regiment, his bags had been packed already.

Two senior officers walked Anton to the gates of the barracks. Then, without a word of good-bye, they turned their backs on him and returned inside the compound. The gates were closed and bolted.

On his first full day as a cadet, Pekkala was summoned to the office of the Commandant. He did not yet know how to present himself to a senior officer, or how to salute. Pekkala worried about this as he walked across the parade square. Platoons of new recruits shambled past him as they learned to march, flanked by shrill-shrieking drill sergeants who cursed them and their families back to the dawn of time.

In the waiting room, a tall, immaculately dressed guard was waiting for Pekkala. The guard's clothes were of a lighter shade than those of the recruits. Over his tunic he wore a belt whose heavy brass buckle was stamped with the double-headed eagle of the Tsar. A short-brimmed cap covered half of his face.

When the guard raised his head and looked him in the eye, Pekkala felt as if lights were shining in his face.

In a voice barely above a whisper, the guard instructed Pekkala to keep his back straight and his heels together when he stood before the Commandant.

"Let's see you do it," said the guard.

Pekkala did the best he could.

"Don't bend over backwards," the guard told him.

Pekkala couldn't help it. All of his muscles were locked so tight he could barely move.

The guard pinched the gray cloth at the tips of Pekkala's shoulders, straightening the rough wool tunic. "When the Commandant speaks, you must not answer 'yes, sir.' Instead, you only say 'sir.' However, if the answer to his question is no, you may say 'no, sir.' Do you understand?"

"Sir."

The guard shook his head. "You do not call me sir. I am not an officer."

The rules of this strange world raced around in Pekkala's brain like bees shaken from a hive. It seemed impossible that he would ever master all of them. At that moment, if someone had offered him the chance to go home, he would have taken it. At the same time, Pekkala was afraid that was exactly why the Commandant had called for him.

The guard seemed to know what he was thinking. "You have nothing to fear," he said. Then he turned, and knocked on the door to the Commandant's office. Without waiting for a reply from inside, he opened the door and, with a jerk of his chin, showed Pekkala that he was to enter.

The Commandant was a man named Parainen. He was tall and thin, with jaw and cheekbones so sharply angled that his skull seemed to be made of broken glass. "You are the brother of Anton Pekkala?"

"Sir."

"Have you heard anything from him?"

"Not lately, sir."

The Commandant scratched at his neck. "He was due back with us a month ago."

"Due back?" asked Pekkala. "But I thought he had been expelled!"

"Not expelled. Rusticated. That's not the same thing."

"Then what does it mean?" asked Pekkala, and then he added, "Sir."

"It is only a temporary dismissal," explained Parainen. "If it happened again, the expulsion would be permanent, but in the case of a cadet's first offense, we tend to show leniency."

"Then why hasn't he returned?"

The Commandant shrugged. "Perhaps he decided that this life was not for him."

"That can't be right, sir. It's all he wanted in the world."

"People change. Besides, now you are here to take his place." The Commandant rose to his feet. He walked over to the window, which looked out over the barracks to the town beyond. The gunmetal gray of a winter's afternoon lit his face. "I want you to know that you will not be held accountable for what your brother did. You will be given the same chances as anybody else. If you fail, as many do, you will fail on your own terms. And if you succeed, it will be because of what you did and no one else. Does that sound fair to you?"

"Sir," said Pekkala. "Yes, it does."

In the weeks that followed, Pekkala learned to march and shoot and to live in a place where there was no such thing as privacy except in those thoughts which he kept locked inside his head. Within the confines of the Finnish Regiment barracks, thrown in among young men from Helsinki, Kauhava, and Turku, it was almost possible to forget that he had left his native country. Many had never dreamed of any other life except to become members of the Finnish Guards. For some, it was a family tradition dating back generations.

Sometimes, Pekkala felt as if he had woken up and found himself clad in the skin of a different man. The person he had been was receding into the shadows like the dead, whose final journeys he had overseen at home.

One day, all that changed.

With the barrel of Anton's gun digging into his temple, Pekkala slowly closed his eyes. There was no terror in his face, only a kind of quiet anticipation, as if he had been waiting for this moment for a long time. "Go ahead," he whispered.

Footsteps sounded in the corridor. It was Kirov, the young Commissar. "That policeman has run away," he said as he walked into the room. He stopped when he saw Anton's gun aimed at Pekkala's head.

With an unintelligible curse, Anton released his grip on his brother's throat.

Pekkala rolled away, choking.

Kirov stared at them in amazement. "When you are done brawling, Commander," he said to Anton, "would one of you mind explaining to me why the hell your brother is making everybody so nervous?"

Pekkala's career began with a horse.

Midway through their training in the regiment, cadets were brought to the stables for instruction in riding.

Although Pekkala knew well enough how to handle a horse which had been hitched to his father's wagon, he had never ridden in the saddle.

The idea did not trouble him. After all, he told himself, I knew nothing about shooting or marching before I came here, and those things have not been more difficult for me than they were for anybody else.

The training went smoothly at first, as recruits learned to saddle a horse, to mount and dismount, and to steer the animal around a series of wooden barrels. The horses were themselves so familiar with this routine that all Pekkala had to do was not fall off.

The next task was to jump a horse over a gate set up in a large indoor ring. The Sergeant in charge of this exercise was new to his job. He had ordered several strands of barbed wire to be stretched across the top of the gate and nailed to the posts at either end. It was not enough, he told the assembled cadets, simply to hang on to a horse while it performed tasks it could just as easily have accomplished without a rider.

"There needs to be," he told them, pleased at the boom of his voice within the enclosed space of the ring, "a bond between horse and rider. Until you can demonstrate this to me, I will never permit you to be members of this regiment."

As soon as the horses saw the glint of barbs along the top of the gate, they grew nervous, shying and sidestepping and clanking the bits with their teeth. Some refused to jump. Rearing up before the wire, they threw the cadets who rode them. Pekkala's horse turned sideways, slammed its flank into the gate, and sent Pekkala flying. He landed on his shoulder, rolling on the hard-trampled ground. By the time he got to his feet, covered with flecks of old straw, the sergeant was already making marks in his notebook.

Only a few animals made it across the first time. Most of these were injured by the wire, which cut them on their shins or on their bellies.

The sergeant ordered the cadets to try again.

An hour later, after several attempts, only half of the class had succeeded in getting their horses to jump the gate. The ground was sprinkled with blood, as if a box of red glass buttons had been tipped over.

The cadets stood at attention, holding the reins of their trembling horses.

By now, the sergeant realized he had made a mistake, but there was no way for him to back down without losing face. His voice was shredded from all the shouting he had done. Now, when he yelled, his shrillness sounded less like a man in charge than like someone on the edge of hysterics.

Each time a horse collided with the gate—the hollow boom of the animal's side connecting with the wooden planks, the scuffling of hooves and the grunt of the rider falling hard—the remaining horses and cadets would flinch in unison as if an electric current had arced through their bodies. One young man wept silently as he waited for his turn. It would be his sixth attempt. Like Pekkala, he had not cleared the gate even once.

When it was time for Pekkala to try again, he swung himself up into the saddle. He looked over his horse's head and at the distance between them and the gate. He could see gashes in the lower planks, where hooves had torn into the wood.

The sergeant stood off to one side, notebook at the ready.

Pekkala was about to dig his heels into the horse's side and begin another run towards the gate. He had no doubt that he would be thrown; he was resigned to it. He was ready and then suddenly he was no longer ready to ride his horse against that gate, with its garland of bloodied iron barbs. As fluidly as he had climbed into the saddle, he climbed back down again.

"Get back on your horse," said the sergeant.

"No," said Pekkala. "I will not." From the corner of his eye, Pekkala saw what looked to him like relief in the eyes of the other cadets. Relief that this could not go on, and relief that they would not be held responsible if it did not.

This time, the sergeant did not scream and curse as he'd been doing all day long. As calmly as he could, he shut his notebook and slid it into the top pocket of his tunic. He tucked his hands behind his back and walked over to Pekkala, until their faces almost touched. "I will give you one more chance," he said, his raw voice no stronger than a whisper.

"No," Pekkala said again.

Now the sergeant came even closer, bringing his lips to Pekkala's ear. "Listen," he said, "all I am asking of you is to attempt your jump. If you fail, I will not hold it against you. I will even end the day's exercise after your jump. But you will get on that horse, and you will do as you are told, or I will see to it that you are washed out of the cadets. I will personally walk you through the gates and see them bolted at your back, just as they were for your brother. That's why it will be easy for me, Pekkala. Because people are expecting you to fail."

At that moment, a tremor passed through Pekkala. It was the strangest thing he had ever felt, and he was not the only one to feel it.

Both Pekkala and the sergeant turned at the same time, and saw a man standing in the shadows, near the stable entrance to the ring. The newcomer wore a dark green tunic and blue trousers with a red stripe running down the side. It was a simple uniform, and yet the colors seemed to vibrate in the still air. The man was not wearing a hat. Because of this they could see clearly that it was the Tsar himself.

A small fire crackled in the grate of the police chief's office.

"Detective?" Kirov paced the room, raising his hands and letting them fall again. "Do you mean your *brother* worked for the Tsar's Secret Police?"

Pekkala sat at the desk, reading through the muddy brown case file with its red stripe running diagonally across the page. Written in black on the red stripe were the words VERY SECRET. The word *secret* alone had lost all meaning. These days, everything was secret. Carefully, he turned the pages, his face only a hand's length from the desk, so lost in thought that he did not seem to hear the Commissar's ranting.

"No." Anton sat by the fire, hands stretched out towards the flames. "He did not work for the Okhrana."

"Then who did he work for?"

"I told you. He worked for the Tsar."

They spoke of Pekkala as if he was not in the room.

"In what branch?" asked Kirov.

"He was his own branch," Anton explained. "The Tsar created

a unique investigator, a man with absolute authority, who answered only to himself. Even the Okhrana could not question him. They called him the Eye of the Tsar and he could not be bribed, or bought or threatened. It did not matter who you were, how wealthy or connected. No one stood above the Emerald Eye, not even the Tsar himself."

Pekkala looked up from his reading. "Enough," he muttered.

But his brother kept on talking. "My brother's memory is perfect! He remembered the face of every person he'd ever met. He put the devil Grodek behind bars. He killed the assassin Maria Balka!" He pointed at Pekkala. "This was the Eye of the Tsar!"

"I've never heard of him," said Kirov.

"I don't suppose," said Anton, "that they would teach cooks about the techniques of criminal investigation."

"A chef!" Kirov corrected him. "I was training to be a chef, not a cook."

"And there's a difference?"

"There is if you're a chef, which I would have been by now if they hadn't closed the school."

"Well, then, Comrade Almost-Chef, the reason you don't know about him is because his identity was suppressed after the Revolution. We couldn't have people wondering what had happened to the Eye of the Tsar. It doesn't matter. From now you can simply refer to him as the Eye of the Red Tsar."

"I said *enough*!" growled Pekkala.

Anton smiled and breathed out slowly, satisfied with the effect of his tormenting. "My brother possessed the kind of power you see once in a thousand years. But he threw it all away. Didn't you, brother?"

"You go to hell," said Pekkala.

The sergeant sprang to attention.

The cadets, in a single motion, crashed their heels together in salute. The sound echoed like a gunshot through the horse ring.

Even the horses became strangely still as the Tsar walked out across the ring to where the men were standing.

It was the first time Pekkala had ever seen the Tsar. Recruits in training did not usually set eyes on him until the day of their graduation, when they would parade before the Romanov family in their new, fine-cut gray uniforms. Until then, the Tsar remained distant.

But there he was, without his usual bodyguards, without an entourage of officers from the regiment—a man of medium height, with narrow shoulders and a tight stride, placing one foot directly in front of the other as he walked. He had a broad, smooth forehead, and his beard was close-trimmed and sculpted on his chin in a way which gave his jaw a certain angularity. The Tsar's narrowed eyes were hard to read. His expression was not unkind, but neither was it friendly. It seemed to hover between contentment and the desire to be somewhere else.

More of a mask than a face, thought Pekkala.

Pekkala knew he was not supposed to look directly at the Tsar. In spite of this, he couldn't help but stare. It was like watching a picture come to life, a two-dimensional image suddenly emerging into the third dimension of the living.

The Tsar came to a stop before the Sergeant and offered a casual salute.

The Sergeant returned the salute.

Now the Tsar turned to Pekkala. "Your horse seems to be bleeding." He did not raise his voice, but still it seemed to carry through the wide space of the training ring.

"Yes, Excellency."

"It looks to me as if most of these animals are bleeding." He looked at the Sergeant. "Why are my horses bleeding?"

"A part of the training, Excellency," the Sergeant replied breathlessly.

"The horses are already trained," replied the Tsar.

The Sergeant spoke at the ground, not daring to raise his head. "Training for the recruits, Excellency."

"But the recruits are not bleeding." The Tsar ran his hand through his beard. His heavy signet ring stood out like a knuckle made of gold.

"No, Excellency."

"And what seems to be the trouble with this particular recruit?" asked the Tsar, casting a glance at Pekkala.

"He refuses to jump."

The Tsar turned to Pekkala. "Is this true? Do you refuse to go over that gate?"

"No, Excellency. I will go over the gate, only not on this horse."

The Tsar's eyes opened wider for a moment, then returned to their normal squint. "I'm not sure that's what your Sergeant had in mind."

"Excellency, I will not continue to injure this horse in order to prove that I am capable of doing so."

The Tsar took one long breath, like a man preparing to dive underwater. "Then I regret that you find yourself in a dilemma." Without another word, the Tsar walked past Pekkala and down the line of horses and riders standing at attention. The only sound was of his footsteps.

When the Tsar's back was turned, the Sergeant raised his head and looked Pekkala in the eye. It was a stare of pure hatred.

The Tsar continued past the gates, where he paused to study the bloody strands of barbed wire.

When he reached the far end of the ring, he spun on his heel and faced the soldiers again. "This exercise is finished," he said. Then he stepped back into the shadows and was gone.

As soon as the Tsar was out of sight, the Sergeant snarled at Pekkala, "You know what else is finished? Your life as a member of this Regiment. Now return to the stables, brush down your horse, wipe the saddle, fold the blanket, and get out."

As Pekkala led his horse away, the Sergeant's shrill commands to the other cadets echoed across the ring.

He led his horse into the stable. The horse moved willingly into its pen, where Pekkala unbuckled the saddle and removed the reins. He brushed down the animal, seeing its muscles quiver beneath the silky brown coat. He was stepping out to fetch a bucket of water and a cloth for dressing the horse's injured shins when he saw the silhouette of a man standing at the opposite end of the stable, where it opened out onto the barracks grounds.

It was the Tsar. He had come back. Or maybe he had never left. Pekkala could see nothing of the man beyond an inky outline. It was as if the Tsar had returned to the two-dimensional form in which Pekkala had imagined him before. "That was an expensive gesture," he said. "Your Sergeant will have you kicked out."

"Yes, Excellency."

"If I were in your place, I would also have refused," said the Tsar. "Unfortunately, it is not my place to argue with the methods of your training. If you had to do it over again, would you take your horse over the gate?"

"No, Excellency."

"But you would clamber over it yourself."

"Yes."

The Tsar cleared his throat. "I look forward to telling that story. What is your name, cadet?"

"Pekkala."

"Ah, yes. You came here to take your brother's place in the regiment. I read your file. It was noted that you have an excellent memory."

"That comes without effort, Excellency. I can take no credit for it."

"Nevertheless, it was noted. Well, Pekkala, I regret that our acquaintance has been so brief." He turned to leave. Sunlight winked off the buttons on his tunic. But instead of walking away, the Tsar came full circle, turning back into the stable's darkness. "Pekkala?"

"Yes, Excellency?"

"How many buttons are on my tunic?"

"The answer is twelve."

"Twelve. A good guess, but . . ." The Tsar did not finish his sentence.

The silhouette changed as he lowered his head in disappointment. "Well, good-bye, Cadet Pekkala."

"It was not a guess, Excellency. There are twelve buttons on your tunic, including the buttons on your cuffs."

The Tsar's head snapped up. "Good heavens, you are right! And what is on those buttons, Pekkala? What crest did you see?"

"No crest at all, Excellency. The buttons are plain."

"Hah!" The Tsar walked into the stable. "Right again!" he said.

Now the two men stood only an arm's length apart.

Pekkala recognized something familiar in the Tsar's expression—a kind of hardened resignation, buried so deep that it was now as much a permanent part of the man as the color of his eyes. Then Pekkala realized that the Tsar, like himself, was on a path not of his own choosing, but one which he had learned to accept. Looking at the Tsar's face was like studying his own reflection in some image of the future.

The Tsar seemed to grasp this connection. He looked momentarily bewildered, but quickly regained his composure. "And my ring?" he asked. "Did you happen to notice . . . ?"

"Some kind of long-necked bird. A swan, perhaps."

"A crane," muttered the Tsar. "This ring once belonged to my grandfather, Christian the Ninth of Denmark. The crane was his personal emblem."

"Why are you asking me these questions, Excellency?"

"Because," replied the Tsar, "I think your destiny is with us, after all."

ANTON WAS STARING INTO THE FIRE. "MY BROTHER GAVE UP EVERYthing he had, but still he did not give up everything."

"What's that supposed to mean?" Kirov snapped.

"He is rumored to be the last man left alive who knows the location of the Tsar's secret gold reserves."

"That's not a rumor," said Pekkala. "That's a fairy tale."

"What gold reserves?" asked Kirov, looking more confused

than ever. "I learned in school that all of the Tsar's property was seized."

"Only what they could get their hands on," said Anton.

"How much gold are you talking about?" asked Kirov.

"Nobody seems to know exactly," Anton replied. "Some people say there are more than ten thousand bars of it."

Kirov turned to Pekkala. "And you know where it is?"

With a look of exasperation, Pekkala rocked back in his chair. "You can believe what you want, but I am telling the truth. I do not know where it is."

"Well," said Kirov, injecting his voice with authority, "I am not here to oversee a search for gold. I am here, Inspector Pekkala, to see that you obey the protocols."

"Protocols?"

"Yes, and if you do not, I have been authorized to use deadly force."

"Deadly force," Pekkala repeated. "And have you ever shot anyone before?"

"No," replied Kirov, "but I've fired a gun at the range."

"And the targets. What were they made of?"

"I don't know," he snapped. "Paper, I suppose."

"It's not as easy when the target is made of flesh and blood." Pekkala slid the report across the desk towards the Junior Commissar. "Read this report and, afterwards, if you still feel like shooting me"—he reached inside his coat, drew out the Webley revolver, and laid it on the desk in front of Kirov—"you can borrow this for the occasion."

On the Tsar's orders, Pekkala began work with the Petrograd Regular Police, later switching to the State Police, known as the Gendarmerie, and finishing with the Okhrana at their offices on Fontanka Street.

There, he served under Major Vassileyev, a round-faced, jovial man who had lost both his right arm below the elbow and his left leg below the knee in a bomb attack ten years earlier. Vassileyev did not so much walk as lurch about, constantly on the verge of falling, then righting himself just before he crashed to the floor. The artificial leg caused Vassileyev great pain on the stump of his knee, and he often removed the prosthetic when sitting in his office. Pekkala grew accustomed to the sight of the fake limb, dressed in a sock and shoe, propped against the wall along with Vassileyev's walking stick and umbrella. The Major's replacement right hand was made of wood with brass hinges, which he adjusted with his left hand before putting it to use, primarily for holding cigarettes. The brand he smoked was called Markov. The cigarettes came in a red and gold box, and Vassileyev kept a whole shelf of them behind his desk.

Also on the wall behind Vassileyev's desk, displayed in a black shadow box, was a cut-throat razor opened halfway to form a V.

"It's Occam's razor," explained Vassileyev.

Pekkala, feeling foolish, admitted that he had not heard of Occam, whom he assumed to be a great criminal put behind bars by Vassileyev's detective work.

Vassileyev laughed when he heard this. "It's not really Occam's razor. The razor is just an idea." Seeing Pekkala's confusion, he went on to explain. "In the Middle Ages, a Franciscan monk named William of Occam formulated one of the basic principles of detective work, which is that the simplest explanation that fits the facts is usually right."

"But why is it called Occam's razor?" asked Pekkala.

"I don't know," admitted Vassileyev. "Probably because it cuts straight to the truth, something you will need to learn how to do if you ever hope to survive as an investigator."

Vassileyev liked to test Pekkala, sending him into town with instructions to walk a certain route. Vassileyev, meanwhile, would have planted people along the way, noted down advertisements pasted on walls, the headlines of newspapers hawked on the street corners by boys with floppy hats. No detail was too small. When Pekkala returned, Vassileyev would quiz the young man about everything he had seen. The point, Vassileyev explained, was that there was too much to note down, especially when he might not even know what he was looking for. The purpose of the exercise was to train Pekkala's mind to catalogue it all and then to permit his subconscious to sift through the information. Eventually, Vassileyev explained, he would be able to rely solely on his instincts to tell him when something was not right.

Other times, Pekkala was instructed to evade capture by traveling in disguise across the city while different agents searched for him. He learned to pose as a cabdriver, a priest, and a bartender.

He studied the effects of poisons, the disarming of bombs, the business of killing with a knife.

In addition to instructing Pekkala on how to shoot a variety of weapons, all of which he had to disassemble, reassemble, and load while blindfolded, Vassileyev taught him to recognize the sounds made by different-caliber guns and even the varying sounds made by different models of the same caliber. Pekkala would sit on a chair behind a brick wall while Vassileyev, perched on a chair on the other side of the wall, fired off various guns and asked Pekkala to identify each one. During these sessions, Vassileyev was rarely without a cigarette wedged between his wooden fingers. Pekkala learned to watch the thin gray line of smoke rising from behind the wall, and the way it would ripple as Vassileyev bit down on the cigarette, just before he pulled the trigger of the gun.

At the beginning of his third year of training, Vassileyev called Pekkala into his office. The artificial leg was on the desk. Using a chisel, Vassileyev had begun to hollow out the solid block of wood from which his prosthetic limb had been constructed.

"Why are you doing that?" Pekkala asked.

"Well, you never know when you might need a hiding place for valuables. Besides, this damned thing is too heavy for me." Vassileyev set down the chisel and carefully swept the wood shavings into his palm. "Do you know why the Tsar chose you for this job?"

"I never asked him," replied Pekkala.

"He told me that he chose you because you have the closest thing to

perfect memory as he has ever seen. And also because you are a Finn. To us Russians, the Finns have never quite seemed human."

"Not human?"

"Warlocks. Witches. Magicians," explained Vassileyev. "Do you know that many Russians still believe the Finns are capable of casting spells? That's why the Tsar surrounded himself with a regiment of Finnish Guards. And that is why he picked you. But you and I both know that you are not a magician."

"I never claimed to be one."

"Nevertheless," replied Vassileyev, "that is how you are likely to be seen, even by the Tsar himself. You must not forget the difference between who you are and who people believe you to be. The Tsar needs you even more than he realizes. Dark times are coming, Pekkala. Back when I got blown to bits, crooks were still robbing money from banks. Now they have learned how to steal the whole bank. It won't be long before they are running the country. If we let them get that far, Pekkala, you and I will wake up one day and find we are the criminals. And then you'll need the skills I've taught you just to stay alive."

THE NEXT MORNING, AS RED STREAMERS OF DAWN UNFURLED ACROSS the sky, Pekkala, Kirov, and Anton climbed into the Emka staff car.

The houses all around were still shuttered, their occupants not yet emerged. The slatted shutters made the buildings look as if they were asleep, but there was something sinister about them, and each man felt that he was being watched.

Kirov got behind the wheel. Having stayed up half the night reading the secret report, the young Commissar now seemed in a state of total shock.

Pekkala had decided that they should proceed directly to the mine shaft where the bodies had been dumped. According to Anton, who had the place marked on his map, the mine was on the outskirts of Sverdlovsk, approximately two days' drive away.

They had only been on the road a few minutes when a figure came stumbling out of an abandoned house on the outskirts of the town. It was the policeman. His clothes were filthy from hiding out all night.

The Emka skidded to a stop.

The policeman stood ankle deep in a puddle in the middle of the road. He was drunk. He moved like a man on the deck of a ship in rough seas. "I don't care if he's the Emerald Eye or not!" he shouted. "You're taking me with you." He staggered over to the car, hauled out his service revolver, and tapped the glass with the barrel of the gun.

"Everybody out," said Anton, in a low voice.

The three men piled into the muddy road.

"We have to get out of here!" shouted the policeman. "Word is all over town that Pekkala is investigating me!" He brandished the gun back towards the rooftops of the village. "But they're not going to wait for that."

"We have more important things to do than put you under investigation," said Anton, not taking his eyes from the gun.

"It doesn't matter now!" insisted the policeman. "If I go back into town, those people will tear me to pieces!"

"You should have thought about that," said Anton, "before you started kicking the teeth out of old men. Your job is to stay at your post. Now get out of the road and go back to work."

"I can't." The policeman's finger locked inside the trigger guard. All he had to do was clench his hand and the gun would go off. The way the man looked, he seemed just as likely to accomplish that by accident as on purpose. "I won't let you leave me here!"

"I will not help you to desert," replied Anton.

"I wouldn't be deserting!" His voice rippled thinly through the still morning air. "I could come back with reinforcements."

"I can't help you," said Anton. "We have other work to do."

"This is your fault! You brought that ghost into my town"—he jerked his head towards Pekkala—"and woke up things which should have stayed asleep."

"Return to your post," Anton ordered. "You are not coming with us."

The policeman trembled, as if the ground beneath his feet were shaking. Then suddenly his arm swung out.

Anton found himself staring down the blue eye of a gun barrel. His holster was strapped to his waist, but he would never be able to reach it in time. He stood motionless, hands by his sides.

"Go on," the policeman challenged. "Give me an excuse."

Now Kirov grabbed for the flap of his holster, drew the gun, but lost his grip on the handle. The pistol slipped through his fingers. Kirov's empty hands clawed at nothing as the Tokarev cartwheeled into the mud. A look of terrified amazement spread across his face.

The policeman did not even notice. He kept his gun aimed at Anton. "Go on," he said, "I'm going to shoot you either way, so—"

A stunning crash filled the air.

Kirov cried out in shock.

Anton watched in confusion as the drunken policeman dropped to his knees. A white gash showed across his neck, followed instantly by a torrent of blood which poured from the hole in his throat. Slowly and deliberately, the policeman raised a hand to cover the wound. The blood pulsed out between his fingers. His eyes blinked rapidly, as if he was trying to clear his vision. Then he tipped forward into a puddle on the road.

Anton looked across at his brother.

Pekkala lowered the Webley. Smoke still slithered from the cylinder. He slid the gun back into its holster under his coat.

Kirov retrieved his own gun from the mud. He wiped some of

the dirt away, then tried to put the pistol back in its holster, but his hands were shaking so much that he gave up. He looked from Anton to Pekkala. "I'm sorry," he said. Then he walked to the side of the road and threw up in the bushes.

The engine of the Emka was still running. Exhaust smoke puffed from the tailpipe.

"Let's go." Anton motioned for them to get back in the car.

"We should file a report," said Pekkala.

"It never happened," Anton said. Without looking Pekkala in the eye, he walked past him and got into the car.

"What should we do with the body?" Kirov wiped his mouth with his sleeve.

"Leave it!" shouted Anton.

Kirov climbed behind the wheel.

Pekkala stared at the corpse in the road. The puddle had turned red, like wine spilled out of a bottle. Then he got back in the car.

They drove on.

For a long time, nobody talked.

None of the roads were paved, and they encountered few cars along the way. Often they sped past horses harnessed to carts, leaving them in clouds of yellow dust, or slowed to navigate around places where puddles had merged to form miniature ponds.

In this wide, deserted countryside, they eventually became lost. The rolling hills and valleys all began to look the same. All road markers had been forcibly removed, leaving only the splintered stumps of posts on which the signs had once been nailed. Kirov had a map, but it did not appear to be accurate.

"I don't even know what direction we are heading in," sighed Kirov.

"Pull over," said Pekkala.

Kirov glanced at him in the rearview mirror.

"If you stop the car, I can tell you where we are going."

"Do you have a compass?"

"Not yet," replied Pekkala.

Grudgingly, Kirov eased up on the gas. The car rolled to a stop in the middle of the road. He cut the engine.

Silence settled on them like the dust.

Pekkala opened the door and got out.

All around them, wind blew through the tall grass.

Pekkala opened the trunk.

"What is he doing?" demanded Kirov.

"Just leave him alone," replied Anton.

Pekkala fished out a crowbar from the tangle of fuel containers, towing ropes, and assorted cans of army rations rolling loose around the trunk of the car.

He walked out into the field and jammed the bar into the earth. Its shadow stretched long on the ground. Then, sweeping his fingers through the grass, he pulled a couple of dusty pebbles from the earth. One of these he laid at the end of the shadow. The other one he put inside his pocket. Turning to the men who waited in the car, he said, "Ten minutes." Then he sat down cross-legged by the crowbar, resting his elbow on his knee and his chin in the palm of his hand.

Both men stared out the window at the figure of Pekkala, his dark shape like some ancient obelisk out in the blankness of that desolate land.

"What's he doing?" Kirov asked.

"Making a compass."

"He knows how to do that?"

"Don't ask me what he knows."

"I pity him," said Kirov.

"He does not want your pity," replied Anton.

"He is the last one of his kind."

"He is the only one of his kind."

"What became of all the people he knew before the Revolution?"

"Gone," replied Anton. "All except one."

"She is a beauty," said the Tsar.

Pekkala stood beside him on the veranda of the Great Ballroom, squinting in the sunlight of an early summer afternoon.

Ilya had just led her students through the Catherine Palace. Now the dozen children, holding hands in pairs, made their way across the Chinese Bridge.

Ilya was a tall woman with eyes the blue of old Delft pottery and dirty-blond hair which trailed over the brown velvet collar of her coat.

The Tsar nodded approvingly. "Sunny likes her." That was what he called his wife, the Tsarina Alexandra. She, in turn, had given him the curious name of "Blue Child," after a character in a novel they'd both enjoyed by the author Florence Barclay.

Once across the Chinese Bridge, Ilya steered the small but orderly procession towards the Gribok gardens. They were headed for the Chinese Theater, its windows topped with gables like the mustaches of Mongol Emperors.

"How many of these tours does she give?" asked the Tsar.

"One for each class, Excellency. It is the highlight of their year."

"Did she find you sleeping in a chair again, with your feet up on one of my priceless tables?"

"That was last time."

"And are you engaged to be married?"

Flustered by the question, Pekkala cleared his throat. "No, Excellency."

"Why not?"

He felt the blood run to his face. "I have been so busy with the training, Excellency."

"That may be a reason," replied the Tsar, "but I would not call it an excuse. Besides, your training will soon be complete. Are you planning to marry her?"

"Well, yes. Eventually."

"Then you had better get on with it before someone else beats you to the finish line." The Tsar appeared to be wringing his hands, as if tormented by some memory jostled to the surface of his mind. "Here." He pressed something into Pekkala's hand.

"What is this?" asked Pekkala.

"It's a ring."

Then Pekkala realized that what the Tsar had been doing was removing the signet ring from his finger. "I can see what it is," he said, "but why are you handing it to me?"

"It's a gift, Pekkala, but it is also a warning. This is no time to hesitate. When you are married, you will need a ring to wear. This one, I think, will do nicely. She will need a ring as well, but that part I leave to you."

"Thank you," said Pekkala.

"Keep it somewhere safe. There! Look." He pointed out the window.

Ilya had seen them standing in the window. She waved.

Both men waved back and smiled.

"If you let her get away," the Tsar said through the clenched teeth of his grin, "you'll never forgive yourself. And neither will I, by the way."

Anton glanced at the white face of his oversized wristwatch and leaned his head out the window. "Ten minutes!" he shouted.

Pekkala climbed to his feet. The shadow of the crowbar had drifted to the right. He withdrew the second pebble from his pocket and laid it at the end of where the shadow had now reached. Then he dug his heel into the dirt and carved a line between the two pebbles. Positioning himself at the end of the second shadow, he held his arm out straight along the line he had dug in the sand. "That way is to the east," he said.

Neither man questioned this result, conjured from thin air with skills beyond their reckoning, a thing both strange and absolute.

Having driven all day, stopping only to refuel from one of several gas cans they carried in the trunk, they stopped that night under the roof of an abandoned barn.

They parked the Emka on the dirt floor of the barn, to keep it out of sight in case this place was not as empty as it seemed. Then they lit a fire on the floor, feeding the flames with wooden planks prised out of old horse stalls.

Anton opened up a can of army ration meat with the word TUSHONKA stamped on the side. With a spoon pulled from his boot, he took a mouthful, jammed the spoon into the can, and passed it on to Kirov, who gouged out a clump of meat and packed it into his mouth, then turned and spat it out.

"This is atrocious!"

"Get used to it," Anton told him. "I have three cases of the stuff."

Kirov shook his head violently, like a dog shaking water from its fur. "If you'd thought to bring some decent food, I would gladly have cooked it for us."

Anton pulled a flask from his pocket. It was made of glass wrapped in leather and had a pewter cup which fitted to the bottom of the glass. He unscrewed the metal cap and took a swig. "The reason they shut down your cookery class—"

"Chef! A school for chefs!"

Anton rolled his eyes. "The reason they closed it, Kirov, was because there isn't enough decent food left in this country to make a proper meal. Trust me, you're better off working for the government. At least you won't starve."

"I will," said Kirov, "if I have to keep eating this." He held the can out to Pekkala. "What did the Tsar like to eat?"

Up in the rafters, pigeons peered down at the men, flames reflected in their wide and curious eyes.

"Simple food mostly," replied Pekkala. "Roast pork. Boiled cabbage. Blinis. Shashlik." He remembered the skewers of meat, red peppers, onions, and mushrooms, served next to beds of rice and washed down with heavy Georgian wine. "I'm afraid you might have found his tastes a little disappointing."

"On the contrary," said Kirov, "those meals are the hardest to make. When chefs meet for a meal, they choose the traditional recipes. The mark of a good chef is whether he can create a simple meal and have it taste the way everyone expects it to."

"What about cooks?" asked Anton.

Before Kirov could reply, Anton tossed the flask into his lap.

"What's in here?" Kirov eyed the flask as if it were a grenade about to blow up in his face.

"Samahonka!" said Anton.

"Home brew," muttered Kirov, handing back the flask. "You're lucky you haven't gone blind."

"I made it in my bathtub," said Anton. He took another drink and put the flask back in his pocket.

"Aren't you going to offer some to your brother?"

Anton lay back, resting his head on the secret report. "A detective is not allowed to drink when he's working. Isn't that right, brother?" He pulled his heavy greatcoat over him and curled up in a ball. "Get some rest. We still have a long way to go."

"I thought we were just stopping here for a meal," said Kirov. "You mean we're spending the whole night? On this bare floor?"

"Why not?" Anton muttered through a veil of fading consciousness.

"I used to have a bed," said Kirov indignantly. "I used to have a room to myself." He pulled the pipe from his pocket. With jerky and impatient hands, he stuffed it with tobacco.

"You're too young for a pipe," said Anton.

Kirov held it out admiringly. "The bowl is made from English briar wood."

"Pipes are for old men," yawned Anton.

Kirov glared at him. "Comrade Stalin smokes a pipe!"

But the comment was lost on Anton. He had fallen asleep, his steady breaths like the sound of a pendulum swinging slowly through the air above them.

Pekkala dozed off, hearing the click of Kirov's teeth on the pipe stem and breathing the smell of Balkan tobacco, which smelled to him like a new pair of leather shoes when they're just taken out of the box. Then Kirov's voice jolted him awake.

"I was wondering," the young man said.

"What?" growled Pekkala.

"If it is the Romanovs down at the bottom of that mine, those bodies have been lying there for years."

"Yes."

"There will be nothing left of them. How can you investigate a murder when you have no remains to investigate?"

"There is always something to investigate," replied Pekkala, and as he spoke these words the face of Dr. Bandelayev rose from the darkness of his mind.

"He is the best there is," Vassileyev had told Pekkala, "at a job no sane man would ever want to do."

Dr. Bandelayev was completely bald. His head resembled a shiny pink lightbulb. As if to compensate, he sported a thick walrus-like mustache.

On a hot, muggy afternoon in late July, Vassileyev brought Pekkala to Bandelayev's laboratory.

There was a smell he recognized instantly—a sharp, sweet odor that cut right through his senses. He knew it from his father's basement, where the work of undertaking was carried out.

Vassileyev held a handkerchief over his mouth and nose. "Good God, Bandelayev, how can you stand it in here?"

"Breathe it in!" ordered Bandelayev. He wore a knee-length lab coat embroidered in red with his name and the word OSTEOLOGIST. *"Breathe in the smell of death."*

Vassileyev turned to Pekkala. "He's all yours," the Major said, his voice muffled by the handkerchief. Then he strode out of the room as quickly as he could.

Pekkala looked around the laboratory. Although one wall of windows looked out onto the main quadrangle of the University of Petrograd, the view had been blocked by shelves of glass jars containing human body parts, preserved in a brownish fluid that looked like tea. He saw hands and feet, the raw ends frayed, with stumps of bone emerging from the puckered flesh. In other jars, coils of intestine wound together like miniature tornadoes. On the other side of this narrow corridor, bones had been laid out on metal trays, looking like puzzles which had been abandoned.

"Indeed they are puzzles!" said Bandelayev, when Pekkala mentioned this to him. "All of this, everything I do, is the discipline of puzzles."

In the days ahead, Pekkala struggled to keep up with Bandelayev's teaching.

"The stench of a rotting human is no different than that of a dead deer lying by the side of a road," said Bandelayev, "and that is why I don't believe in God." The doctor spoke quickly, his words sticking together, depriving him of breath until he was forced to pause and gasp in a lungful of fresh air.

But there was no fresh air in Bandelayev's lab. The windows remained closed, and plumber's tape had been used to seal them.

"Insects!" said Bandelayev, by way of explanation. "This is not merely a shop of rotten meat, as some of my colleagues have described it. Here, all facets of decay are controlled. One fly could ruin weeks of work." Bandelayev did not like to sit. It seemed an act of laziness to him. So when he lectured Pekkala, he stood behind a tall table littered with bones,

which he would lift from their trays and hold out for Pekkala to identify. Or he would plunge his hand into a jar and remove a pale knot of flesh, commanding Pekkala to name it, while brown preserving fluid ran the length of his fingers, trickling down his sleeve.

Once, Bandelayev held up a skull pierced through the forehead by a small, neat round hole, the result of a bullet fired point-blank into the victim. "Do you know that in the summer months, blowflies will settle on a body in a matter of minutes. They will concentrate in the mouth, the nose, the eyes, or in the wound." Bandelayev stuck his pinkie into the hole in the forehead. "In a few hours, there can be as many as half a million eggs laid on the corpse. In a single day the maggots which hatch from these eggs can reduce a full-grown man to half his body size. In a week"—he jerked his head to the side, a movement he used for emphasis but which appeared more like an involuntary nervous twitch—"there might be nothing left but bones."

Having seen many bodies laid out on his father's marble work slab, Pekkala was not squeamish. He did not flinch when Bandelayev thrust a lung into his hands or handed him a box of human finger bones. The hardest part for Pekkala, accustomed to his father's quiet reverence for the bodies in his care, was Bandelayev's total disregard for the people whose corpses he alternately pulled apart and reassembled, allowed to rot or pickled in preserving fluid.

His father would not have liked Bandelayev, Pekkala decided. There was something in Bandelayev's breathless enthusiasm which would have struck his father as undignified.

When Pekkala mentioned that his father had been an undertaker, Bandelayev seemed equally unimpressed. "Quaint," the doctor said dismissively, "and ultimately irrelevant."

"And why is that?" asked Pekkala.

"Undertaking," said Bandelayev, "is the creation of an illusion. It is a magic show. Make the dead appear at peace. Make the dead appear asleep." He glanced at Pekkala, as much as if to ask—and what could be the point of that? *"Osteology is the exploration of death." Bandelayev*

wrapped his lips around those words as if no person could resist the urge to pull apart a corpse with bare hands and a blade.

"Alive," he continued, "you are of little interest to me, Pekkala. But come back to me dead, and then I promise you we will become properly acquainted."

Pekkala learned to differentiate between the skulls of women—narrow mouth, pointed chin, streamlined forehead, sharp edges where the eye sockets met the forehead—and the skulls of men, immediately identifiable by the bony bump at the base of the skull.

"Identity!" said Bandelayev. "Sex, age, stature."

He made Pekkala chant it like a spell.

"The external occipital protuberance!" announced Bandelayev, as if introducing a dignitary to a gathering of royals.

Pekkala learned to tell the forward-angled teeth of an African from those of a Caucasian, which grew perpendicular to the jaw.

He studied the zigzag lines of cranial sutures, rising like lightning bolts over the dome of a skull, while Bandelayev leaned over his shoulder, muttering, "What is it saying? What is it telling you?"

At the end of each lesson, Bandelayev assigned Pekkala books by such men as the Roman Vitruvius, from which he learned that the length of a person's outstretched arms corresponded to his height and that the length of a hand corresponded to one-tenth of a body's length.

Another day, Bandelayev sent him home with a translation of the thirteenth-century Chinese doctor Sung Tz'u's book, The Washing Away of Wrongs, *in which the devouring of a body by maggots was described in language Pekkala had previously thought was reserved only for religious rapture.*

Soon the reek of death no longer bothered him, even though it lingered in his clothes long after he had left Bandelayev's laboratory.

Throughout the weeks they spent together, Bandelayev returned over and over to the question "What is it saying?"

One day, Bandelayev was teaching a lesson on the effect of fire upon a corpse. "The hands will clench," he said, "arms bend, knees bend. A body on fire resembles the stance of a boxer in a fight. But suppose you find a body which has been burned but discover that the arms are straight. What does that say?"

"It says," answered Pekkala, "that perhaps his hands were bound behind his back."

Bandelayev smiled. "Now you are speaking the language of the dead."

To Pekkala's surprise, he realized that Bandelayev was right. Suddenly from every jar and tray, voices seemed to clamor at him, telling the story of their deaths.

The flames had burned down on the floor of the barn. Poppy-colored embers glowed among the ashes.

Outside, lightning flashed across the sky.

"Who is Grodek?" asked Kirov.

Pekkala breathed in sharply. "Grodek? What do you know about him?"

"I heard your brother say you put a man named Grodek behind bars."

Facing away from Kirov, Pekkala's eyes blinked silver in the dark. "Grodek was the most dangerous man I ever met."

"What made him so dangerous?"

"The question is not 'what' but 'who.' And the answer to that is the Tsar's own Secret Police."

"The Okhrana? But that would mean he was working for you, not against you."

"That was the plan," replied Pekkala, "but it went wrong. It was General Zubatov, head of the Moscow Okhrana, who came up with the idea. Zubatov wanted to organize a terrorist group whose sole purpose was to be the assassination of the Tsar."

"But Zubatov was loyal to the Tsar!" Kirov protested. "Why on earth would Zubatov want to assassinate him?"

As the sound of Kirov's voice echoed around the barn, Anton grumbled, muttered something unintelligible, and then fell back asleep.

"The group would be a fake. Zubatov's plan was to draw in as many would-be assassins as he could. Then, when the time was right, he would have them all arrested. You see, in ordinary police work, it is necessary to wait until a crime has taken place before taking people into custody. But in organizations like the Okhrana, the task is sometimes to anticipate the crimes before they have happened."

"So all the time these people believed they were working for a terrorist cell, they would in fact be working for Zubatov?"

"Exactly."

The young Commissar's eyes looked glazed as he struggled to fathom the depth of such deception. "Was Grodek a part of this cell?"

"More than a part of it," replied Pekkala. "Grodek was the one in charge. He was younger than you. His father was a distant cousin of the Tsar. The man had failed in business many times, but instead of accepting responsibility for his failures, he chose to blame the Tsar. Grodek believed that his family had been denied the privileges they deserved. When his father committed suicide after piling up more debts than he could ever repay, Grodek held the Tsar responsible."

"Why wouldn't he," said Kirov, "if he only knew what his father had told him?"

"Precisely, and as Grodek grew into a young man, he made no secret of his hatred for the Romanovs. He was the perfect candidate for leading an assassination attempt."

"But how could a person like that be persuaded to work for the Okhrana? That seems impossible to me."

"That is exactly why Zubatov chose him. First, he had Grodek arrested in a public place. News of this soon spread. A young man, grabbed off the street and roughly shoved into a waiting car. Anyone witnessing such a thing, and Zubatov made sure there were many of these, would feel sympathy for Grodek. But once Zubatov had him in custody, the real work began."

"What did he do to the boy?"

"He blindfolded Grodek, put him in a car, and drove him to a secret location. When Zubatov removed Grodek's blindfold, the Tsar himself was standing there in front of them."

"What was the point of that?" asked Kirov.

"Zubatov brought Grodek face-to-face with a man who had become only a symbol to him. But to see him there, as a man of flesh and blood, instead of what Grodek's father had made him out to be, that was the beginning of the process. The Tsar explained his own version of events. Together, they looked over his father's record books, which showed, in the father's own handwriting, how his family's wealth had been squandered. Of course, Grodek had never seen any of these things before. It left a deep impression on them both to be reminded that they were part of the same family."

"And was Grodek convinced by all this?"

"Yes," replied Pekkala. "And it was then that Zubatov explained his plan to Grodek. He was to be what is known as an 'agent provocateur' and would act as the ringleader of this fake terrorist cell. It was extremely dangerous. If any of these assassins caught wind of the fact that Grodek was really working for the Okhrana, his life would have been over in a second. But young men are attracted to danger, and when Grodek agreed to lead this band of terrorists, Zubatov believed that he had chosen wisely. In reality, it turned out to be the greatest mistake of his life."

"Why?" Kirov was fascinated.

"Over the next year," continued Pekkala, "Grodek underwent training with the Special Section of the Okhrana. In order to be convincing as a terrorist, he had to be able to behave like one. They taught him how to make bombs, how to shoot, how to fight with a knife, just as they taught me. Soon after the terrorist cell was activated, people came forward to enlist. Grodek was a natural. He possessed a kind of energy that drew people to him. In the months ahead, while the membership of this cell continued to grow, Grodek surpassed every goal Zubatov had set for him. He never missed a meeting with his contacts, and the information he supplied was so accurate that Zubatov spoke of Grodek as the person who would one day take his place at the head of the Okhrana. But Zubatov had made one great miscalculation. After proving to Grodek that the blame for his family's misfortune belonged entirely with his father, Zubatov had assumed that Grodek's hatred of the Tsar had been extinguished. What Zubatov did not realize was that Grodek, after seeing the evidence laid before him, had decided to blame them both.

"In the meantime, Grodek had also made a mistake. He had fallen in love with one of the women he recruited. Her name was Maria Balka. She was fifteen years older than Grodek and, in many ways, more dangerous than Grodek himself. She had already carried out several killings in the name of various anarchist groups. Grodek kept their relationship a secret from Zubatov, and when Zubatov mentioned to Grodek that Maria Balka would certainly receive the death penalty after she was arrested along with the other members of Grodek's organization, it made what happened next almost inevitable."

"What did happen?" asked Kirov.

"Zubatov decided that the trap could only be sprung after an attempt on the life of the Tsar. This would provide justification for the arrests which would follow. Of course, it was arranged that Grodek would carry out the attempt. It would be made to appear that the Tsar had actually been assassinated. Other members of the terrorist cell would be stationed nearby, in order to witness the staged killing. The assassins would then rendezvous at their safe house, where they would be arrested by agents of the Okhrana.

"The attack was to take place as the Tsar took an evening walk around the grounds of the Summer Palace. Zubatov made sure that the Tsar stuck to a regular route on these walks, in order to make the terrorists confident of success. The Tsar would be shot as he passed between the gates which surrounded the palace and the Lamski Pond. This was a relatively narrow area, which offered the Tsar no protection. Firing through the gates, Grodek would only be a few paces from the Tsar."

"But wouldn't it seem suspicious that the Tsar would be out walking by himself?"

"Not at all," replied Pekkala. "He set aside a portion of each day to exercise. Sometimes it was riding, sometimes swimming, but often he would walk the grounds of the palace, whatever the weather, and at those times he insisted on being alone."

"But what about the other assassins? Wouldn't they be armed as well?"

"They were instructed to fire only if Grodek missed his target. The Tsar would be seen to fall, struck by several rounds, but of course only blank ammunition would be used.

"At this point, no one had any doubts about Grodek's loyalty to the Okhrana. After all, he had delivered the names of every member of the organization he had helped to create. He had betrayed them all, as he had promised to do from the beginning.

"What nobody in the Okhrana knew was that Grodek had switched out the blanks for real bullets.

"The night of the shooting, everything went like clockwork. The terrorists were allowed to approach the palace grounds. They hid. The Tsar set out on his walk. Meanwhile, dozens of Okhrana agents waited to swoop down on the safe house. The Tsar reached the narrow walkway between the gates and the Lamski Pond.

The sun had set. A cool wind blew across the pond. Grodek stepped out of the shadows. The Tsar paused. He had heard the sound of branches rustling. Grodek stepped up to the gate, reached between the bars, the gun in his hand. The Tsar never moved. He stood there, as if he didn't understand what was happening."

"And he missed?" stammered Kirov. "Grodek missed at a range of three paces?"

Pekkala shook his head. "Grodek did not miss. He emptied the cylinder. All six shots found their mark."

Now Kirov jumped to his feet. "Do you mean to tell me that he shot the Tsar six times and did not kill him?"

"The man Grodek killed was not the Tsar."

"Then who . . ." Kirov narrowed his eyes as the truth dawned on him. "You mean a double? Grodek shot a double?"

"Zubatov made many mistakes, but he would not go so far as to actually endanger the life of the Tsar. That was the one part of the plan Zubatov never discussed with Grodek. When Grodek pulled the trigger, he did not know he was killing a double."

"But still a man died," Kirov insisted.

"Somebody usually does," replied Pekkala.

Pekkala and the Tsar stood in the darkness on the balcony of the Palace, looking out over the grounds. They could see the Chinese Bridge and Parnassus Hill. In the Gribok gardens, straight ahead of them, leaves rustled in the night breeze.

At that moment, they knew, the Tsar's double would be walking just inside the gates of the Palace grounds, between the Great Pond and the Parkovaya Road.

Neither man had spoken for a while.

The air was tense as they waited for the shooting to begin.

"Can you imagine how it is," asked the Tsar, "that I cannot venture out beyond the gates of this palace without knowing I would probably be

killed? I am the ruler of a country along whose streets I cannot walk alone." He waved his hand back and forth out over the grounds, in a way which reminded Pekkala of a priest swinging an incense holder. "Is it worth all this? Is it worth anything at all?"

"It will be over soon, Excellency," said Pekkala. "By tomorrow, the terrorists will have been arrested."

"This is about more than just one group of terrorists," replied the Tsar. "It's the war which has brought us to this. I think back to the day it was declared, when I stood on the veranda of the Winter Palace, looking out across that sea of people who had come to show their support. I felt that we were indestructible. The notion of surrender had not even crossed my mind. I could never have imagined the defeats we would suffer. Tannenburg. The Masurian Lakes. The names of those places still echo in my mind. I should have listened to Rasputin."

"What has this to do with him?" Pekkala had met the Siberian mystic, who supposedly possessed the magical ability to cure the hemophilia that afflicted the Tsar's only son, Alexei. In Pekkala's judgment, Rasputin was a man who understood his limitations. It was the Tsar, and even more so the Tsarina, who had demanded from Rasputin a wisdom he did not possess. He had been called upon to judge matters of state about which he had little knowledge. The best he could do, most of the time, was to offer vague words of comfort. But the Romanovs had fastened on those words, stripping them of vagueness, turning them to prophecy. It was no wonder Rasputin had become so hated by those who sought the favor of the Tsar.

Pekkala had been there, on a bitterly cold morning in December of 1916, when the Petrograd police fished Rasputin's body from the Neva River. Rasputin had been invited to a private party at the house of Prince Yusupov. There he was fed cakes which, with the help of a doctor named Lazoviert, had been laced with enough potassium cyanide to have killed an elephant. When the poison appeared to have no effect, Yusupov's accomplice, a government minister named Purishkyevich, shot Rasputin several times and stabbed him in the throat. Then they both rolled him in a heavy carpet and dumped him in the water where, in spite of everything which had been done to him, Rasputin died by drowning.

"Grief without end," said the Tsar. "That is what Rasputin said the war would bring us. And look how right he was."

"All wars bring grief, Excellency."

The Tsar turned to him, trembling. "God spoke through that man, Pekkala! Who speaks through you, I'd like to know."

"You do, Excellency."

For a moment, the Tsar looked stunned. "Forgive me, Pekkala," he said. "I did not have the right to speak to you that way."

"Nothing to forgive," replied Pekkala. It was the only lie he ever told the Tsar.

KIROV'S VOICE SNAPPED PEKKALA BACK TO THE PRESENT.

"What about Grodek?" asked Kirov. "What became of him?"

"When Okhrana agents surrounded the safe house, a gunfight broke out. The Okhrana found themselves under fire from weapons they themselves had supplied to Grodek. After the battle, of the thirty-six members of the terrorist cell, the Okhrana found only four survivors among the dead. Grodek was not one of them, and neither was Maria Balka. The two of them had simply disappeared. That was when the Tsar sent for me, with orders to arrest Balka and Grodek before they had the chance to kill again." He let out a long sigh. "And I failed."

"But you did find him!"

"Not before he had killed again. I tracked them down to a small lodging house on Maximilian Lane in the Kasan district of Petersburg. The owner of the house had remarked on the difference in age between the woman and the man. He assumed they were simply having an affair, a thing proprietors of places like that are sometimes obliged to overlook. But they kept bringing boxes into their room, and when the owner asked what was in them, Balka told him it was only books. Now people who are having an affair do not spend their days shut away and reading books. That was when the landlord notified the police. Soon we had the house surrounded. I waited at the back of the house. Okhrana agents went in the front, expecting that Balka and Grodek would try to leave through the rear, where I would apprehend them.

"Unfortunately, having been trained in police work, Grodek noticed the agents moving into place. When the agents kicked down the door to the room, they set off a bomb which tore away the whole front of the building. Grodek had made it, killing the same people who had trained him in the art of bomb making. We lost four agents and sixteen civilians in the blast. I myself was knocked almost unconscious. By the time I got up, Balka and Grodek were running out of the back of the building.

"I chased them along Moika Street, by the banks of the Neva. It was the middle of winter. The streets were ankle deep in slush, and snow had piled up on the sides of the road. I could not get a clear shot at them. Eventually, Balka slipped. She must have broken her ankle. I caught up with them on the Potsuleyev Bridge. Police were coming from the other way. There was no cover. I had them in my sights. They had no place to go." Pekkala paused. He closed his eyes and pinched the bridge of his nose. "And what I saw next, I have never been able to get out of my head. They stopped at the crest of the bridge. I could hear the police shouting at them from the other side. Balka was obviously hurt. Grodek had been alternately carrying her and dragging her for several blocks, and he had become exhausted. It was clear that they couldn't go on. I called to them. I said it was time to give up. Grodek looked at me for a long time. Balka stood beside him with her arm over his shoulder. Then Grodek embraced her, lifted her up and set her on the stone rail of the bridge. The water below was choked with ice. I told him there was no escape that way."

"What did he do?" asked Kirov.

"He kissed her. And then he pulled a gun and shot her in the head."

Kirov rocked back. "He shot her? I thought he was in love with her."

"I did not understand how far he was prepared to go. Maria Balka fell into the river and drifted under the ice."

"And Grodek? Did he surrender?"

"Only after he had failed to kill himself. He put the gun to his own head and pulled the trigger, but the cylinder had jammed."

"Why didn't he jump?" Kirov asked. "He might have been able to escape."

"Grodek was afraid of heights. Even though the distance to the water was only three or four times the height of a man, Grodek became paralyzed by fear. He tried to rush past me, and I knocked him out with the butt of my gun. It put a gash in his forehead. For the entire length of his trial, he refused to wear a bandage. The scar, with its line of dark stitches, looked like a purple centipede crawling up into his hairline. Every day as he left the proceedings on the way back to his holding cell, Grodek would shout to the journalists who had gathered outside the courthouse that the police had tortured him."

"And Balka? What happened to her body?"

"We never found it. In the winter that river runs fast below the ice. The current must have carried her out into the Baltic Sea. I had a team of divers search that river more than a dozen times." Pekkala shook his head. "She had vanished without a trace."

"And Grodek? After what he had done, why did they put him behind bars? Why did he not receive the death penalty?"

"He did, at first, but the Tsar overruled the decision of the judges. He believed that Grodek had been a pawn, first of his father and then of Zubatov. Grodek was still a young man. In a different world, the Tsar felt, it might have been his own son facing execution. But it was clear to the Tsar that Grodek could never go free. So he was locked up for the rest of his life with no chance of parole in the Trubetskoy Bastion of the Peter and Paul Fortress."

"But I thought all prisoners were released during the Revolution."

"Political prisoners, yes, but even the Bolsheviks would have known better than to set free a man like Grodek."

"What made Grodek so different from the other killers they set free?"

Pekkala thought for a moment before answering.

"Almost anyone," said Pekkala, "can be driven to kill if the circumstances are forced upon them. But there is a difference between those people who react to situations and those who create the situation for which murder is the outcome. Those are the ones we have to fear, Kirov, because they enjoy the act of killing. And in all my years as a detective, I never met a killer who enjoyed what he did more than Grodek."

The fire wheezed and crackled.

"Where will you go when you are free?" asked Kirov.

"Paris," he replied.

"Why there?"

"If you have to ask that question, you have never been to Paris. Besides, I have unfinished business there." It felt strange to think of the future. Each time he watched the sun go down in the valley of Krasnagolyana, he knew he had outpaced the odds of his survival. He had measured his survival in increments of days, not daring to hope for more. The idea that he might stretch those increments from days to weeks, to months and even years, filled him with confusion. It took Pekkala a moment to realize that what he was feeling was actually hope, an emotion he had once believed that he would never feel again.

At last, Kirov's breathing grew heavy and deep.

Lightning flashed in the distance.

Pekkala slipped away into the river of his dreams, while thunder rolled across the clouds.

BY SUNRISE THE NEXT MORNING, THEY WERE ON THE MOVE AGAIN.

Their route intersected with a road known as the Moscow Highway which, in spite of its grand name, was only a two-lane strip of dirt laid out across the undulating steppe.

While turmeric-colored dust blew in through the open windows, Anton sat with the map, squinting at the thumbprint whorls of hills, the veins and arteries of roads, and the dense bone mass of forests.

By noon, they had reached the intersection Anton was looking for. Without any signposts, it resembled nothing more than a horizontal crucifix of mud. "Turn here, Kirov," he ordered. "Turn here." And then again. "Turn here."

Their course took them away along the edge of a shallow stream and through a grove of white birch trees before the ground opened out into a field. The woods which ringed the field were dark and gloomy-looking. Kirov eased the car along an old wagon track which cut across the field, the Emka's bumper swishing through the tall grass.

An old shack stood in the middle of this field, a tin chimney leaning drunkenly out of its roof.

Anton turned his map one way and then another, struggling to get his bearings. "It's over by that house, I think."

The car's springs creaked as it lumbered over the bumpy ground. When they reached the far end of the field, the three men got out and started looking for the mine shaft.

It did not take them long to find it. The shaft was little more than a hole in the ground, about five paces wide, above which perched a rusted metal pulley. Clumps of luminous green grass hung over the edges of the hole. The first section of the mine shaft had been neatly bricked, like the sides of a well. Beneath that was bare rock and earth, from which tiny rivulets of water seeped down into the black. Bolted to the walls on either side were two rusted iron ladders. Most of the rungs were missing. The bolts which held the ladders to the wall were loose. There was no hope of using them to get down into the mine.

"Are you really going down there?" asked Kirov. "It's pitch-black."

"I have a flashlight," said Anton. He removed it from the glove compartment of the car. The flashlight had a leather casing around its metal frame and a goggle-eyed crystal for its lens. He slung it from a cord around his neck.

Searching for a way to lower Pekkala into the shaft, Anton examined the pulley. The twisted threads of cable wound onto it were rusted together, beads of water resting in places where oil still clung to the metal. Sticking from the side of the drum was a large, two-man hand crank for raising and lowering the cable into the mine shaft. He took hold of the crank, pulled it, and the lever snapped off in his hands. "So much for that," he muttered.

But Kirov was already removing a length of hemp rope from the trunk of the car, which had been placed there in case the vehicle broke down and needed to be towed. He looped one end around the Emka's bumper, then walked to the edge of the pit and threw the rest of the coil down into the shaft.

The three men listened as the rope unraveled into the darkness. Then they heard a wet slap as it reached the ground.

Pekkala stood at the edge of the pit, the rope in his hand. He seemed to hesitate.

"Are you sure you want to do this?" Anton asked.

"Give me the flashlight," Pekkala said.

After Anton had handed it to him, Pekkala leaned back on the rope, testing its strength. The hemp creaked around the bumper but held firm. While Kirov lifted the rope, so that it would not drag at the edge of the mine shaft, Pekkala stepped to the edge, then leaned out backwards over the emptiness. With his hands white-knuckled around the line, he stepped down into the shaft. In a moment he was gone.

The two men on the surface watched the flashlight's glow yawing back and forth across Pekkala's chest, one moment illuminating his feet, then the rope, then the slippery sides of the mine shaft. The light grew smaller and smaller, and the sound of Pekkala's breaths faded to a hollow echo.

"He looked afraid," said Kirov.

"He is afraid," replied Anton.

"Of the bodies?"

"The bodies don't scare him. It's being closed in that he can't stand. And he'll never forgive me for that."

"Why is it your fault?"

"It was a game," said Anton. "At least it started out that way. Once, when we were children, we went to a place our father had made us promise never to go. Deep in the woods behind our house, there was a crematory oven which he used for his funeral business. It had a tall chimney, as tall as the tops of the trees, and the oven itself was like a huge iron coffin built up on a pedestal of bricks. On those days when he used the oven, I would go to my bedroom window and see smoke rising above the tops of the trees. Our father had described the oven to us, but I had never seen it for myself. I wanted to, but I was far too scared to go alone. I persuaded my brother to come with me. He would never have gone otherwise. He was too obedient for his own good, but he is younger than me, and at that age I was able to convince him.

"It was an autumn day when we went to see the oven. We knew no one would miss us. We often disappeared for hours at a time.

"The ground was hard. The first snow had fallen, just a dusting of it, collecting in the shells of dried-out leaves. We kept looking back, expecting to see our father coming down the trail behind us, but after a while we realized we were alone.

"There was a bend in the trail and then the oven was suddenly in front of us. It was smaller than I'd thought it would be. And the area around it was very tidy. Wood for the fuel had been neatly cut and stacked. The ground was even swept, and my father had left a broom to prop open the oven door. Even though the sun was out, the oven stood beneath the trees and it seemed dark in there, and cold.

"I took the broom and opened the door to the oven. Inside, I saw a long tray, like the frame of a stretcher. The chamber was gray with dust, but it had been swept as clean as it could be.

"That sort of thing mattered to my father. Even though nobody else ever came to the oven, as far as he knew anyway, he needed the place to be orderly and dignified.

"Almost as soon as we arrived, my brother wanted to go back. He was sure our father would figure out that we'd been here.

"That was when I suggested that one of us should go inside the oven, just to see what it was like.

"At first my brother refused.

"I called him a coward. I said we would draw straws for it. I told him if I was willing to do it, he should be willing, too.

"Eventually, I got him to agree."

"And Pekkala drew the short straw?" asked Kirov.

"He thought he did," replied Anton. "The truth is, after I saw that he had drawn the long straw, I squeezed it so hard between my fingers that it broke in half, so what he drew was only half the proper length.

"I told him he couldn't back down or else he'd spend the rest of his life knowing that he'd proved himself to be a coward.

"He crawled into the oven. I made him go headfirst. And then I closed the door on him."

"You did what?"

"It was only going to be for a second. Just to give him a scare. But there was a spring lock on the door and I couldn't get it open. I tried. I honestly did. But I wasn't strong enough.

"I could hear him shouting and banging on the door. He was trying to get out. I panicked. I ran home. It was getting dark. I arrived home just as my mother was putting supper on the table.

"At the supper table, when my parents asked me where my brother was I said I didn't know.

"My father was looking at me. He must have known I was hiding something.

"Hold out your hands, he said, and when I held them out he grasped them hard and stared at them. I remember he even lowered his face to my fingertips and smelled them. Then he ran out of the house.

"I watched the lantern he was carrying disappear down the trail towards the oven.

"An hour later he was back with my brother."

"What happened to you then?" asked Kirov.

"Nothing," replied Anton. "My brother said he had shut the door on himself. Of course, it wasn't even possible to lock that door from the inside. My father must have known it, but he pretended to believe my brother. All he did was make us swear never to go back to the oven."

"And your brother? He never took revenge for what you'd done?"

"Revenge?" Anton laughed. "His whole life since he joined the Finnish Regiment has been vengeance for what happened between us."

"I would have killed you," said Kirov.

Anton turned to look at him. His face was layered in shadow. "That would have been less cruel than what my brother did to me."

Halfway down the mine shaft, Pekkala clung to the rope.

It was cold down there and damp and musty-smelling, but the sweat was coursing off his face. The walls appeared to spin around him, like a whirlpool made of stone. Memories of being in the oven swirled inside his head. He remembered reaching out into the darkness, his fingers brushing against the blunt teeth of the burner nozzles which hung from the ceiling of the oven. He had pressed his hands against them, as if to stop the flames from shooting out. At first, he had tried not to breathe the smell in, as if his lungs might filter out those particles of dust. But it was no use. He had to breathe, and as the air grew thin inside that metal cylinder, Pekkala had to fill his lungs as deeply as he could, and all the while that smell poured into him, sifting through his blood like drops of ink in water.

Pekkala looked up. The mouth of the mine shaft was a disk of pale blue surrounded by the blackness of the tunnel walls. For minutes, he fought against the urge to climb out again. Waves of panic traveled through him, and he hung there until they subsided. Then he lowered himself down to the mine floor.

His feet touched the ground, sinking into decades of accumulated dust. Pieces of rotting wooden support beams, toothed with nails, littered the floor.

Pekkala let go of the rope and kneaded the blood back into his hands. Then he took hold of the flashlight and shone it into the darkness.

The first thing he saw was a section of ladder which had fallen to the ground. It stood propped against the wall, the rusted metal glistening black and orange.

The space was wide here, but the way into the belly of the mine soon narrowed to a point where the tunnel split into two and pairs of rusty iron rails curved into blackness. Both of the tunnel entrances were blocked by walls of rock. Pekkala knew that mines were sometimes closed before they had been completely dug out. The miners had probably collapsed the tunnels on purpose, to protect whatever minerals remained in the ground in case they ever returned. The wagons which had run along these rails were parked in an alcove. Their sides showed dents from hard use, the metal smeared with whitish-yellow powder. Pekkala felt a tremor of pity for the men who had worked in these tunnels, starved of daylight, the weight of the earth poised above their crooked backs.

Pekkala played the flashlight around this stone chamber, wondering where these bodies were. It occurred to him that perhaps his brother had been wrong. Perhaps the madman had worked in this mine years before and had invented the whole story, simply to get attention. This train of thought was still unraveling in his head, when he turned, sweeping the beam into the darkness, and realized he was standing right beside them.

They lay as they had fallen, piled in a grotesque heap of bones and cloth and shoes and hair. There were multiple corpses. In such a jumble of decay, he could not tell how many.

He had come down on one side of the mine opening. The bodies must have landed on the other side.

As the flashlight's beam wavered, like a candle flame boxed by the wind, Pekkala's instincts screamed at him to get out of this place. But he knew he couldn't leave, not yet, even with fear sucking the breath out of his lungs.

Pekkala forced himself to hold his ground, reminding himself that he had seen many bodies in the past, plenty of them in worse condition than these. But those corpses had been anonymous to him, in death as they had been in life. If this sad tangle of limbs did indeed belong to the Romanovs, then this was unlike anything he'd witnessed before.

A sound startled him, echoing off the stone walls. It took Pekkala a moment to realize that it was his brother's voice, calling down from above.

"Did you find anything?"

"Yes," he called up.

There was a long pause.

"And?" his brother's voice came down.

"I don't know yet."

Silence from above.

Pekkala turned back to the bodies. Down here in the mine, the process of decomposition had been slowed. The clothing was largely intact and there were no flies or other insects, whose larvae would have eaten the corpses down to the bone if the bodies had been left above ground. Neither was there any evidence of rats or mice having gnawed upon the dead. The depth of the mine and the vertical entrance had prevented them from reaching the bodies. He did not know what had been mined here. Whatever it was might also have had a preserving effect.

The victims appeared to be partially mummified. Their skin had turned a greenish brown, nearly translucent, drawn tight over the bones and filmed with mold. He had seen corpses like this before—people frozen in ice or buried in soil with a high acid content, like peat bogs. Pekkala also recalled a case in which a killer stuffed a body up a factory chimney. Over the years in which the victim remained hidden, the body became smoked to the consistency of shoe leather. It was remarkably well preserved, but as soon as police removed it, the corpse decayed at an astonishing rate.

While these bodies remained intact in their present state, he knew that they would also deteriorate very quickly if any attempt was made to move them above ground. He was glad that the decision had been made to leave them here until a properly equipped removal team could be brought in.

At first, Pekkala touched nothing.

On the top of the pile was a woman, lying on her back with her arms thrown out to the sides. From the way she had landed, Pekkala judged that the fall would probably have killed her, but he could see clearly that she'd been dead before she fell. Her skull had been shattered by a bullet between the eyes and the base of the nose, penetrating that part of the brain known as the dura oblongata. The woman would have died instantly. Whoever did this, Pekkala realized, had known exactly what they were doing. But there was more to it than simply knowing how to kill a person. As Vassileyev had drilled into him, the way a murder was committed told a great deal about the killer. Even in cases in which bodies were horribly mutilated, usually with knives, most murderers avoided harming the faces of their victims. Those who used guns to kill their victims usually shot them several times, and most often aimed at the chest. In cases where a pistol was used by someone inexperienced with firearms, the bodies often showed multiple and random impact wounds, the shooters having underestimated how inaccurate those weapons were. Pekkala knew of people who had escaped from shots unleashed at almost point-blank range by untrained marksmen.

Killings carried out by skilled gunmen were usually classified as executions. These, too, left a particular signature. Between a man's ears at the back of the head was a small knot of bone—the external occipital protuberance. Executioners were taught to press the muzzle of their guns exactly over that place, allowing them to kill with a single shot. Pekkala had seen many such executions, carried out by both sides during the opening stages of the Revolution. The killers left their victims facedown in fields, in ditches, or in banks of snow, hands tied behind their backs, their foreheads blown away by the exiting bullet.

One reason for this method was that executioners did not have to look into the faces of their victims. But whoever killed this woman had stood directly in front of her. Pekkala knew that such a method required a particular coldness of blood.

Already, in his mind, he began to draw a portrait of the killers, assuming there had been more than one. They were almost certainly male. Women were not usually employed in execution teams, although there were exceptions to this. The Reds had made use of women in their death squads, and these particular women had proven to be more bloodthirsty than any of their male counterparts. He recalled the Bolshevik assassin Rosa Schwartz, responsible for the deaths of hundreds of former Tsarist officers. After her killing spree, she was declared a national hero and toured the country as "Red Rosa," carrying a bunch of roses and wearing a white dress, like a virgin on her wedding day. Another detail which pointed towards these killers being men was the fact that the skulls all bore exit marks, indicating the use of a large-caliber pistol. Women, even those in death squads, tended to use guns of small caliber.

Now Pekkala examined the clothing, bringing the flashlight close to the woman's body so that he could examine the material of her clothes. The first thing which caught his eyes was the tiny mother-of-pearl buttons on her dress, which must once have been red but now appeared as a blotchy pink. His heart sank. These were the garments of wealthy people. Otherwise those buttons would have been made of bone or wood. Long, clumped strands of hair draped over the clothing.

On the bared arms, he could see where fat deposits had turned into adipocere, the soapy, grayish-yellow substance known as grave wax.

He saw shoes, the leather crimped and twisted, the tiny nails which had once held them together jutting now like little teeth from the soles. Again he felt the weight of growing certainty.

This was not the footwear of a laborer, not the type that one would find out in the countryside and far too elegant for the wilds of Siberia.

At that moment, the flashlight shuddered and died.

The darkness that enveloped him was so complete it seemed to him that he had suddenly gone blind. Pekkala's breathing grew rapid and shallow. He fought against the panic which swirled around him like a living thing.

Swearing, he shook the flashlight and the light popped back on again.

Wiping the sweat from his face, Pekkala returned to his work.

Having examined all he could without disturbing the scene, he now reached out and touched what lay before him.

The tips of his fingers were shaking.

He tried to maintain emotional distance from the corpses, as Dr. Bandelayev had taught him. "Think of them as puzzles, not as people," the doctor had said.

Working his hands in under the back of the woman, fingers inching between the layers of damp and moldy cloth which separated the corpses, he lifted her body. The weight of it was still significant, unlike the corpse he'd pulled from the chimney, which had felt so light it reminded him of a Japanese lantern.

As he shifted the body to the floor, so that he could lay the corpses side by side, the woman's skull snapped off the spine. It rolled off the other side of the pile and cracked against the stone floor with a sound like a dropped earthenware pot. He walked around the side of the pile and retrieved the skull, lifting it gently from the ground. It was there, in the beam of the flashlight, that he saw the sleeve of a man's garment, a shriveled hand hanging from it like the claw of a bird.

He was not able to immediately identify the woman who lay at the top of the heap. Her corpse bore no distinguishing marks. But as he stared at the hand, he felt a shudder of certainty. Pekkala had learned to trust his instinct, even if it had not yet been tested against the checklist of rational thought.

Pekkala placed the skull of the woman with the rest of her body and moved on to the next one.

Over the next half hour, he untangled the bodies of three more women from the pile and laid them out. All had been shot in the face.

By now, there was little doubt in his mind that these were the Romanov sisters—Olga, Maria, Anastasia, and Tatiana.

Beneath lay a fifth woman, undoubtedly the Tsarina, due to the size of her body and the more mature cut of her clothes, who had also been shot in the head. Unlike the others, however, she had been shot from behind. The exiting bullet had blown away the forehead, exposing a massive cavity in the skull. She had died this way, he reasoned, as she sought to shield one of her children from the killer's gun.

For all of them, Pekkala knew, death would have been instantaneous. He tried to draw some comfort from that fact.

Pekkala noted the obvious lack of resistance by the women. The shots had all been carefully aimed, which would not have been possible if the victims had put up a fight.

Then Pekkala came to the last body.

By then, the batteries of his flashlight were beginning to die. The light through the bubble-eyed crystal had gone from a blinding white to a dull brass yellow. The thought that it might die altogether, leaving him sightless among these corpses, filled his brain with mutterings of dread.

The last body was that of a man, lying on its side. His bones had been partially crushed by the weight of the other corpses which had been thrown down upon it. The rib cage and collarbone had collapsed. Beneath him, and spreading out in a pool on either side, the ground was black and oily.

The whole body was covered with a layer of dry, yellowy-brown mold. The coat buttons protruded like little mushrooms from the cloth. Pekkala reached out and brushed his thumb over the dust which covered the buttons, revealing the double-headed eagle of the Romanovs.

The man's left arm was broken, probably by the fall. The right arm lay across his face. Pekkala wondered if the man had survived the fall and tried to protect himself from the bodies which were thrown down after him.

In addition to riding breeches and tall boots, the dead man wore a tunic in the *gymnastyrka* style. The tunic had been modified to open down the front and the stand collar was decorated with two thick bands of silver brocade. The color of the tunic had originally been a pale greenish brown, the front and hem trimmed with the same silver brocade as the collar. Now it was the color of a rotten apple. He had seen this tunic before.

Now there was no doubt in Pekkala's mind that this was indeed the body of the Tsar. The Tsar had owned dozens of different uniforms, each representing different branches of service of the Russian military. This particular uniform, which the Tsar put on when reviewing his regiments of Guards, had been one of the most comfortable to wear. Because of that, it was also one of his favorites.

Four bullet wounds were clearly visible in the chest of the tunic. Pekkala studied the faded stains of blood that radiated from the wounds. Powder burns revealed that the shots had come from extremely close range. Gently, Pekkala moved the arm, to better see the dead man's face. He fully expected the skull to have been shattered like the rest, but was surprised: it was still intact. No bullet had penetrated the dura oblongata. He stared in confusion at the remains of the neatly trimmed beard, the hollow where the nose had been, the shriveled lips pulled back around a set of strong, straight teeth.

Pekkala stood back, gasping in a breath not filled with the dust of decay. He glanced upwards, to where a velvet disk of night sky showed the mouth of the mine shaft. At that moment, as if jolted from the scaffolding of his own body, Pekkala found himself looking through the eyes of the Tsar as those last seconds of his life played out on the floor of the mine. From far above, spears of light stabbed down towards him. They glinted off a tunnel of wet stone. Illuminated raindrops flickered like jewels all around. Then he saw silhouettes of the Tsar's wife and children come tumbling down towards him, fingers spread like wing tips, the dresses of the women thrumming with the speed of their descent. Pekkala felt them pass right through him, trailing the night behind them like black comets, and he heard their bones shatter like glass.

Pekkala shook the nightmare from his head. He forced himself to focus on the work that lay before him. Why, he asked himself, would the killer execute the women with a shot to the head but leave the Tsar's face intact? It would have made more sense if things had been done the other way around, particularly if the killings had been done, as he suspected, by a male. Such a killer would have been more likely to disfigure someone of his own gender.

Suddenly Pekkala's heart began to thunder in his chest. He had been so focused on this detail that he had completely forgotten something far more important.

The Tsar's corpse was the last one in the pile.

Hoping he might somehow be mistaken, Pekkala glanced at the bodies of the women laid out on the dirt floor of the mine.

But there had been no mistake. One body was missing.

Alexei was not among the dead.

Every time Pekkala thought about the boy, he felt a constriction in his throat. Of all the members of that family, Alexei had been his favorite. The daughters were charming, particularly the eldest daughter, Olga, but all four of them remained aloof. They were beautiful, although in a melancholy way, and rarely acknowledged his presence. Pekkala knew he made them nervous, towering above them in his black overcoat and seemingly immune to the kind of frivolity which occupied much of their lives. He lacked the refinements of the seemingly endless procession of visitors received by the Romanov family. The stylishly dressed barons, lords, and dukes—there was always a title in there somewhere—tweaking their trim mustaches and peppering their speech with French exclamations, considered Pekkala too coarse for their company.

"Don't mind them, Pekkala!" said Alexei.

Following reports of an explosion in the streets of Petersburg, Pekkala had been summoned by the Tsar to the royal estate, known as Tsarskoye Selo and located on the outskirts of the city.

As he entered the Tsar's study, in the north wing of the Alexander Palace, a cluster of guests barged past him without so much as a glance in his direction.

The Tsar was sitting at his desk.

Alexei sat beside him, his head in a white bandage which bulged with some concoction of herbs prescribed to him by Rasputin.

Alexei's expression was always the same—both warm and sad. The hemophilia which afflicted the boy had come so close many times to taking his life that the Tsar, and the Tsarina Alexandra in particular, seemed almost to have absorbed the disease into their own bodies. Alexei could have bled to death from the kind of nick or scrape a normal boy might expect to receive every day. This frailty had required him to live as a person might if they were made of glass. And so the parents lived as if they too were as fragile, like the tens of thousands of pieces of amber which plated the walls of the Catherine Palace's Amber Room, or the extraordinarily intricate Fabergé eggs the Tsar gave to his wife as birthday presents.

Even Alexei's friends were hand-selected by his parents for their ability to play gently. Pekkala remembered the soft-spoken Makarov brothers—thin and nervous boys whose ears stuck out and who carried their shoulders in a perpetual hunch, like children do when they are waiting for a firework to explode. In spite of his frailty, Alexei outlived them: both had died in the war.

No matter what precautions they took with their son, his parents seemed always to be waiting for that moment when Alexei would simply fade away. Then they, too, would crumble to dust.

"Alexei is right," the Tsar said. "You mustn't mind those people." Dismissively, he flipped his hand in the direction of the guests.

"They did not give you the welcome you deserve," said Alexei.

"They do not know me," replied Pekkala.

"Lucky for you, eh?" The Tsar smiled. He always seemed to cheer up when Pekkala was around.

"But we know you, Pekkala," said Alexei, "and that's what matters most."

"Now then, Pekkala! See what I have here!" The Tsar gestured towards a red handkerchief which lay upon the desk. The handkerchief looked out of place beside the neatly arranged pens, scissors, inkwell, and jade-handled letter opener. The Tsar required his desk to be kept in perfect order. When speaking to people in his study, particularly those whose company he did not care for, he would often make minute adjustments to these items, as if the distance of a millimeter between objects was the absolute margin of his sanity.

Now, with the flourish of a magician performing a trick, the Tsar whisked away the handkerchief to reveal what lay beneath.

To Pekkala, it looked like some kind of large egg. Its colors were luminous—a blur of flaming greens and reds and oranges. He wondered if it might be another one of Fabergé's creations.

"What do you think, Pekkala?" asked the Tsar.

Pekkala knew how to make the most of these games. "It appears to be"—he paused—"some sort of magic bean."

The Tsar burst out laughing, showing his strong white teeth.

Alexei laughed too, but he always bowed his head and kept a hand against his mouth.

"Magic bean!" shouted the Tsar. "Now I have heard everything!"

"It's a mango," said Alexei. "Those people who just left brought it to us as a present. It's come all the way from South America by the fastest ships and boats and trains. According to what they said, that mango was hanging from a tree not even three weeks ago."

"A mango," repeated Pekkala, struggling to recall if he had ever heard that word before.

"It's a fruit of some sort," said the Tsar.

"Pekkala has no time for mangos." Alexei was trying to make him smile.

"Unless"—Pekkala held up a finger—"it is guilty of a crime."

"A crime!" laughed the Tsar.

Pekkala held out his hand for the mango, and when the Tsar had given it to him, Pekkala pretended to examine it closely. "Suspicious," he muttered. "Deeply suspicious."

Alexei rocked back in his chair, delighted.

"Well, then," said the Tsar, playing along, "it must pay the ultimate price. There's only one thing to be done." He opened the drawer to his desk and pulled out a large folding knife with a stag-horned handle.

The Tsar freed the blade, which locked with a sharp click. *Taking the fruit in one hand, he proceeded to slice open the luminous skin, revealing a vivid orange flesh inside. Carefully, he cut into the mango. Keeping the slice pinned between the flat edge of the blade and the side of his thumb, he offered one to Pekkala and to his son and then took one for himself.*

In silence, the three of them chewed.

The cold sweetness of the fruit seemed to jump around in Pekkala's mouth. He could not repress small grumbling noises of appreciation.

"Pekkala likes it," said Alexei.

"I do," agreed Pekkala. Looking out over the Tsar's shoulder, he watched snow falling on the grounds of the palace.

They finished the mango.

The Tsar wiped the knife blade on the red handkerchief and then returned the knife to his desk. When he looked up to meet Pekkala's gaze, the Tsar's face had hardened into that expression which always came to him when the troubles of the outside world intruded.

He had already guessed that reports of the bomb blast in Petrograd were true. And even if the Tsar did not know who had been killed, he had no doubt that someone loyal to him had met their end. It was as if he could actually see the splintered body of Minister Orlov, whom he would later learn had died in the attack, so torn apart that almost the entire length of his spine lay like a white snake beside the dead man's rib cage.

These attacks were growing more frequent.

No matter how many terrorist plots were uncovered, there always seemed to be others which slipped through the wire undetected.

"I do not wish to discuss the recent unpleasantness in Petrograd," said the Tsar. It was more of a request than a command. In a gesture of fatigue, he rested his face in his hands, kneading his fingertips into his closed eyelids. "We'll sort it out later."

"Yes, Excellency."

Oblivious to the real reason for Pekkala's visit, Alexei was still smiling at him.

Pekkala winked.

Alexei winked back.

Pekkala backed up three paces, turned, and headed for the door.

"Pekkala!" the Tsar called.

Pekkala stopped and turned again and waited.

"Don't ever change," said the Tsar.

"Ever!" shouted Alexei.

When Pekkala left the Tsar's study, he closed the door behind him. Just as he was doing this, he heard Alexei's voice.

"Why does Pekkala never smile, Papa?"

Pekkala paused. He did not mean to eavesdrop, but the question had caught him by surprise. He did not think of himself as a man who never smiled.

"Pekkala is a serious man," he heard the Tsar reply. "He views the world with gravity. He does not have time for the games which you and I enjoy."

"Is he unhappy?" asked Alexei.

"No, I don't think so. He just keeps to himself how he feels."

"Why did you choose him to be your special investigator? Why not just choose another detective in the Okhrana or the Gendarmerie?"

Pekkala glanced up and down the empty corridor. Laughter came from distant rooms. He knew he should move on, but the question Alexei had asked was one he'd often asked himself, and it seemed to him that if he did not learn the answer now, he never would. So he stayed, barely breathing, straining to hear their voices through the thick slab of the door.

"A man like Pekkala," said the Tsar, "does not realize his own potential. I knew that the first time I set eyes on him. You see, Alexei, it is necessary for people in our walk of life to understand with a single glimpse the character of those we meet. We have to know whether to trust someone or to keep them at arm's length. What a person does matters more than what they say. I saw Pekkala refusing to jump his horse over a barbed-wire fence which some sadist of a drill instructor had constructed, and I watched how he behaved when the sergeant was dressing him down. And you know, he did not show a trace of fear. If I had not been there to witness it, that sergeant would have had Pekkala expelled from the ranks for insubordination. And it wouldn't have mattered to Pekkala."

"But why not?" asked the boy. "If he didn't want to be in the regiment . . ."

"Oh, but he did, only not on those terms. Most of those cadets would simply have sacrificed the horse and done as they were told."

"But isn't it important," asked Alexei, "to be obedient no matter what?"

"Sometimes, yes, but not for what I had in mind."

"You mean, you chose him because you thought he might not do as he was told?"

"What I needed, Alexei, was a man who could not be threatened or beaten or corrupted into surrendering his sense of what was right or wrong. And that will never happen to a person like Pekkala."

"But why not?"

"Because it would not occur to him. Men like that, Alexei, are fewer than one in a million. When you find them, you will know them at first sight."

"Why would he choose to do the job he does? Do you think he enjoys such a life?"

"It is not a question of enjoying it or not. He is built for it, like a greyhound is built for running. He does the thing he was put on this earth to do, because he knows that it matters."

As he listened to the Tsar, Pekkala was reminded of his father, doing the job which no one else would do. There had been times in the past months when Pekkala felt overwhelmed by the extraordinary coincidences which had led to him working for the Tsar. Now, hearing those words, what had once seemed the result of impossible randomness appeared to him almost inevitable.

"Did you really need someone like him?" asked Alexei.

"It is an unfortunate truth that the Okhrana is filled with spies. So is the Gendarmerie. The two branches are spying on each other. We send spies into the ranks of the terrorists. We even create spy rings which appear to be working against us, but are in fact controlled by the government. There is no end to the deception. When people reach a point where they do not expect to be ruled by leaders they can trust, that country is headed for ruin. With this going on, Alexei, what the people needed was one person they knew they could depend on."

"Even more than you, Papa?"

"I hope not," replied the Tsar, "but the answer is yes, all the same."

"Are you all right?" Kirov's voice ricocheted down the mine shaft.

Looking up, Pekkala glimpsed the silhouettes of Anton and Kirov, looking like paper cutouts as they leaned over the hole.

"I'm fine," he stammered.

"Is it who we thought?" asked Anton.

"Yes, but one of them is gone." Until now Pekkala had considered only three possibilities—one: that there would be no bodies; two: that bodies would be there but they would not be the Romanovs; and three: that the Romanovs would indeed be found dead at the bottom of that mine shaft. Pekkala had not factored in the chance that one of the Romanovs would be missing.

"Gone?" shouted Kirov. "Who?"

"Alexei," answered Pekkala.

The flashlight was almost extinguished now, reduced to a coppery haze which barely reached beyond the bubble lens. The darkness was crowding in around him.

"Are you sure?" As it traveled down the mine shaft, Anton's voice was amplified as if through a megaphone.

Pekkala glanced back to where the tunnel entrances had been sealed off. "Yes. Quite sure." Even if Alexei had survived the fall, he would not have been able to make his way into the tunnels, and with his hemophilia the young man would certainly have died of his injuries.

Up at the top of the shaft, the two men held a whispered conversation. Their words grew harsh, the sound like a hissing of snakes.

"We're bringing you up," shouted Anton.

A moment later, the Emka's engine growled into life.

"Take hold of the rope," called Anton. "Kirov will back up slowly. We'll pull you up."

Light flickered on the walls, like ghosts emerging from the rock.

He gripped the rope.

"Ready?" asked Anton.

"Yes," replied Pekkala.

The engine revved and Pekkala felt himself lifted slowly towards the surface. As he rose, he glanced down at the bodies, laid out side by side. The mouths gaped wide, as if in some terrible and silent chorus.

Keeping a firm grip on the rope, Pekkala walked his way up the sheer walls of the mine shaft. Finally, when he was almost at the top, Anton waved to Kirov and the car came to a halt. Anton reached down. "Take hold," he commanded.

Pekkala hesitated.

"If I'd wanted to kill you," said Anton, "I would have done it before now."

Pekkala released one hand from the rope and clasped his brother's forearm.

Anton hauled him to the surface.

While Kirov coiled the rope, Pekkala walked over to the car and leaned against the hood, arms folded, lost in thought.

Anton offered him his flask of Samahonka.

Pekkala shook his head. "You realize that there are two investigations now. One to find who killed the Romanovs and one to find the prince. He might still be alive."

Anton shrugged and took a drink himself. "Anything's possible," he muttered.

"I will help you to find Alexei's body," continued Pekkala, "but if it turns out he's alive, you'll have to find someone else to track him down."

"What do you mean?"

"I mean I will not deliver Alexei to you so you can assassinate him or throw him in prison for the rest of his life."

"I have something to tell you." Anton dropped the flask back in his pocket. "It might help you change your mind."

"I doubt that very much."

"Listen," said Anton, "don't forget we have been chasing rumors for years now that some of the Romanovs might have survived. We were well aware that the rumors might actually be true. It is Comrade Stalin's intention to offer amnesty to any of the Tsar's immediate family who can be found alive."

"You expect me to believe that?" rasped Pekkala.

"I've told you before that it was never Moscow's intention to kill all of the Romanovs. The Tsar was to be put on trial and, yes, he would have been found guilty and, yes, he almost certainly would have been executed. But there was never any mention of wiping out his entire family. They were to be used as bargaining tools. They were too valuable a resource simply to kill them."

"But Moscow already announced that the entire family were killed!" said Pekkala. "Why would Stalin acknowledge that he had made a mistake? It would make more sense for him to kill the Prince, rather than admit that he had lied."

"Perhaps one of the guards took pity on Alexei. Perhaps he was saved from execution and hidden away until he could be smuggled to safety. If that was the case, there would have been no lie. Moscow could say they had simply been misinformed. For Stalin to let Alexei live means that we are no longer afraid of our past. The Romanovs will never rule this country again. There will never be another Tsar. Alexei no longer stands as a threat, and that is why Alexei is worth more to us alive than dead."

Kirov had finished loading the tow rope into the car. He slammed the trunk and walked over to the brothers. He said nothing, but it was clear he had been listening.

"What do you think?" Pekkala asked him.

At first, Kirov seemed surprised to have been asked. He thought for a moment before he replied. "Alive or dead, Alexei is just another human being now. Just like you and me."

"The Tsar would have wanted that for his son," said Pekkala, "as much as he wanted it for himself."

"Well?" Anton reached out and tapped his brother on the arm. "What do you say?"

In spite of his instinctive mistrust, Pekkala could not deny that an offer of amnesty was an important sign. Only a government confident in itself could make such a gesture to a former enemy. Stalin was right. The world would take notice of that.

Pekkala felt himself swept along by the possibility that Alexei might still be alive. He tried to stifle it, knowing how dangerous it was to want a thing too much. It could cloud his judgment. Make him vulnerable. But, at that moment, with the smell of the dead still bitter in his lungs, his hesitation was outweighed by the duty he felt to the Prince.

"Very well," he said. "I will help you to find Alexei, one way or the other."

"Where to now, boss?" asked Kirov.

"The Vodovenko asylum," Pekkala told him. "Obviously that madman is not as crazy as they think he is."

Although they were now within sight of Sverdlovsk, its gold-painted onion dome church rising above rooftops in the distance, they settled on a route which bypassed the main road into town and continued due south towards Vodovenko. On the outskirts of the town, they stopped at a fuel depot to requisition more gasoline.

The depot was little more than a fenced enclosure, inside which stood a hut surrounded by a barricade of dirty yellow fuel drums. The gate was open and when the Emka pulled in, the station manager emerged from the hut, wiping his hands on a rag. He wore a set of blue overalls, torn at the knees and tattooed with grease stains.

"Welcome to the Sverdlovsk Regional Center for Transportation," he announced without enthusiasm as he shuffled over to them through puddles rainbowed with spilled gasoline. "We're also the Regional Center for Contact and Communication." The manager pointed towards a battered-looking phone nailed to the wall inside the hut. "Would you like to know the title they gave me to run this place? It takes about five minutes to say the whole thing."

"We just came for some fuel." Anton pulled a stack of brick-red-colored fuel coupons from his pocket. He flipped through them rapidly, like a bank teller counting money, then handed some over.

Without even glancing at them, the manager tossed the coupons into a barrel of old engine parts and oily rags. Then he turned to a fuel drum which had a pump attached to the top of the barrel. He worked the hand pump to pressurize the fuel drum, lifted the heavy nozzle, and began filling the Emka's fuel tank. "Where are you men going? Not many people pass through here by car. They all take the train these days."

"To the Vodovenko Sanitarium," replied Kirov.

The manager nodded grimly. "Which route are you taking?"

"The road which runs south goes straight to it," Kirov replied.

"Ah," whispered the man. "An understandable mistake, seeing as you're not from around here."

"What do you mean 'a mistake'?"

"I think you'll find that road is . . . ah . . . not there."

"What are you talking about?" asked Anton. "I saw it on the map."

"Oh, it exists," the manager assured him. "Only"—he hesitated—"there is no land to the south."

"No land? Have you completely lost your mind?"

"Do you have your map with you?" asked the manager.

"Yes."

"Then take a look at it and you'll see what I mean," he said.

With the manager standing beside him, Anton spread his map out on the hood of the car. It took him a moment of staring at the chart before he had his bearings.

"There's the road," said Anton, tracing his finger along it.

Now the manager dabbed one diesel-greasy finger at a large white space south of the town, through which the dark blue vein of road became a dotted line.

"I didn't notice that before," said Anton. "What does it mean?"

From the look on the manager's face, it was clear that he knew but had no intention of saying. "Go around," he said, pointing to another road which meandered to the south and then looped around, eventually trailing into Vodovenko.

"But that will take days!" said Anton. "We don't have the time."

"Suit yourself," replied the manager.

"What aren't you telling us?" asked Pekkala.

The manager lifted another fuel can and placed it in Pekkala's arms. "Take this with you, just in case," was all he would say.

IT WAS LATE AFTERNOON WHEN THEY ARRIVED AT THE EDGE OF THAT emptiness on the map. They came upon a roadblock made from a tree trunk set across the road at waist height, supported on either side by two X-shaped wooden structures. A small hut had been built beside the road.

A guard stood in the middle of the road, holding out his arm for them to stop. In his other hand, he held a revolver attached to a lanyard which hung around his neck. His ears were pressed back close against his skull, giving him a predatory look. On his collar he wore the red enameled rectangles of an officer.

Another man dozed in the darkness of the hut, arms folded and head lolling.

Pekkala noticed that beyond the roadblock, the fields were

green and cultivated. In the distance, the thatched rooftops of a village seemed to glow in the midday sun.

Anton had seen it too. "According to the map," he said, "that village does not exist."

Kirov stopped the car but kept the engine running.

The officer stepped over to his window. "Out," he snapped. "All three of you." By now the second guard had emerged from the hut. He had wide, deep-set eyes and a dark beard which straggled across his face. He buckled on a gun belt and joined his companion at the car.

While Anton, Pekkala, and Kirov stood by the roadside, the two guards searched the vehicle. They opened the fuel containers and sniffed the liquid inside. They inspected the cans of army ration meat. They pawed through the coils of bristling hemp rope. Finding nothing, the first guard finally addressed himself to the three men. "You are lost," he said.

"No," replied Kirov. "We are on our way to Vodovenko."

"I am not asking you if you are lost. I am telling you."

"Why is there nothing on the map?" asked Anton.

"I am not allowed to answer that question," the officer said. "You are not even permitted to ask it."

"But how do we proceed?" Anton asked. "This is the only road heading south."

"You will have to turn around," said the officer. "Go back the way you came. Eventually, you will reach a crossroads. From there, you can go north. And then"—he rolled his hand in the air—"after some hours, you will find another road heading east."

"Hours?" shouted Kirov.

"Yes, so the sooner you get started..."

Anton rummaged in the pocket of his tunic.

As he did this, the second guard reached slowly down and undid the flap on his gun holster.

Anton removed a sheaf of orders typed on thin, waxy paper,

grayishly transparent, the last one signed at the bottom with ink which had soaked through the page. "Read this," he said.

The officer snatched the papers. He glanced at each of the three men in turn.

The Emka's engine burbled patiently, filling the air with a smell of exhaust.

The second guard leaned over the officer's shoulder, reading the orders Anton had given them. He made a faint choking sound. "The Emerald Eye," he said.

One late September afternoon, Pekkala was summoned to the Catherine Palace, which was on the grounds of the Tsarskoye Selo estate.

Pekkala arrived late. That afternoon, in Petrograd, he had testified at Grodek's trial. The hearings lasted longer than expected. By the time the tribunal had released Pekkala from the witness stand, he was already overdue.

He guessed that the Tsar would not have waited up, but would already have returned to his quarters for the night. Without any way to confirm this, and with no idea what the Tsar wanted, Pekkala decided to make his way to the palace. In his two years as the Tsar's Special Investigator, he had often been summoned without knowing the purpose of his visit until after he arrived. The Tsar did not like to be kept waiting. He was a man of disciplined habits, his days rigidly scheduled between meetings, meals, exercise, and time with family. Anyone who upset this balance was not dealt with kindly.

To Pekkala's surprise, the valet who met him as he entered the Catherine Palace explained that the Tsar had waited after all. The next surprise came when the valet told him the Tsar was expecting him in the Amber Room.

The Amber Room was unlike any other place on earth. Pekkala had heard it described as the Eighth Wonder of the World. Few people outside the immediate family were allowed inside. It was not a large room, a little over six paces wide by ten paces long and the height of two tall men. Nor, in comparison with other rooms in the Catherine Palace, did it have the most spectacular view from the windows which lined one of its walls. What made the room remarkable was the walls themselves. Covering them from floor to ceiling were panels inlaid with over half a million pieces of amber. Wooden mosaics on the floor mirrored this dizzying collage of fragments, and a glass case in the corner contained trinkets made from the fossilized sap—cigar cases, music boxes, hairbrushes, an entire chess set whose pieces were carved from amber.

When light poured through the windows, the walls would glow as if they were on fire, radiating heatless flame from somewhere deep inside. At moments like this, the amber appeared to be like a window into a world of perpetual sunset.

In spite of finding himself so often surrounded by the priceless possessions of the Tsar, Pekkala did not covet them. He had grown up in a house where beauty had been found in simplicity. Tools, furniture, and cutlery were appreciated for their lack of frivolousness. To Pekkala, so much of what the Tsar owned struck him as merely impractical.

Pekkala's lack of interest in such wealth confused the Tsar. He was used to people being jealous, and the fact that Pekkala didn't envy him troubled the Tsar. He would try to interest Pekkala in the ivory and ebony inlay of a desk, or a damask-barreled set of dueling pistols, even going so far as to offer them to Pekkala as gifts. Pekkala usually refused, accepting only small tokens and then only when the Tsar would not take no for an answer. In the end, it was the Tsar who envied Pekkala, and not the other way around, not because of what the younger man had, but because of what he did not need.

But the Amber Room stood apart from all the other treasures of the Tsar. Even Pekkala could not deny the spell it cast on those who saw it.

As he passed through the White and Crimson Dining Rooms, Pekkala noticed a tall man in military uniform emerging from the Amber Room.

The man closed the door behind him and, with a spring in his step, strode through the Portrait Gallery.

As the man approached, Pekkala recognized the close-tailored uniform and slightly bowlegged gait of a cavalry officer. The Major's face was thin and accented by a rigid waxed mustache.

He walked right past Pekkala without so much as a greeting, but then he seemed to change his mind and he stopped. "Pekkala?" he said.

Pekkala turned and raised his eyebrows, waiting for the man to identify himself.

"Major Kolchak!" said the man, his voice louder than it needed to be in the gallery's confined space. He held out his hand. "I'm glad we have a chance to meet."

"Major," said Pekkala and shook his hand. He did not want to offend the man by admitting that he'd never heard of him before.

"You are expected, I believe." Kolchak nodded towards the Amber Room.

Pekkala knocked at the door and walked into the room.

Without the sunlight through the open windows, the amber walls seemed mottled and dull. In the half-light, the polished surfaces made the walls appear wet, as if he had stumbled into a cave and not a room inside the Catherine Palace.

The Tsar sat in a chair by the window. Beside the chair stood a small table, on which a candle burned in a holder. The holder was shaped like a dog howling up at the moon, with the candle clenched in its teeth. Two books lay neatly stacked beside the candle.

Only in that sphere of the candle's reach did the amber seem to glow. The Tsar himself appeared more like an apparition, floating in the darkness. On his lap was a stack of documents—a common sight, since he acted as his own secretary. This meant that, in spite of his fastidiousness, the Tsar was often overwhelmed with paperwork.

"You met Major Kolchak?" asked the Tsar.

"Briefly," Pekkala replied.

"Kolchak is a man of great ingenuity. I gave him the unusual task of

protecting my private financial reserves. In the event of an emergency, he and I have arranged to hide them in a place where, God willing, they will not be found until I need them." The Tsar lifted the stack of documents and let them fall with a slap to the floor. "So," he said. "You are late."

"I apologize, Excellency," said Pekkala, and was about to explain why when the Tsar cut him off.

"How was the trial?"

"Long, Excellency."

The Tsar gestured towards the two books. "I have some things for you."

Now that he looked more closely, Pekkala realized they were not books at all but wooden boxes.

"Go on and open them," said the Tsar.

Pekkala lifted up the first box, which was smaller than the one below. Opening it, he caught his first glimpse of the emblem which was to become his trademark in the years ahead.

"I have decided," said the Tsar, "that the title of Special Investigator lacks . . ." He twisted his hand in the air, like the claw of a barnacle sweeping through an ocean current. "Lacks the gravitas of your position. There are other Special Investigators in my police force, but there has never been a position quite like yours before. It was my grandfather who created the Gendarmerie and my father who established the Okhrana. And you are my creation. You are unique, Pekkala, and so is that badge you will wear from now on. I noticed, as others have done, that certain silvery quality to your gaze. I have never known anything like it. One might think you suffered from a type of blindness."

"No, Excellency. My sight is not impaired. I know what you are speaking of." Pekkala reached one hand towards his eyes, as if to touch the light which seemed to emanate from them. "But I do not know why it is there."

"Let us call it Fate," said the Tsar. He rose from his chair and, taking the badge from its velvet cushion, pinned it to the cloth beneath the right lapel of Pekkala's jacket. "You will be known from now on as the

Emerald Eye. You shall have absolute authority in the fulfillment of your duties. No secrets may be withheld from you. There are no documents you cannot see upon request. There is no door you cannot walk through unannounced. You may requisition any mode of transport on the spot if you deem it necessary. You are free to come and go where you please and when you please. You may arrest anyone whom you suspect is guilty of a crime. Even me."

"Excellency . . ." he began.

The Tsar held up a hand to silence him. "There can be no exceptions. Otherwise, it is all meaningless. I entrust you with the safety of this country and also with my life and the lives of my family, which brings us to the second box."

Setting aside the now empty container in which the badge had rested, the Tsar opened the larger box.

Inside its fitted case lay a brass-handled Webley revolver.

"This was given to me by my cousin, George V."

Pekkala had seen a picture of the two of them together hanging on the wall of the Tsar's study—the King of England and the Tsar of Russia, two of the most powerful men in the world. The photo had been taken in England, with both men in formal boating clothes, after the Tsar had sailed there in his yacht, the Standart. *The two men looked almost identical. Their expressions were the same, the shapes of their heads, their beards, their mouths, noses, and ears. Only their eyes showed any difference; the King's more round than the Tsar's.*

"Go on," the Tsar instructed. "Take it out."

Pekkala lifted the gun gently from its box. It was heavy, but superbly balanced. The brass grips felt cold against his palm.

"The Empress won't have it around," the Tsar told him. "She says it is too sauvage *for a man like me, whatever that means."*

Pekkala knew exactly what it meant, coming from a woman like the Empress, and he suspected the Tsar did as well.

"It was she who had the idea of presenting this to you. And do you know what I told her? I said that for a man like Pekkala, it might not be

sauvage *enough." The Tsar laughed, but his face became abruptly serious. "The truth is, Pekkala, if my enemies came close enough to require that I use a gun like this, it would already be too late. That's why it should belong to you."*

"It is very fine, Excellency, but you know how I feel about gifts."

"Who said anything about a gift? That weapon and the badge are the tools of your trade, Pekkala. I am issuing them to you the same as any soldier in the army is issued what he needs for his work. I'll have five thousand rounds of the correct ammunition delivered to your quarters tomorrow. That should keep you going for a while."

Pekkala nodded once and was about to take his leave when the Tsar spoke to him again.

"This business with Grodek will make you famous, Pekkala. It cannot be avoided. There has been too much publicity since you brought him into custody. Some people thirst for fame. They will do anything to have it. They will betray anyone. They will humiliate themselves and those around them. To be hated or loved makes no difference to them. What they want is to be known. It is a sad addiction, and such people wallow in it all their lives, like pigs in filth. But if you are the man I think you are, you will not like the taste of it."

"Yes, Excellency."

The Tsar reached out and grasped Pekkala by the forearms. "And that is why I consider you a friend."

The officer flipped through the orders. "Special Operations," he muttered.

"Did you see who signed those papers?" asked the second guard.

"Shut up," said the officer. He folded the orders and thrust them back at Anton. "You may pass through."

The second guard holstered his gun.

"Tell no one what you see beyond this barricade," said the

officer. "You must drive straight through. You may not stop. You may not speak to anyone. It is important that you give the appearance of normality. Once you have passed through the village, you will come to another roadblock. You must never speak of what you have seen here. Do you understand?"

"What on earth is out there?" asked Kirov. His face had turned pale.

"You will know that soon enough," replied the officer, "but there is still time to change your mind."

"We don't have time," said Anton.

"Very well," said the guard, nodding. He turned to his partner. "Fetch some of the apples," he said.

The second man disappeared inside the hut and reappeared carrying a wooden box, which he set on the hood of the car. Inside, nestled on a padded black cloth, were half a dozen perfect apples. He handed one to each of the men.

It was only when Pekkala felt the apple in his hand that he realized it was made of wood which had been carefully painted.

"What is going on?" asked Kirov.

"When you drive through the town," said the guard, "you must hold these apples in your hands as if you are about to eat them. Make sure they are seen. The apple is a sign to those people in the town that you have been cleared to pass through. You will be shot if you do not do exactly as I say."

"Why can't we just talk to them?" Kirov tried again.

"No more questions," said the officer. "Just make sure they see the apples in your hands."

The two guards lifted the heavy beam blocking the road.

Kirov drove the Emka past the barricade.

Pekkala stared at the apple. There was even a little green leaf hand-painted beneath a wooden stem.

They passed fields dazzling yellow with sunflowers. Far out in green tides of barley, they could make out the white headscarves of women standing on carts and gathering baskets handed up to them by men down on the ground.

"Those baskets are empty," muttered Kirov.

When they entered the village, they found it bustling with people. The place looked clean and prosperous. Women carried babies on their hips. Shop windows were piled with loaves of bread and fruit and slabs of meat. The village bore no resemblance at all to the muddy streets and miserable inhabitants of Oreshek.

As they were driving by, a cluster of men and women spilled out of the meeting hall. They were foreigners. Their clothes and hairstyles were those of Western Europeans and Americans. Some carried leather satchels and cameras. Others had notebooks open and were scribbling in them as they walked.

Leading the group was a small man with round glasses and a dark suit which, by the length of the jacket and the wide sweep of its lapel, was clearly Russian in origin. He smiled and laughed. He gestured first one way and then another, and the heads of the foreigners swayed back and forth, following his outstretched hands as if caught in a trance by the swing of a hypnotist's watch.

"Journalists," whispered Anton.

The man in the dark suit turned away from the flock he was leading and stared at the car as it drove by. Once his back turned to the journalists, the smile sheared off his face. It was replaced by a menacing glare.

Anton waved, the wooden apple clenched in his fist.

Raising a small camera to his eye, one journalist snapped a picture of the car as it sped past.

The other journalists bent forward, craning their necks like birds to get a glimpse inside the vehicle.

The man in the suit spun back to face the journalists. As he turned, the smile reappeared on his face like the sun coming out from behind a cloud.

Pekkala stared at the people milling about in the street. They all appeared so happy. Then he caught the eye of a man sitting by himself on a bench, smoking his pipe. And there was nothing but fear in his gaze.

A railway station stood on the other side of the town. The single track ended in a siding and a turnaround, so that the engine could go back the way it had come in. The train had been readied for its return journey, wherever that was. Black curtains covered the windows of the two carriages, whose olive green sides were trimmed with navy blue paint. The side of each carriage was emblazoned with a hammer and sickle, surrounded by a large red star.

Four men who had been sitting on the edge of the platform, legs dangling down towards the tracks, suddenly jumped to their feet when they saw the car approaching, grabbing brooms and sweeping the platform busily. Their sweeping paused as they gaped at the car's occupants. The men appeared confused. They were still staring at the car as it sped out of sight towards the second roadblock.

The road dipped down into a hollow, where they suddenly came up against another heavy wooden beam straddling the road.

Kirov jammed on the brakes and the car skidded to a stop.

More guards were waiting for them.

"Did you stop in town?" asked the man in charge.

"No," replied Kirov.

"Did you speak to anyone?"

"No."

Kirov held out his wooden apple. "Do you want this back?" he asked.

The apples were collected. When the barricade was lifted, Kirov hit the pedal so hard the wheels of the Emka spun in the dirt.

Emerging from the hollow, Pekkala looked back and saw now why that location had been chosen. From the train tracks, the roadblock was invisible, in case any of the foreigners managed to get a look past the black curtains hiding their view. He wondered what story the authorities had cooked up for keeping the windows covered. He wondered, too, if the journalists from the West believed what they were being shown.

Beyond, the land returned to the way it had been before—with fields gone fallow, rows of dead fruit trees clawing the sky with leafless skeleton branches, and houses whose roofs drooped saddlebacked from neglect.

Suddenly, Kirov swerved off the road.

The two brothers collided and swore.

As soon as the car had come to a stop, Kirov got out and walked into the field, leaving his door open. He stood there, staring out across the empty countryside.

Before Pekkala could ask, Anton began to explain. "After the Revolution, the government ordered all of the farms to be collectivized. The original landowners were either shot or sent to Siberia. The people who were left in charge did not know how to run the farms, so the crops failed. There was a famine. Five million people died of starvation."

Pekkala breathed out through his teeth.

"Maybe more than five," continued Anton. "Exact numbers will never be known. When word of the famine reached the outside world, our government simply denied it. They have built several of these model towns. Foreign journalists are invited to tour the country. They are well fed. They receive gifts. They see these model villages. They are told that the famine is a fabrication of anti-Soviet propaganda. The location of these villages is secret. I didn't realize this was one of them until we reached it."

"Do you think those journalists believed what they were seeing?" asked Pekkala.

"Enough of them do. People can sympathize with the death of one person, five people, ten people, but to them a million deaths is only a statistic. As long as there is doubt, they will choose what is easiest to believe. That is why you and your Tsar didn't stand a chance against us in the Revolution. You wanted too badly to believe that the human capacity for violence has limitations. The Tsar went to his death believing that because he loved his people, they would love him back. And look where it has gotten you."

Pekkala said nothing. He looked down at his hands and slowly clenched them into fists.

When Kirov returned to the car, Pekkala and Anton were both surprised to see that he was smiling.

"Glad to see you looking so inspired," sneered Anton, when Kirov had them on the road again.

"Why wouldn't I be?" Kirov replied cheerfully. "Don't you understand the genius in what we saw back there? We were taught at the Institute that sometimes it is necessary to portray the truth in a different light."

"You mean to lie," corrected Pekkala.

"A temporary lie," explained Kirov. "Someday, when the time is right, the record will be set straight."

"You believe that?" Pekkala asked.

"Of course!" the Commissar replied enthusiastically. "I just never thought I'd actually get to see it for myself."

Pekkala reached into his pocket and removed the wooden apple he had been given at the checkpoint and which he had failed to return. He tossed it into Kirov's lap. "Here's a little souvenir, from your visit to the town of temporary lies."

Anton reached across and bounced a fist off his brother's shoulder. "Welcome to the Revolution," he said.

But Pekkala was not thinking about the Revolution. His thoughts had drifted back to an earlier time, when apples like that had been real.

He found the Tsar chopping firewood outside the greenhouses of the Tsarskoye Selo estate, which were known as the Orangeries.

When he emerged onto the terrace of the Catherine Palace, having failed to locate the Tsar in any of its rooms, he'd heard, in the distance, the rhythmic sound of an axe cutting into dry wood.

From the way that axe was being handled—rapidly, without hesitation, and without the heavy thump of someone using more strength than was necessary to split logs into kindling—Pekkala knew it was the Tsar.

The Tsar liked to exercise, but not for its own sake. He preferred to be doing something he considered useful, such as shoveling snow, clearing rushes from the edges of the ponds. But his favorite occupation was simply to hide himself away behind the Orangeries and lose himself in the meditation of swinging an axe.

It was a cold day in late September. The first snow of the winter had fallen and the ground was hard with frost. In a few days the snow would probably melt again. Roads and paths would turn to mud. Pekkala had noticed that these first snowfalls were a special time for people in Petrograd. It filled them with new energy, replenishing what had been sapped from them by the muggy summer months.

The Tsar was stripped to the waist. On his left rose a pile of neatly stacked logs, each one about half the length of a man's leg. On his right lay the jumble of logs which had been quartered for use as kindling. In the middle, the Tsar used a tree stump as a cutting platform. Pekkala admired the precision of the Tsar's work, the way he placed each log for cutting, the effortless rise of the axe, its ash handle sliding through his grip until it reached the height of its arc. Then came the sharp downward swing, almost too swift to see, and the log would split apart like segments of an orange.

Pekkala waited at the edge of the clearing until the Tsar had paused to wipe sweat from his face. Then he stepped forward and cleared his throat.

The Tsar wheeled about, surprised. At first, he looked annoyed to have been disturbed, but his expression softened when he realized who it was.

"Oh, it's you, Pekkala." He let the axe drop onto the tree stump. Its blade bit into the wood, and when he let go, the axe stayed where it was, jutting at an angle from the cutting platform. "What brings you here today?"

"I have come to ask for a favor, Excellency."

"A favor?" The Tsar slapped his hands together, as if to brush away the redness in his palms. "Well, it's about time you asked me for something. I was beginning to think you had no use for me at all."

"No use for you, Excellency?" He had never thought about it like that.

The Tsar smiled at Pekkala's confusion. "What is it that you would like, my friend?"

"A boat."

The Tsar raised his eyebrows. "Well, I think we can manage that. What sort of boat? My yacht, the Standart? Or something bigger? Do you need some sort of military vessel?"

"I need a rowboat, Excellency."

"A rowboat."

"Yes."

"Just an ordinary rowboat?" The Tsar failed to hide his disappointment.

"And some oars, Excellency."

"Let me guess," said the Tsar. "You would like two of those."

Pekkala nodded.

"Is that all you want from me?"

"No, Excellency. I also need a lake to put it in."

"Ah," growled the Tsar, "now that's more like it, Pekkala."

Two days later, just after the sun had set, Pekkala rowed out into the lake known as the Great Pond, at the southern edge of the Tsarskoye Selo estate. Ilya sat in the back of the boat, a blindfold over her eyes.

It was a cool evening, but not cold. In a month this whole lake would be frozen.

"How much longer do I have to wear this?" Before he could respond, she asked another question. "Where are we going?"

He opened his mouth to reply.

"Is there anyone else in this boat?" she asked. "Why don't you give me an answer?"

"I will if you'll let me," he said. "The answers are 'not long,' 'not telling,' and 'no.' "

Ilya sighed and folded her hands in her lap. "What if one of my students sees me? They'll think I'm being kidnapped."

"I love you," said Pekkala. He had meant to save that for later, but it just slipped out on its own.

"What?" she asked, her voice growing suddenly soft.

"You heard me."

She was silent.

He wondered if he had made a mistake.

"Well, it's about time," she said, softly.

"You're the second person who's said that to me recently."

"I love you, too," she told him.

The bow of the rowboat nudged up against the shore of an island called the Hall, which stood in the middle of the Great Pond. A large pavilion had been built on the island, taking up most of its space, so that the pavilion itself seemed to float upon the water.

Pekkala drew in the oars, droplets falling from the Turk's head knots which had been laced just forward of the oar grips. Then he helped Ilya out of the boat. She was still wearing the blindfold, but now she no longer complained. Holding her hand, he led her up to the pavilion, under which there was a single table with two chairs. A lantern on the table cast a pool of light around the space, and the backs of the chairs made shadows like the loops of twisted vines.

Once she was seated, he lifted the silver domes which had been placed over their plates. He had made the meal himself—chicken Kiev, its center stuffed with a knot of butter and parsley, mushrooms stirred into a sauce of cream and brandy, string beans no thicker than a sewing needle, and potatoes broiled with rosemary. The Tsarina had contributed a bottle of Grande Dame Veuve Clicquot. Beside the lantern sat a bowl of perfect apples, which they would eat with cheese for their dessert.

The plates had been set in silver rings, raising them just above the level of the table, and the meal kept warm by candles placed beneath.

Now Pekkala removed the candles and the silver rings, so that the plates were resting on the table.

He breathed in, his eyes scanning the place settings to make certain everything was in perfect order. For the past two days, he had been so busy with the details of this meal that he hadn't had time to get nervous. But now he was very nervous. "You can take off the blindfold now," he said.

She looked at the meal and then at him and then around her at the pavilion, darkness like velvet curtains all around.

Pekkala watched her anxiously.

"You did not need to go to all this trouble," she told him.

"Well, I know, but—"

"You had me at the first creak of the oars."

Now Kirov held the wooden apple as he drove, his other hand gripping the wheel. "Isn't it beautiful!" he exclaimed. "Don't we live in a wonderful time!"

The Vodovenko Sanitarium stood by itself on the top of a windswept hill. Only one road led to and from the towering stone structure. The entire hill was stripped of vegetation and all the land around it had been ploughed.

"Why did they do that?" asked Kirov. "Are they planting crops?"

It was Anton who replied. "They do that so the footsteps of anyone who escapes can be tracked across the ground."

They arrived at a checkpoint at the base of the hill.

Armed guards inspected their papers, raised the yellow-and-black barrier pole, and allowed them to proceed.

Two steel doors at the entrance to Vodovenko swung open. The Emka rolled into a courtyard.

The walls of the sanitarium seemed to lean out over them.

In front of each window, secured by bolts a hand's length from the wall, large metal plates blocked any view.

Kirov cut the engine.

They had not expected the silence, but it was not the silence of an empty place. Instead, it seemed as if everything contained within that massive building was holding its breath.

At the front desk, an attendant reexamined their documents. He was a wide-faced man with a tangle of red hair and rust-colored freckles constellationed on his cheeks. His nose had been broken and healed crookedly. The attendant pulled out a file and slid it across the counter.

Pekkala saw a photograph of a haunted-looking man stapled at the top left corner, and a name written across the top—*Katamidze.*

The attendant picked up a phone and ordered the patient to be brought to a secure room.

Pekkala wondered what he meant by *secure,* in a place which was already a prison.

"You will need to surrender your weapons," the attendant told them.

Two Tokarevs and the Webley clanked down on the countertop.

The attendant behind the desk looked at the Webley. He glanced at Pekkala but said nothing. The guns were placed in a metal cabinet. Then the attendant walked around to a set of metal doors, slid back a dead bolt, and nodded for them to go through.

Pekkala turned to Anton and Kirov. "Wait here," he said.

Anton looked relieved.

"I don't mind coming in," said Kirov. "I would actually—"

"No," said Pekkala.

Anton tapped Kirov on the shoulder. "Come on, Junior Man. Let's go outside and you can smoke that fancy little pipe of yours."

Kirov glared at him, but did as he was told.

When Pekkala stood on the other side of the armored door,

the attendant followed him in and dead-bolted it with a key which he kept on his belt.

With his first step into the corridors of Vodovenko, Pekkala began to sweat. It started with the floors, which were covered with thick gray felt. They drank up the noise of their footsteps and seemed to leach from their bodies even the patient drumming of their hearts. Flooding his senses were the smells of coal tar soap, of food boiled into a pulp, of excrement. Fusing it all together was the distinctive reek of sweat from people living in fear.

The corridors were lined with doors. Duck-egg blue paint clung in layers to the metal. All of them were closed and each had an observation slit, covered with a slide. Beneath the observation slit, like an unsmiling mouth, each door also had a slot for passing through food.

Pekkala stopped. His legs refused to move. Perspiration dripped off his jawline. His breath felt hot as cinders in his throat.

"Are you all right?" asked the attendant.

"I think so," replied Pekkala.

"You have been here before," the attendant said. "Here or some place like it. I know the look you people get when you come back."

The attendant led him to a room two stories underground. It had a low ceiling, barely a handsbreadth above the top of Pekkala's head. A metal chair stood in the exact center of the room. It was anchored to the concrete floor with L-shaped brackets, through which bolts had been driven into the floor.

The only light in the room came from the ceiling directly above the chair, where a naked bulb hung in a metal cage.

A man sat in the chair, chained by each wrist to the forward legs. He was a tall man, and the way he had been chained caused him to stoop over in a manner which reminded Pekkala of a sprinter crouched before the beginning of a race.

Dirty, graying hair stuck out on the sides of his head, leaving a wide sweep of baldness in between. His ears were large, as was his soft, round chin, speckled with a two days' growth of beard. The man's eyes, set into a shallow brow, were as smoky blue as those of a newborn baby.

Katamidze wore the same beige cotton pajamas which Pekkala had worn at the outset of his journey to the Gulag. He recalled the humiliating thinness of the cloth, the way it stuck to the backs of his legs when he sweated, and the perverse absence of a drawstring, so that a prisoner had to hold up his pants all the time.

"Katamidze," said the attendant, "I have someone to see you."

"This isn't my usual cell," replied the man.

"Now then, Katamidze," crooned the attendant. "Do you see the man I've brought to meet you?"

"I see him." His gaze fixed on Pekkala. "So you are the Emerald Eye?"

"Yes," said Pekkala.

"Prove it," said Katamidze.

Pekkala turned up his lapel. In the glare of the metal-caged bulb, the emerald flashed.

"They told me you were dead."

"A slight exaggeration," replied Pekkala.

"I said I'd only speak to you." Katamidze looked at the attendant. "In private."

"Very well," said Pekkala.

"I am not authorized to leave you alone with the patient," the attendant protested.

"I won't talk to anyone but the inspector," said Katamidze. After he had finished speaking, his mouth continued to move, but without making any sound.

Pekkala watched the words which formed upon the prisoner's lips and realized that Katamidze was repeating the last few words of every sentence, like an echo of himself inside his head. He also noticed that the right ankle and left wrist of the prisoner were badly swollen where he had been chained to the wall of his cell.

"It's against regulations," the attendant persisted.

"Go," replied Pekkala.

The attendant looked as if he were about to spit on the floor. "Fine, but this man is classified as dangerous. Stay away from him. I won't be held responsible for what he'll do to you if you come too close."

When the two men were finally alone, Pekkala sat down on the floor with his back to the wall. He did not want Katamidze to feel as if he were being interrogated.

"What season is it now?" asked Katamidze.

"Nearly autumn. The leaves are beginning to turn."

A smile flickered across Katamidze's face. "I remember the smell of the leaves on the ground after the first frost. You know, I had begun to believe them when they told me you were dead."

"I was, in a manner of speaking."

"Then you should thank me, Inspector Pekkala, for bringing you back from the world of the dead! And now you have something to live for."

"Yes," said Pekkala, "I do."

Ilya and Pekkala stood on the crowded railway platform of the Nikolaevsky station in Petrograd.

It was the last week of February 1917.

Entire army regiments—the Volhynin, the Semyonovsky, the Preobrazhensky—had mutinied. Many of the officers had already been shot. The clattering of machine-gun fire sounded from the Likjeiny Prospekt. Along with the army, striking factory workers and sailors from the fortress island of Kronstadt began systematically looting the shops. They stormed the offices of the Petrograd Police and destroyed the Register of Criminals.

The Tsar had finally been persuaded to send in a troop of Cossacks to battle the Revolutionaries, but the decision came too late. Seeing that the Revolution was gaining momentum, the Cossacks themselves had rebelled against the government.

This was the point at which Pekkala knew he had to get Ilya out of the country, at least until things quieted down.

Now the train was ready to depart, heading east towards Warsaw. From there it would travel to Berlin and on to Paris, which was Ilya's final destination.

"Here," said Pekkala, and reached inside his shirt. He pulled a leather cord from around his neck. Looped into the cord was a gold signet ring. "Look after this for me."

"But that was going to be your wedding ring."

"It will be," he replied, "and when I see you again, I'll put on that ring and never take it off again."

The crowd ebbed and flowed, as if a wind was blowing them like grain stalks in a field.

Many of those fleeing had come with huge steamer trunks, sets of matching luggage, even birds in cages. Hauling this baggage were exhausted porters in their pillbox hats and dark blue uniforms with a single red stripe, like a trickle of blood, down the sides of their trousers. There were too many people. Nobody could move without shoving. One by one, passengers abandoned their baggage and pressed forward to the train, tickets raised above their heads. Their shouts rose above the panting roar of the steam train as it prepared to move out. High above, beneath the glass-paned roof, condensation beaded on the dirty glass. It fell back as black rain upon the passengers.

A conductor leaned out of a doorway, whistle clenched between his teeth. He blew three shrill blasts.

"That's a two-minute warning," said Pekkala. "The train won't wait. You have to go, Ilya."

The crowd began to panic.

"I could wait for the next train," she pleaded. In her hands, she

clutched a single bag made out of brightly patterned carpet material, containing some books, a few photographs, and a change of clothes.

"There might not be a next train. Please. You must leave now."

"But how will you find me?"

He smiled faintly, reaching up and running his fingers through her hair. "Don't worry," he said. "That's what I'm good at."

"How will I know where you are?"

"Wherever the Tsar is, that's where I'll be too."

"I should stay with you."

"No. Absolutely not. It's too dangerous now. When things settle down, I will come for you, and I will bring you back."

"But what if they don't settle down?"

"Then I will leave this place. I will find you. Stay in Paris if you can, but wherever you are, I will find you. Then we will start a new life. One way or the other, I promise we will be together soon."

The roar of those who could not get aboard had risen to a constant shriek.

A pile of luggage stacked too high suddenly lurched and fell. Fur-coated passengers went sprawling. The crowd closed up around them.

"Now!" said Pekkala. "Before it's too late."

"All right," Ilya said at last. "Don't let anything happen to you."

"Don't worry about me," he told her. "Just get aboard the train."

She moved away into the sea of people.

Pekkala remained where he was. He watched her head above the others. When she was almost at the carriage, she turned and waved to him.

He waved back. And then he lost sight of her, as a tide of people poured past him, pursuing the rumor that another train had pulled in at the Finland station on the other side of the river.

Before he knew it, he had been swept out into the street.

Pekkala ran around the side of the station, and from a street just off the Nevski Prospekt, he watched the train pulling out. The windows were open. Passengers leaned out, waving to those they had left behind on the platform. The carriages rattled past. Then suddenly the tracks were empty and there was only the rhythmic clatter of the wheels, fading away into the distance.

It was the last train out.

The next day, the Reds set fire to the station.

"WHAT IS IT YOU WANT TO TELL ME, KATAMIDZE?"

"I know where they are," he replied. "The bodies of the Romanovs."

"Yes." Pekkala nodded. "We have found them." For the moment, he said nothing about Alexei.

"And did you find my camera?"

"Camera? No. There was no camera in the mine shaft."

"Not in the mine shaft! In the basement of the Ipatiev house!"

Pekkala's face went suddenly numb. "You were in the Ipatiev house?"

Katamidze nodded. "Oh, yes. I'm a photographer," he said, as if that would explain everything. "I'm the only one in town."

"But how did you come to be in the basement?" According to Anton, that was where the bodies of the guards had been found. Pekkala tried to sound calm, even though his heart was racing.

"For the portrait!" said Katamidze. "They called me. I have a telephone. Not many people in town have one of those."

"Who called you?"

"An officer of the Internal Security, the Cheka. They were the ones guarding the Tsar and the family. The officer said they wanted me to take a formal portrait, to prove to the rest of the country that the Romanovs were being well treated. He said it was going to be published."

"Did he give his name?"

"No. I didn't ask. He just said he was Cheka."

"Did you know the Tsar was staying at the Ipatiev house?"

"Of course! Nobody saw them, but everyone knew they were

there. You can't keep a secret like that. The Guards built a temporary fence around the house and painted the windows so that no one could look in. Afterwards, they tore the fence down, but when the Romanovs were there, if you so much as stopped and *looked* at the place, the soldiers would pull a gun on you. Only the Red Guards came and went. And I got the call! A portrait of the Tsar. Imagine it. One minute I am taking pictures of prize cows and farmers who have to pay me in apples because they don't have the money for a picture, and then next minute I am photographing the Romanovs. It would have made my career. I planned on doubling my fees. The officer said to come right over, but it was already after dark. I asked if it couldn't wait until morning. He said he had just received orders from Moscow. You know how those people are. You can't get them to do anything but, when they want something, it all has to happen yesterday. He told me there was a room in the basement which had been cleared out and that this would be a good place for taking the family portrait. Fortunately, I knew that the Ipatievs had electricity in their house, so I would be able to use my studio lights. I barely had time to pack. There's all sorts of things involved. Tripod. Film. I had just received a new camera. Ordered it from Moscow. Only had it for a month. I would like to have it back."

"What happened when you arrived at the Ipatiev house?"

Katamidze puffed his cheeks and exhaled noisily. "Well, I almost got run over on the way there. One of their trucks went racing past me. They had two, you know. I was carrying all my photography equipment. I barely had time to get out of the way. It's a miracle nothing got broken."

"Where was the other truck?"

"It was in the courtyard behind the house. I couldn't see it, because the courtyard has high walls, but I could hear the engine running. I smelled the smoke of its exhaust. When I knocked on the door, two Cheka guards came to answer it. Both had their guns drawn. They looked very nervous. They told me to go away, but when I explained about the photo, and that the order to take it had come from one of their own officers, they let me inside."

"What did you see when you walked in?"

Katamidze shrugged. "I'd been in there before. I'd done portraits for the Ipatiev family. It looked about the same, except there was less furniture on the ground floor. I never made it upstairs. That's where the Romanovs were staying. There's a staircase to the right of the front door, and a big room to the left."

"Did you see the Romanovs?"

"Not at first," said Katamidze, and in the silence which followed his lips continued to shape the words. *At first. At first. At first.* "I could hear them upstairs. Muffled voices. There was music, too. It was playing on a gramophone. Mozart. Sonata number 331. I used to play that tune when I was studying piano."

Mozart had been one of the Tsarina's favorite composers. Pekkala remembered the way she tilted her head while she listened. She would hold the thumb and index finger of her right hand joined in an O, tracing seagulls in the air as if conducting the music herself.

"I carried my equipment down to the basement," continued Katamidze. "Then I brought down some chairs from the dining room. I set up my light and the tripod. I was just checking the film in the camera when I heard a noise behind me and a woman appeared at the bottom of the stairs. It was the Princess Maria. I recognized her right away from pictures I had seen. I didn't know what to do, so I got down on my knees! Then she laughed at me and said I should get to my feet. She said she had been told about the portrait and wanted to know if everything was ready. I told her it was. I said they should come right away. Then she went back up the stairs."

"What did you do then?"

"What did I do? I checked the camera about twenty times to make sure it was working, and then I heard them coming down the stairs. Soft as mice. They filed into the room, and I bowed to each one and they nodded their heads at me. I thought my heart was going to stop!

"I arranged the Tsar and the Tsarina in the two middle chairs, then the two youngest, Anastasia and Alexei, on either side. Behind them stood the three eldest daughters."

"How did they seem to you?" asked Pekkala. "Did they look nervous?"

"Not nervous. No. I wouldn't say that."

"Did they speak to you?"

Katamidze shook his head. "Only to ask if I wanted them to move or if the way they were standing was acceptable. I could barely answer them, I was so nervous."

"Go on," said Pekkala. "What happened then?"

"I had just taken the first picture. I was planning on several. Then I heard someone knocking on the front door of the house, the same one I'd used to come in. The guards opened the door. There was some sort of conversation. I couldn't hear what they were saying. Then there was shouting. That's the first time I saw the Tsar looking nervous. And the next thing I heard was a gun going off! Once! Twice! I lost count. There was a regular battle going on upstairs. One of the princesses screamed. I don't know which one. I heard the Tsarevich Alexei ask his father if they were going to be rescued. The Tsar told them all to be quiet. He got out of the chair and walked past me to the door and closed it. I was frozen to the spot. He turned to me and asked if I knew what was happening. I couldn't even speak. He must have known that I had no idea. The Tsar said to me—'Do not let them see you are afraid.' "

"And then?"

"Footsteps. Coming down the stairs. Somebody stopped outside the closed door. Then the door flew open. Another Cheka guard came into the room."

"A different one?"

"Yes. I hadn't seen this man before. At first, I thought he had come to tell us that we were safe."

"Just the one man? Can you describe him?"

Katamidze screwed up his face, trying to recall. "He was neither tall nor short. He had a thin chest. Narrow shoulders."

"What about his face?"

"He had one of those caps which the officers wear, the kind where the brim comes down over their eyes. I couldn't see him very well. He was holding a revolver in each hand."

Pekkala nodded. "And then?"

"The Tsar told the man to let me go," continued Katamidze. "At first, I didn't think he would, but then the man just told me to get out. As I stumbled from the room, I heard the man talking to the Tsar."

"What were they speaking about?"

"I couldn't hear. Their voices were muffled."

"Did you hear the Tsar call him by name?"

Katamidze stared up at the lightbulb in the ceiling, teeth gritting with the exertion of remembering. "The Tsar called out a word when the man first entered the room. It could have been a name. I remembered it for a while, but then it went out of my head."

"Try, Katamidze. Try to remember it now."

The prisoner laughed. "After so long trying to forget..." He shook his head. "No. I don't recall. The next thing I remember is that the Tsar and the guard began to argue. Then the guns went off. There was screaming. The room filled with smoke."

"Why didn't you run?" asked Pekkala.

"I was so petrified I couldn't get my legs to take me up the stairs. I just stood there and watched. I couldn't believe what was happening."

"What did you do then?"

"The shooting stopped suddenly. The door was half open. I could see the guard reloading the guns. Bodies were writhing on the floor. I heard groaning. A woman's arm reached out through the smoke. I could see Alexei. He was still sitting in his chair. He had his hands held up by his chest. He was just staring straight ahead. When the guns were loaded again, the guard moved from one person to the next." He fell silent, his jaw locked open, unable to find the words.

"Did you see him shoot Alexei?"

"I saw him shoot the Tsarina," whispered Katamidze.

Pekkala flinched, as if the sound of that blast had just ripped through the air. "But what about Alexei? What happened to him?"

"I don't know. I don't see how anyone could have survived. Finally, I came to my senses and ran. Up the stairs. Out the front door. As I left the house I nearly fell over the two guards who had let me in. They'd both been shot and were lying on the floor. There was a lot of blood. I assumed they were dead. I didn't stop to check. I don't understand it. If the Cheka were supposed to be guarding the Romanovs, why would one of them have murdered the Tsar and even some of his own people?"

"What happened next, Katamidze?"

"I ran out into the dark," the man replied, "and I just kept running. First I went home, but then I realized it was only a matter of time before someone came looking for me, either the gunman or people who thought I'd committed the murders. So I left. I ran away. In the woods outside of town I have a little cabin, the kind they call a Zemlyanka."

Pekkala thought of his own cabin, deep in the forest of Krasnagolyana, now only a silhouette of ash and rusted nails.

"I knew I'd be safe there," continued Katamidze, "for a while at least. I had been on the move for about an hour when I passed by the old mine at the edge of town. It is a bad place. In the old language, it is called Tunug Koriak. It means 'the place where the birds have stopped singing.' The locals stay away from there. The people who worked in that mine had to be brought in from somewhere else. They all got sick. Most of them died."

"What was mined there?"

"Radium. The stuff they use on watches and on compasses. It glows in the dark. The dust is poisonous."

"What did you see at the mine?"

"One of the Cheka trucks. The same man who killed the Romanovs. He had unloaded the bodies next to the mine shaft. He was throwing them down one by one."

"Are you sure it was him?"

Katamidze nodded. "The headlights of the truck were on. When he passed in front of the beam, I knew it was him."

"But are you sure he threw in all of the bodies?"

"By the time I arrived, the truck was already there. I don't know how many bodies he threw down."

"Did he see you?"

"No. It was dark. I hid behind the old buildings where the mine workers lived. I waited until he climbed back in the truck and drove off. Then I started running. When I got to my cabin, I stayed there for a while. But I didn't feel safe. I moved again. And again. Somewhere along the way, I read in the paper that the Romanovs had been executed on orders from Moscow. All nice and official. But that's not what it looked like to me. After I read that, I realized I knew something I wasn't supposed to know. Who can you trust after that? I kept moving, until I ended up in Vodovenko."

"How did you end up here, Katamidze?"

"I was living on the streets in Moscow, in the sewers. Some tunnel workers found me. I don't know how long I had been down there. It was the only place where I thought I might be safe. Do you know what that feels like, Inspector? Never feeling safe, no matter where you are?"

"Yes," replied Pekkala. "I do."

On the 2nd of March 1917, with riots in the streets of Petrograd and soldiers at the front in open mutiny against their officers, the Tsar gave up his power as absolute ruler of Russia.

One week later, with negotiations under way to have the Romanovs exiled to Britain, the Tsar and his family were placed under house arrest at the Tsarskoye Selo estate.

General Kornilov, the Revolutionary Commander of the Petrograd district, informed the staff at Tsarskoye Selo that they had twenty-four hours to leave. Any who chose to remain behind would be placed under the same conditions of arrest as the royal family.

Most of the staff departed immediately.

Pekkala chose to stay.

The Tsar had given him the use of a small cottage on the outskirts of the estate, not far from the horse enclosure known as the Pensioner's Stables. It was here that Pekkala waited, with a growing sense of helplessness, for events to unfold. The confusion outside the palace gates was made worse by the fact that within the imperial household, no one seemed to have any sense of direction.

Pekkala's only instructions, which he had received on the same day the Tsar had abdicated, had been to stand by for more orders. In this time of uncertainty, what Pekkala found most difficult was the ordinary, everyday tasks which he had once carried out so fluidly that he never gave them any thought. Things like boiling water for tea, or making his bed, or washing his clothes became suddenly monumental in their complexity. With nothing else to do, anticipation gnawed at him as he tried to imagine what events were taking place beyond the confines of his rapidly shrinking world.

Pekkala did not hear from the Tsar. Instead, he picked up fragments of gossip when he went each day to pick up rations from the kitchen.

He learned that negotiations had begun to move the Romanov family into exile in Britain. They were to sail, under armed Royal Navy escort, from the arctic port of Murmansk. At first, the Tsar had been reluctant to travel, since his children were recovering from measles. The Tsarina, fearing a long sea journey, had requested that they sail only as far as Denmark.

With crowds of armed factory workers arriving daily to jeer at the Romanovs through the gates of the Royal Estate, Pekkala knew that if the Romanovs were to escape, they would have to be smuggled out. Since no news of this plan had reached Pekkala, he came to the conclusion that he was being left behind to fend for himself.

Soon afterwards, however, he learned that the British had withdrawn their offer of asylum. From then on, until the Revolutionary Committee figured out what to do with them, the Romanovs were trapped inside their own estate.

For the sake of the children, the Tsar and Tsarina were trying to carry on as normal an existence as they could. Alexei's tutor, Pierre Gilliard—known to the Romanovs as Zhilik—who had also chosen to remain behind, taught his daily classes in the study of French. The Tsar himself taught history and geography.

Pekkala always found the kitchen filled with off-duty guards warming up after their foot patrols around the estate. They knew who he was, and Pekkala could not help being surprised at their lack of hostility towards him. Unlike the teachers and personal servants who had stayed behind, they considered him separate from the Romanovs. His decision to remain at Tsarskoye Selo baffled them. Privately, they encouraged him to leave and even offered to help him slip out through the perimeter of guards.

The guards themselves seemed to have no clear orders about how to treat the royal family. One day, they confiscated Alexei's toy gun. Then they gave it back. Another day, they banned the Romanovs from swimming in the Lamski Pond. Then that order was rescinded. Without clear direction, their hostility towards the Romanovs grew more open. Once, as the Tsar was bicycling around the estate, one guard jammed a bayonet into the spokes and sent the Tsar sprawling in the dust.

When he heard about that, Pekkala realized it was only a matter of time before the lives of the Romanovs would be at risk. Soon, the family would not be any safer within the confines of the estate than they were on the outside. If they didn't leave soon, they would never leave at all, and his own life would be swallowed up along with theirs.

"I HAVE ONE LAST QUESTION FOR YOU," PEKKALA SAID.

Katamidze raised his eyebrows.

"Why speak up now? After all these years?"

"For a while," said Katamidze, "I knew that the only way for me to stay alive was for people to think I was crazy. So no one would believe a word I said. The trouble is, Inspector, you stay here long enough, and you really do go crazy. I wanted to tell what happened, before even I stopped believing it."

"Are you not afraid that the man who killed the Tsar might track you down?"

"I want him to find me," Katamidze said softly. "I am tired of living in fear."

IT WAS LATE WHEN THEY REACHED SVERDLOVSK.

The tires of the Emka popped and rumbled over the cobblestones which paved the main street running through the town. With the night mist glistening on them, the road looked like the cast-off skin of some giant snake.

Neatly planted trees formed a barrier between the part of the street intended for horses and cars and the part set aside for people going on foot. Beyond the pedestrian walkway stood large, well-maintained houses, with gardens closed off by white picket fences and shutters bolted for the night.

Anton's orders were to present his papers to the local police chief as soon as they arrived, but the station had closed. They decided to wait until morning.

Only the tavern was open, a low-roofed place with benches set out in front of whitewashed walls. A line of old and bearded men sat with backs slumped against the wall. Large copper mugs, each with two handles, were being passed from one man to the next. Some of the men smoked pipes, cobras of smoke rising from the pipe bowls, their faces lit by the glow. They watched the Emka drive past, eyes sharpened with suspicion.

Following Anton's directions, Kirov steered the car into a courtyard at the back of a large two-story house. High stone walls surrounded the courtyard, obscuring any view from the outside. Pekkala could tell at a glance that no one lived here now. Paint around the window frames had flaked away; weeds grew from the gutters. The courtyard walls had once been covered with mortar and painted, but chunks had fallen, revealing the bare stones beneath. The structure seemed to radiate a hostile emptiness.

"Where are we?" asked Kirov, as he climbed out of the car.

"The Ipatiev place," replied Anton. "What we called the House of Special Purpose."

With a key which he took from his pocket, Anton opened the kitchen door and the three men went inside. He found a switch for electric lights and flipped it on, but the dust-covered light fixtures above him stayed dark. Hanging from nails by the door were several storm lanterns, which Kirov filled from a can of kerosene they carried in the Emka. Each man carried a lantern as they passed through the kitchen avoiding a few rickety chairs tipped over on the floor. They emerged into a hallway, with narrow-planked wooden floors and a tall ceiling, from which hung the remains of a crystal chandelier. Their shadows loomed across the walls. Ahead of them was the front door, leading out into the street, and to the left, a staircase to the second floor, its bannister thick with dust. On the right, a stone fireplace dominated the front room.

Pekkala breathed the stagnant air. "Why isn't anyone living here now?"

"The house was closed down as soon as the Romanovs disappeared. Nikolai Ipatiev, the man who owned it, left for Vienna and never came back."

"Look." Kirov pointed to bullet gashes in the wallpaper. "Let's get out of here. Let's go to the hotel."

"What hotel?" asked Anton.

Kirov blinked at him. "The one where we are staying while we conduct the investigation."

"We're staying here," replied Anton.

Kirov's eyes widened. "Oh, no. Not here."

Anton shrugged.

"But this place is empty!" protested Kirov.

"It won't be when we're in it."

"I mean there's no furniture!" Kirov pointed into the front room. "Look!"

Along one wall of the empty room, tall windows looked out into the street. Curtains made of heavy dark green velvet had not only been closed, they had also been stitched together so that there was no way to open them.

Kirov pleaded with them. "There's got to be a hotel in town, one with a decent bed."

"There is," said Anton, "but it's not in the budget."

"What's that supposed to mean?" Kirov demanded. "Can't you just wave those orders around and get us whatever we want?"

"The orders say that this is where we are to make our headquarters."

"Maybe there are beds on the second floor," suggested Pekkala.

"Yes," said Kirov. "I'll check." He raced up the stairs, the lantern swinging in his hand, long shadows trailing after him like snakes.

"There are no beds," muttered Anton.

"What happened to them?" Pekkala asked.

"Stolen," Anton replied, "along with everything else. When the Ipatiev family moved out, they were allowed to bring some of their possessions—pictures and so on. By the time the Romanovs arrived, only the essentials remained. When we left town, the good people of Sverdlovsk came in before the Whites arrived and stripped the place bare. By the time they got here, there was probably nothing left worth stealing."

Kirov stomped around upstairs. As he moved from room to room, the floorboards creaked under his weight. His curses echoed through the house.

"Where is the basement?" asked Pekkala.

"This way," said Anton. Carrying a lantern, he led Pekkala through the kitchen to a pale yellow door, greasy fingerprints smudged around its old brass handle.

Anton opened the door.

A plain wooden staircase led down into the dark.

"Down there," Anton told him, "is where we found the guards."

The two men descended to the basement. On their left, at the bottom of the stairs, they came upon a coal storage chamber. A trapdoor in the ceiling opened to allow the coal to be poured in from ground level. What remained in the chamber was mostly dust, heaped in the corners. Only a few nuggets of coal lay strewn around the floor. It seemed as if even the coal had been stolen. To their right was a room which would normally have been closed off with a double set of doors, but the doors were open, revealing a space four paces wide by ten paces long, with a low, arched ceiling. Stripes of white and pinkish red papered the walls. On the pink stripes, Pekkala saw a repeating image which reminded him of a stylized design of a small tortoise. Rooms like this were used for the storage of clothing during the seasons when it was not being used.

Tidy as the place must once have been, it was now destroyed. Huge chunks of the wallpaper were missing, revealing a latticework of plaster, earth, and stone, much of which was now strewn across the floor. Bullet holes pocked the walls. Large stains of dried blood patched the ground, mixing with crumbs of mortar to form crusts like dark brown shields lying scattered on an ancient battlefield. Streaks of blood appeared to hang suspended in the air, and only by focusing hard could Pekkala see that they had, in fact, been splashed across the walls.

"Based on what Katamidze told me," he said, "the guards were killed upstairs and dragged down here, probably to confuse investigators about where all this blood came from."

"If you say so." Anton looked around nervously. The bullet holes in the walls seemed to peer at them like eyes.

Pekkala spotted the lips of cartridge rims lying in the dust. Bending down, he picked one up and turned it over in his fingers. He used his thumb to rub away dust from the base and saw a tiny dent in the center where the gun's firing pin had ignited the percussion cap. The markings around the base were Russian, dated 1918, indicating that the ammunition had been new when it was fired. Gathering up a handful of other cartridges, he noted that they were all made by the same manufacturer and all bore the same date.

"I have been meaning to talk to you," said Anton.

Pekkala turned to his brother, who stood like a statue, lantern raised above his head to light the room. "About what?"

Anton glanced over his shoulder, to check that Kirov was nowhere around. "About that thing you called a fairy tale."

"You mean the Tsar's treasure?"

Anton nodded. "You and I both know it exists."

"Oh, it exists," agreed Pekkala. "I won't argue with that. The fairy tale is that I know where it's hidden."

Anton struggled to contain his frustration. "The Tsar kept no secrets from you. You may be the only one on earth he really trusted. He must have told you where he hid his gold."

"Even if I did know where it was," Pekkala said, "it's precisely because the Tsar did trust me that I would not think of taking it."

Anton reached out and gripped his brother's arm. "The Tsar is *dead*! His blood is on the floor beneath your feet. Your loyalty now is to the living."

"If Alexei is alive, that gold belongs to him."

"And after what your loyalty has cost you, don't you think that you deserve some of it as well?"

"The only gold I need is what the dentist put in my teeth."

"And what about Ilya? What does she deserve?"

At the mention of her name, Pekkala shuddered. "Leave her out of this," he said.

"Don't tell me you've forgotten her," Anton taunted.

"Of course not. I think about her all the time."

"And you think perhaps she has forgotten you?"

Pekkala shrugged. He seemed to be in pain, as if his shoulder blades had grown too heavy for his back.

"You waited for her, didn't you?" Anton insisted. "Then who's to say she did not wait for you? She paid a price for her loyalty, too, but her loyalty was not to the Tsar. It was to *you*. And you owe it to her, when you find her again, to make sure she doesn't end up begging in the street."

Pekkala's head was spinning. The patterns on the wallpaper danced before his eyes. It seemed to him the dull brown stains upon the floorboards were shining once again with the glimmer of fresh blood.

It was March 1917.

Pekkala heard a knocking at the door of his cottage on the Tsarskoye Selo estate, where he had been confined for months.

When he answered the door, he was astonished to see the Tsar standing there. Even though they were both prisoners here, the Tsar had never come to visit him before. In the peculiar balance of their lives, and even in a time like this, Pekkala's privacy was more sacred than the Tsar's.

The Tsar had aged in the past two months. The skin under his eyes sagged. The color was leached from his cheeks. He wore a slate gray tunic with plain brass buttons and a collar buttoned tight against his throat. "May I come in?" he asked.

"Yes," Pekkala answered.

The Tsar waited a moment. "Then perhaps you could step aside."

Pekkala almost tripped over himself getting out of the way.

"I can't stay long," the Tsar said. "They have me under constant surveillance. I must get back before they notice I am gone." Standing in the low-ceilinged front room, the Tsar glanced at the pale yellow walls, taking in the little fireplace and the chair set out before it. His eyes roamed around the room until at last his gaze locked on Pekkala's. "I apologize for not contacting you until now. But the truth is, the less you are seen with me, the better. I've heard a rumor that we are to be moved away from here, my family and I, sometime in the next couple of months."

"Where are you going?"

"I heard someone mention Siberia. At least we will stay together. That is part of the agreement." He sighed heavily. "Things have taken a turn for the worse. I was obliged to send a message to Major Kolchak. You remember him, don't you?"

"Yes, Excellency. Your insurance policy."

"Exactly. And in the spirit of taking care of what is valuable to

me"—the Tsar smiled bleakly—"my old friend, I want you to get out of here." He reached into his pocket and pulled out a leather wallet. "Here are the documents for your journey."

"Documents?"

"Forged, of course. Identity. Train tickets. Some money. They're still taking proper currency. The Bolsheviks have not had time to print their own yet."

"But, Excellency," he protested, "I cannot agree to this—"

"Pekkala, if our friendship has meant anything to you, do not force me to take responsibility for your death. As soon as we have gone from Tsarskoye Selo, they'll waste no time rounding up whoever's left. And I can no more vouch for their safety than I can for my own. Once they realize you are missing, Pekkala, they will begin a search. The more of a head start you can get, the safer you will be. As you know," the Tsar continued, "they have sealed off all entrances except the main gate and the entrance to the kitchen, but there is a section near the Lamskoy Pavilion which has been only partially blocked. It's too narrow for vehicles, but a man alone can get through. A car is waiting for you there. It will take you as far as it can towards the Finnish border. There are no trains coming into the city, but they are still running in the outer districts. With any luck, you can catch one of those bound for Helsinki." The Tsar held out the leather wallet. "Take it, Pekkala."

Still confused, Pekkala removed the wallet from the Tsar's outstretched hand.

"Ah. And there is one more thing," said the Tsar. Reaching into the pocket of his tunic, he removed Pekkala's copy of the Kalevala, *which he had borrowed months before. "Perhaps you thought I had forgotten." The Tsar placed the book in Pekkala's hands. "I enjoyed it very much, Pekkala. You should take another look at it."*

"But, Excellency." Pekkala set the book down on the table. "I know all the stories by heart."

"Trust me, Pekkala." The Tsar picked up the book again and slapped it gently against Pekkala's chest.

Pekkala stared at him in confusion. "Very well, Excellency." To hear the Tsar rambling like this almost brought him to tears. He understood that there was nothing more he could do. "When am I to leave?"

"Now!" The Tsar walked to the open doorway and pointed across the wide expanse of the Alexander Park, in the direction of the Lamskoy Pavilion. "It's time you settled down with that schoolteacher of yours. Where is she now?"

"Paris, Excellency."

"Do you know exactly where she is?"

"No, but I will find her."

"I don't doubt it," the Tsar replied. "That's what you're trained in, after all. I wish I could come with you, Pekkala."

They both knew how impossible that was.

"Now go," the Tsar told him. "Before it is too late."

Helpless to object, Pekkala set out across the park. Before he disappeared among the trees, however, he looked back towards his cottage.

The Tsar was still there, watching him go. He raised one hand in farewell.

In that moment, Pekkala felt a piece of himself die, like darkness turning in upon itself.

"IF YOU COULD JUST BRING US TO IT," ANTON INSISTED. "WE wouldn't have to take it all."

"Enough," said Pekkala.

"Kirov doesn't even need to know about it."

"Enough!" he said again.

Anton fell silent.

Their shadows tilted with the movements of the lantern flame.

"For the last time, Anton, I don't know where it is."

Anton wheeled and started walking up the stairs.

"Anton!"

But his brother did not stop.

Knowing it was useless to pursue him, Pekkala returned to the dusty cartridges in the palm of his hand. Each one was 7.62 mm. They belonged to an M1895 Nagant. The revolver had a flimsy-looking barrel, a handle like a banana, and a large hammer like a thumb bent back on itself. In spite of its ungainly appearance, however, the Nagant was a work of art; its beauty emerged only when it was put to use. It fitted perfectly in the hand, the balance was precise, and for a handgun it was extremely accurate.

It was the unique shape of the cartridges Pekkala had found which betrayed the Nagant's identity. In most types of ammunition, the bullet extended from the end of the cartridge, but in a Nagant's cartridge the bullet nestled inside the brass tube. The reason for this was to form a gas seal which would provide more power when the gun fired. This gave the Nagant the added advantage of being adaptable for use with a silencer. Guns equipped with silencers had quickly become the weapon of choice for murderers: Pekkala had often encountered Nagants at crime scenes, the large cigar-like silencers screwed onto the ends of their barrels, abandoned near the bodies of shooting victims.

The sound of gunfire in an enclosed space like this must have been deafening, Pekkala thought. He tried to imagine the room as it would have been when the shooting finally stopped. The smoke and shattered plaster. Blood soaking into the dust. "A slaughterhouse," he whispered to himself.

More bullet marks gashed the walls on the staircase, showing that the guards had not given up without a fight. On the second floor, where the Romanovs had lived, there were four bedrooms, two large and two small, as well as two studies. One room, its walls papered in dark green with fitted wooden shelves, had obviously belonged to a man. The other, whose walls were peach-colored, held a cushioned bench, upon which the woman of the house could have sat and looked out at people passing by on the road. The bench still lay in the room, tipped over on its side. One of its legs had been torn off by the impact of a bullet. An oval mirror hung crookedly on the wall, one shark's tooth of glass remaining in the frame while the rest of it had fallen to the ground. Cobwebs hung on the light fixture above him. Traces of whitewash were still visible on the windowpanes. The Whites must have cleaned it off when they occupied the house, thought Pekkala.

He stood on the landing, his eye following the mercury-bright line of the polished bannister down to the ground floor. He tried to imagine the Tsar standing in this same spot. He remembered how the Tsar would sometimes pause in the middle of a sentence or when striding down one of the long hallways of the Winter Palace. He would remain motionless, like a man who heard music in the distance and was trying to pick up the tune. Now, as Pekkala made his way downstairs, he remembered times in the forest when he had watched stags, with antlers like forked branches of lightning emerging from their skulls, pause in just that way, waiting for some danger to reveal itself.

The three men sat tired and stony-faced around the bare wood kitchen table. The only sound was the scraping of spoons inside tins of food. They had no plates or bowls. Anton had simply opened half a dozen cans of vegetables and army ration meat and set them in the middle of the table. When one man was tired of eating sliced carrots, he put the tin back on the table and picked up a jar of shredded beets. They drank water from the well outside, poured into a chip-rimmed flower vase which they'd found on the floor of an upstairs room.

Kirov was the first to break. He shoved away his can of meat and snarled, "How much of this do I have to endure?" From his pocket, he pulled out the wooden apple. He thumped it down on the table. The painted red apple seemed to glow from the inside. "It makes my mouth water just to look at it," said Kirov. He reached into his pocket and brought out his pipe. "To make things worse, I am almost out of tobacco."

"Come now, Kirov," Anton said. "What's become of our happy little Junior Man?" He removed a bulging leather pouch from his pocket and inspected its contents. A leafy smell of unburned tobacco wafted across the table. "My own supply is holding out quite nicely."

"Lend me some," said Kirov.

"Get your own." Anton breathed in, ready to say more, but his sentence was interrupted by a sound like a pebble thrown against a window.

The three men jumped.

The pipe fell out of Kirov's mouth.

"What the hell was that?" Anton asked.

The sound came again, louder now.

Anton drew his gun.

"Someone is at the door," Pekkala said.

Whoever it was had come around the back, rather than risk being seen at the front of the house.

Pekkala went to see who it was.

The other two stayed at the table.

When Pekkala reappeared, he was followed by an old man with a wide belly and a side-to-side plod which made him teeter like a metronome as he walked into the room. With small, almond-brown eyes, he peered suspiciously at Anton.

"This is Yevgeny Mayakovsky," Pekkala said.

The old man nodded in greeting.

"He says," continued Pekkala, "he has information."

"I remember you." Anton was staring at the old man.

"I remember you, too." Mayakovsky turned to leave. "Perhaps I should be going now—" he said.

"Not so fast." Anton held up his hand. "Why don't you stay for a while?" He pulled out a chair and patted the seat. "Make yourself comfortable."

Reluctantly, Mayakovsky sat, sweat already dappling his red-veined cheeks.

"How is it you know each other?" asked Pekkala.

"Oh, he tried this little trick once before," Anton replied. "The day the Cheka arrived, he showed up with information to sell. Swore he could make himself useful to us."

"And did he?" Kirov asked.

"We didn't give him the chance," Anton replied.

"They broke my nose," said Mayakovsky, quietly. "It was uncivilized."

"If you were looking for civilization," replied Anton, "you knocked at the wrong door."

"When I saw the lights on here," continued Mayakovsky, ignoring him, "I did not realize it was you." He stirred in his chair. "I'll just be on my way—"

"No one is going to hurt you this time," Pekkala told him.

Mayakovsky eyed him. "Is that so?"

"I give you my word," Pekkala replied.

"I've got something worth knowing," said Mayakovsky, tapping a stubby finger against his temple.

"What are you talking about?" asked Pekkala.

"When the Whites came in, they set up a board of inquiry. They didn't believe the Romanovs had survived. All they were interested in was making sure that the Reds took the blame. Then, when the Reds came back, they set up their own inquiry. Just like the Whites, they figured the Romanovs had all been killed. The difference was that the Reds wanted to be told that the guards in this house had taken matters into their own hands. It seemed like everyone wanted the Romanovs dead, but nobody wanted to be responsible for killing them. And then, of course, there's what *really* happened."

"And what is that?" asked Pekkala.

Mayakovsky clapped his hands together softly. "Well, that is the part which I have come to sell."

Anton snorted. "We don't have money for buying information."

"You could trade," said Mayakovsky, his voice barely above a whisper.

"Trade what?" asked Kirov.

The old man licked his lips. "That's a nice pipe you're smoking."

"Forget it!" Kirov's back straightened. "You're not getting this!"

"Give him the pipe," said Pekkala.

"What?"

"Yes, I would like that pipe," said Mayakovsky.

"Well, you can't have it!" shouted Kirov. "I'm already sleeping on the floor. You can't expect me to—"

"Give him the pipe," repeated Pekkala, "and let's hear what this man has to say."

Kirov appealed to Anton. "He can't make me do that!"

"He just did," said Anton.

"Nobody knows what I know," Mayakovsky said.

Kirov glared at Anton and Pekkala. "You bastards!"

Both men eyed him patiently.

"Well, this is just outrageous!" said Kirov.

Mayakovsky held out his hand for the pipe.

Anton folded his arms and laughed.

"And give him your tobacco." Pekkala nodded at the leather pouch which lay upon the table.

The laughter died in Anton's throat. "My tobacco?"

"Yes." Kirov thumped the table with his fist. "Give him your tobacco."

The old man held out his hand and wiggled his fingers at Anton.

"You'd better have something good." Anton tossed the pouch at the old man. "Or I'm going to adjust your face again."

While the three men watched, Mayakovsky loaded the pipe and set it burning with a fluff-covered match that he pulled from his waistcoat pocket and lit on the sole of his shoe. He puffed contentedly for a minute. And then he began to talk. "I read in the papers that the Romanovs are dead."

"Everybody read that!" Kirov sneered. "The whole world read about it."

"They did," nodded Mayakovsky. "But it isn't true."

Anton opened his mouth to shout the old man down.

Sharply, Pekkala raised a hand to silence him.

With a grumble, Anton settled back in his chair.

"Mayakovsky," said Pekkala, "what makes you think they aren't dead?"

"Because I saw the whole thing!" answered the old man. "I live across the road."

"All right, Mayakovsky," said Pekkala, "you tell us what happened."

"That night the Romanovs were rescued," Mayakovsky continued, "a load of Cheka guards suddenly came running out into the courtyard of the Ipatiev house. They kept two trucks in the courtyard. The guards piled into one of them and drove away."

"A call had just come in," said Anton. "We were ordered to set up a roadblock. The Whites were getting ready to attack. At least that's what we were told."

"Well, only a few minutes after that truck left, that damned fool Katamidze came to the front door of this house! He's the photographer they've got locked up in Vodovenko. I'm not surprised the bastard ended up in there. Calling himself an artist. Well, I saw some of that art. Naked ladies. There's another name for that. And those pictures were expensive—"

"Mayakovsky!" Pekkala cut him off. "What happened when the photographer arrived at the house?"

"The guards let him in. And a few minutes after that, a Cheka officer came to the door. He knocked and the guards let him in. Then the shooting started."

"Then what did you see?" asked Pekkala.

"A regular gun battle," answered Mayakovsky, grimly.

"Wait a minute," Anton interrupted. "There was a tall fence around the whole building. Except for the front door and the entrance to the courtyard, the whole place was surrounded. How did you see anything?"

"I told you. I live across the road," said Mayakovsky. "There's a little window in my attic. If I went up there, I could see over the top of the fence."

"But the windows had been painted over," said Anton. "They'd even been glued shut."

"I could see the flash of guns going from room to room. When the shooting stopped, the front door flew open and I saw Katamidze come tearing out of the house. He went running off into the dark."

"Do you think Katamidze was involved in the gunfight?" asked Pekkala.

Mayakovsky laughed. "If you gave Katamidze a gun, he wouldn't know which end the bullets came out of. If you're thinking he was brave enough to attack the Ipatiev house and rescue the Tsar, you don't know Katamidze."

"What happened after Katamidze left?" Pekkala asked.

"About twenty minutes later, the second Cheka truck pulled out of the courtyard and headed off in the opposite direction from the first truck. That was the Romanovs. They were getting away, along with the man who rescued them. It wasn't long afterwards that the first truck returned. The Cheka realized they'd been tricked. That's when all hell broke loose. The guards had been killed. I heard one of the Cheka yell that the Romanovs had escaped."

"How do you know the guards were killed?"

"Because I saw their bodies being carried out into the courtyard the next day. I didn't see the bodies of the Romanovs. That's how I knew they'd escaped. It's the truth, no matter what the papers had to say about it."

For a moment, there was silence in the room, except for the faint wheeze of Mayakovsky smoking his pipe.

"That man who came to the door," said Kirov. "Did you see his face?"

Pekkala glanced at Kirov.

Kirov's face reddened. "What I meant was—"

Anton interrupted him. "Yes, what did you mean *exactly,* Junior Man? I did not realize you had taken over this investigation."

Mayakovsky watched this, like a man following the ball at a tennis match.

"That's all right." Pekkala nodded at Kirov. "Continue."

Anton threw his hands up in the air. "Now we're *really* making progress."

Kirov cleared his throat. "Can you describe the man you saw that day, Mayakovsky?"

"He had his back to me. It was dark." Mayakovsky picked at something stuck between his front teeth. "I don't know who he was, but I'll tell you who they say rescued the Tsar."

"Who's *they*?" Pekkala interposed.

"They!" Mayakovsky shrugged. "*They* do not have a name. *They* are voices. All different voices. They come together and that's how you know what they say."

"All right," said Kirov. "Who do they say it was?"

"A famous man. A man I wish I'd met."

"And who is that?"

"Inspector Pekkala," said Mayakovsky. "The Emerald Eye himself. That's who rescued the Tsar."

The three men had been leaning forward, but now they slumped back in their seats. All three of them let out a sigh.

"What's the matter?" demanded Mayakovsky.

"The matter," replied Kirov, "is that the Emerald Eye is sitting right in front of you." He gestured vaguely at Pekkala.

The old man took the pipe from his mouth and aimed the stem at Pekkala. "Well, you do get around, don't you?"

Less than twenty-four hours after he had said good-bye to the Tsar, Pekkala was arrested by a detachment of Red Guard Railway Police at a tiny station called Vainikkala. The situation along the border was still chaotic. Some stations were manned by Finnish personnel, while other stations even farther west were under Russian control. One of these was Vainikkala.

It was late at night when the Guards boarded the train. Their uniforms were made of coarse black wool with collars piped in cherry red, and on their right sleeves they wore homemade red armbands on which someone had drawn the sign of a hammer and a plow, soon to be replaced by a hammer and sickle as the symbol of the Soviet Union. They wore black, short-brimmed hats to match their uniforms, with a large red star sewn on the front.

Pekkala's forged papers listed him as a doctor of obstetrics. The papers had been made for him some time ago by the Okhrana's printing service on the orders of the Tsar. Until the Tsar handed him these documents, Pekkala had not even known the Okhrana ran a printing service. The papers were perfect, complete with photograph, all relevant stamps, and handwritten signatures on multiple travel permits. His papers were not why he was stopped.

Pekkala's mistake had been to raise his head and look one of the

Guards in the eye as three of them made their way down the narrow corridor of the train. Snow was melting on the Guards' shoulders and condensation beaded on their weapons.

The lead Guard had tripped on the carrying strap of a bag stuffed under a seat several rows ahead of where Pekkala sat. He stumbled and fell heavily to one knee, swearing coarsely. People in the carriage flinched at the torrent of obscenities. The Guard's head snapped up. He was furious and embarrassed to have tripped. The first person he saw was Pekkala, who just happened, at that moment, to be looking back at him.

"Let's go," snarled the Guard, and hauled Pekkala to his feet.

Pekkala's first breath of cold air as he left the train felt like pepper in his lungs.

A dozen people, most of them men but a few pretty women as well, had been taken off the train. They stood huddled on the platform. The name of the station was barely visible under its coral-like coating of frost.

The train stamped and snorted, impatient to push on into the night, bound for Helsinki.

Pekkala weighed the situation in his head. He knew these men were probably just former soldiers, not professionals who could spot well-forged papers or know what questions to ask to trip up a man who was not who he was supposed to be. One well-aimed question about obstetrics could have punched a hole through Pekkala's disguise. There had been no time for him to research his new profession.

The Webley was strapped against Pekkala's chest. He could easily have shot the one man guarding them and run away into the dark while the others continued their search of the train. But one glance into the thick, snow-filled forests which surrounded the station and Pekkala knew he wouldn't get far. Even if they didn't catch him, he would most likely freeze to death.

There was nothing to do but hope that the Guards had satisfied their curiosity and their need for feeling important. Then they could all just get back on the train.

His plan had been to visit his parents, then press on via Stockholm to

Copenhagen and from there down to Paris. There he would begin his search for Ilya.

The rest of the Guards disembarked.

Passengers rubbed circles on the condensation-soaked windows to see what was happening outside.

The Guard who had tripped made his way down the line of those who had been detained, examining their papers. He was a little too large for his tunic, whose sleeves stopped well above his wrists. A lit cigarette hung from between his lips, and when he spoke he sounded like a man with nerve damage to his face.

"All right," he told one of the passengers. "You can go."

The man did not look back. He ran to get aboard the train.

Two women who had been ahead of Pekkala and who had not been told to get on board stood weeping in the glare of the station lights. It had begun to snow and the shadows of flakes passed huge as clouds over the frozen platform.

The Guard came to Pekkala. "A doctor," he said.

"Yes, sir." Pekkala kept his head lowered.

"What is this bone?" asked the man.

And then Pekkala knew he was trapped. Not because he could not name the bones of the human body. For years a chart of the human body had hung in his father's mortuary room; there were few bones he could not name. The reason Pekkala knew he was trapped was that if he made eye contact with the Guard, there was no chance that he would be allowed to leave. It was no different than if he had been standing in front of a dog. To the Guard, it had become a game.

"This bone here," said the man, and snapped his fingers to draw Pekkala's attention.

Pekkala looked down at his feet. Snowflakes landed on his boots.

The train wheezed impatiently.

A breath of cigarette smoke brushed past his face.

"Answer me, damn you," said the Guard.

At that, Pekkala had no choice but to raise his head.

The Guard grinned at him. His cigarette had burned so low that the ember almost touched his lips. He held his hand up beside his head, moving his fingers slowly in some mockery of a greeting.

Their eyes met.

When the train pulled out, only Pekkala and one of the women stayed behind. Pekkala was handcuffed to a bench. The Guards dragged the woman into the waiting room beside the station house.

Pekkala heard her screaming.

Half an hour later, the woman ran out naked onto the platform.

By then, the snow had stopped. A full moon shone through passing shreds of cloud. The snow which had fallen no longer melted on Pekkala's coat. Instead, it collected upon him like a mantle of polar bear fur. He could not feel his hands. The bars of the handcuffs were so cold they seemed to burn his skin. His toes became as hard as bullets hammered into the soft flesh of his feet.

The naked woman reached the platform edge. Her feet skidded in the slush. For one second, she turned and looked at Pekkala.

Twisted into her face was the same expression of terror he had once seen in the eyes of an old horse which had collapsed by the side of the road. The owner had pulled out a long puukko knife and was preparing to cut the animal's throat. He sat down beside the horse and sharpened the knife on a small whetstone he had set upon his knee. The horse watched him the whole time, its eyes gone hollow with fear.

The woman leaped off the platform and fell heavily onto the rails half a body's length below. Then she picked herself up and began running away down the tracks in the direction of Helsinki.

The Guards shambled out onto the platform. One was dabbing his fingers against a bloody lip. They looked around, laughing and confused.

"Hey!" A Guard kicked Pekkala's leg. "Where did she go?"

Before he could answer, the leader of the Guards had spotted her. She was still running. Her naked back shone white as alabaster in the moonlight. Silky puffs of breath rose from her head.

The Guard took out a revolver. It was a 9 mm broomhandle Mauser with a wooden holster which could be converted into a stock, so that the gun could be fired like a rifle. The Guard removed the holster and hooked it up to the butt of the gun. Then he nestled the stock into his shoulder and aimed down the tracks towards the running woman. The gun made a dry snap. A cartridge flipped into the air and skittered across the platform, spinning to a stop next to Pekkala's boot. A wisp of gun smoke slithered from its mouth.

The other Guards clustered at the platform edge, peering into the dark.

"She's still running," one said.

The leader of the Guards aimed again and fired.

The smell of cordite drifted on the frigid air.

"Missed," said a Guard.

The leader spun around. "Then give me some space!"

The other Guards were not within three paces of the leader, but they jostled back obediently.

Leaning forward, Pekkala could vaguely see the woman still on her feet and running, her body like a candle flame shimmering between the silver rails.

The leader of the Guards aimed again. He fired twice.

The flame which had been the woman seemed to flicker for a second and then it went out.

The leader set the gun stock in the crook of his elbow, the barrel aimed now at the sky.

"Should we go get her?" asked one of the Guards.

"Let her freeze," replied the leader. "She won't be there in the morning."

"Why not?"

"There's another train coming through before dawn. When that thing hits her, she'll shatter like a piece of glass."

The following morning, a Guard placed a black cloth over Pekkala's head. When the train from Helsinki arrived, he was shoved across the platform, blind and choking for air. Rough hands hauled him on board.

He lay in the unheated baggage compartment, handcuffed to a replacement tractor engine, until the train pulled into Petrograd.

"What if the Romanovs were in that truck . . ." Pekkala said.

Mayakovsky turned in the doorway. "I already told you they were."

"But what if they were dead when the truck took them away?"

"Listen to me," said the old man impatiently. "Everybody in this town knew that when those Cheka men arrived in town, the only reason for them being there was to make sure the Romanovs were dead before the Whites marched into town. That's why they kicked out the local militiamen who had been guarding the Ipatiev house. Moscow wanted to be absolutely sure that if the Whites came close enough, the Cheka would carry out the executions and wouldn't just run away like the militia might have done. If anybody on the outside wanted the Romanovs killed, all they had to do was wait for the Whites to show up. The only kind of person who would break into that house and risk their life in a gunfight with those Guards was someone who wanted to save the Tsar's family, not kill them off."

After Mayakovsky had gone, the three men returned to the table.

"Why did you let him go on talking?" asked Kirov, "when you knew what he was saying was a pack of lies?"

"For once," said Anton, "I agree with Junior Man here. And the worst part is, the old bastard thinks he got away with it."

"Mayakovsky didn't think he was lying," Pekkala told them. "He's convinced that the only reason you and the other Cheka guards took over from the militia was so that you could murder the family."

"We replaced the militia," replied Anton, "because they were stealing from the Romanovs. The Tsar was being guarded by a gang of petty thieves. It was unprofessional. They could no longer be relied upon for anything."

"But you see how your arrival must have looked to someone on the outside. That's why Mayakovsky believed what he was saying. It's important to know how people have perceived a crime, even if you know it's not the truth."

"Either it's true or it's not." Anton picked up the wooden apple and tossed it to Pekkala. "You're sounding like the men who gave us these."

"The difference," said Pekkala, "is that we're solving a crime, not committing one."

Anton flung up his hands. "You go ahead and run this investigation however you want. I am going to the tavern to see if I can beg for some tobacco, since that's the only chance I have of getting any." He stalked out, slamming the door behind him.

Kirov and Pekkala went to the frigid front room and built a fire. They brought the chairs in from the kitchen and sat in front of the hearth, blankets over their shoulders, and hands held out toward the flames.

From his coat pocket, Pekkala removed the old book he had brought with him. As he read, his expression grew distant. The lines smoothed out in his face.

"What's that?" Kirov demanded.

"The *Kalevala*," murmured Pekkala and kept reading.

"The what?"

Pekkala groaned and set the book down on his knee. "It's a book of stories," he explained.

"What sort of stories?"

"Legends."

"I don't know any legends."

"They are like ghost stories. You don't have to believe them, but it's hard to think there is no truth in them at all."

"Do you believe in ghosts, Pekkala?"

"Why are you asking, Kirov?"

"Because I just saw one," he said.

Pekkala sat up. "What?"

Kirov shrugged awkwardly. "While I was making the fire, someone looked in at that window." He pointed to the curtains in the corner near the fireplace. From where the two men sat, they could see a small piece of window glass which was not covered by the curtain. Through this, the silhouettes of tree branches stirred like strange aquatic creatures in the moonlight.

"It's probably just some drunk on his way home from the tavern who wanted to see why there were lights on in this place. People are bound to be curious."

Embarrassed, Kirov scratched at his blushing cheeks. "It's just that . . . well . . . it just sounds . . ."

"What is it, Kirov? Spit it out so I can get back to reading my book."

"It's just that I could have sworn that man looking in at the window was the Tsar. That beard of his. Those sad-looking eyes. Of course, I've only seen pictures. And it was dark. . . . Maybe I just imagined him."

Pekkala got to his feet and left the room. He opened the front door. The night breeze seeped past him, replacing the still air which had accumulated inside the Ipatiev house. For a long time, he stood there, staring at the shuttered windows of houses across the street, searching for any sign which might give away the presence of an observer. He did not see anybody, but he did have the feeling that someone was there.

When at last Pekkala returned to the front room, he found Kirov squatting before the fire, adding pieces of a broken chair.

Pekkala sat down where he had been before.

The flames spat as they rose around the splintered wood.

"I told you I must have imagined it," said Kirov.

"Maybe," Pekkala replied.

Pekkala sat up abruptly.

The crash of breaking glass had woken him.

Kirov was already on his feet. His hair stuck up in tufts. "It came from in there." He pointed to the kitchen. Softly he walked into the next room and lit one of the lanterns.

Pekkala threw back his blanket and rubbed his face. Probably just Anton, he thought. He's got himself locked out and broke a window trying to get in again.

"Damned kids!" said Kirov.

Pekkala got to his feet. He took the Webley from its holster, just in case. On stiff legs, he made his way into the kitchen. The first thing he saw was that the window above the sink had been broken. Shards scattered the floor.

Kirov peered out the broken window. "Go away!" he shouted into the darkness. "Get the hell out of here!"

"What did they throw?" asked Pekkala.

"A piece of a table leg."

Pekkala's breath caught in his throat.

In Kirov's hand was a German stick grenade: a gray-painted metal cylinder like a small soup can attached to a wooden stick a little shorter than a man's forearm, so that the grenade could be thrown a great distance.

"What?" asked Kirov. He looked at Pekkala, then at the stick in his hand. Suddenly, he seemed to understand. "Oh, my God," he whispered.

Pekkala grabbed the grenade from Kirov's hand and threw it back through the kitchen window, shattering another pane of glass. Grabbing Kirov's shirt, he pulled him down to the floor.

The grenade clattered across the courtyard. Glass fragments clinked musically on the cobblestones.

Pekkala put his hands over his ears, his mouth open to equalize the pressure, bracing for the roar. He knew that if the men outside had been properly trained, they would enter the house immediately after the detonation. Pekkala lay as close to the wall as he could get, to avoid being hurt when the windows and the door blew in. These grenades had a seven-second fuse. Vassileyev himself had taught him that. He waited, counting, but there was no explosion. Satisfied at last that the grenade had been a dud, he rose and looked out into the courtyard. Moonlight glinted off the glass shards and off the Emka's windshield, dividing the courtyard into geometric shapes of bluish light and neatly chiseled angles of black shadow. The silence was profound.

"Let's go," he said, nudging Kirov with his toe.

Cautiously, the two men walked out into the courtyard. Stars fanned out across the sky.

The gate was open. It had been closed when they went to sleep.

"Should we try to follow them?" Kirov asked.

Pekkala shook his head. "When they realize the grenade didn't go off, they might come back. We'll be safer if we wait for them here."

As Kirov left to get his gun, Pekkala caught sight of the grenade, lying by the storage shed. As he neared it, he could see what appeared to be a small white button lying beside it. Looking closely, he realized that the button was in fact a ball, the size of a small marble, with a hole drilled into the middle. A string had been threaded through the ball. The other end disappeared into the hollow handle of the grenade. This would have been covered with a metal screw cap until the grenade was to be used. The porcelain ball and the string were stored inside the stick and had to be pulled in order to ignite the fuse. Whoever threw the grenade had unscrewed the cap but forgot to pull the cord.

"Maybe it was just a warning," said Kirov, when Pekkala had explained why the grenade did not go off.

Pekkala weighed the stick grenade in his hand, slapping the metal detonator can gently into his palm. He didn't reply.

While Kirov stood watch at the front of the house, Pekkala remained in the kitchen. In the darkness, he sat with the Webley and the grenade laid out in front of him. Tiny flecks of glass lay scattered across the tabletop. Through the broken window, he stared out into the night until his eyes ached and shadows danced about like people taunting him.

Anton showed up at dawn. He went straight to the pump in the courtyard. Its gracefully curved handle wore an old coat of red paint the same vivid color as a holly berry. Rusted iron showed where the paint had been rubbed away. As Anton worked the lever, a bird-like shriek of grinding metal filled the air.

A moment later, a shapeless explosion of silver emerged from the pump head and Anton stuck his face under the stream. When he raised his head, a plume of silver arced over his shoulder. He smoothed his hair back with both hands, eyes closed, mouth open, droplets falling from his chin.

In that moment, Pekkala realized he had seen that pump before.

It was in a picture, one which Pekkala had discovered in an issue of *Pravda* that was left with his winter's rations at the trailhead in Krasnagolyana. The Tsar and his son, Alexei, were cutting wood with a large two-man saw. Each had hold of one end. A pile of wood stood off to one side. The pump was in the background. The photograph had been taken during the Tsar's captivity in this place. The Tsar wore a plain service tunic, much like his captors would have worn. Alexei wore a heavy coat and fur hat, bundled up against a chill his father did not seem to feel. By the time Pekkala saw that picture, the paper was so out of date that the Tsar had been dead more than a year.

Pekkala thought about the face Kirov had glimpsed in the window. Maybe this place is haunted after all, he thought.

Anton barged into the kitchen. His eyes were bloodshot, the whites turned sickly yellow. One of his cheeks was bruised purple, the color almost black where his cheekbone nudged against the skin.

"What happened to you?" Pekkala asked him.

"Let's just say that Mayakovsky isn't the only one in this town who remembers me."

"We had another visitor last night." Pekkala set the grenade on the table.

Anton whistled quietly. He walked over and peered at it. "A dud?"

"They didn't pull the cord."

"That's not something a person does by mistake."

"Then it's a warning," said Pekkala, "and next time we won't be so lucky."

"I have to present my papers at the police station before you can officially begin your investigation," Anton told him. "You can come along and see if they know anything."

ALEXANDER KROPOTKIN, THE SVERDLOVSK POLICE CHIEF, WAS A SQUAT, broad-shouldered man with a thick head of blond hair which he combed straight down over his forehead.

While Pekkala and Anton stood waiting, Kropotkin sat behind his desk, leafing through the papers which Anton had presented to him. He got to the last page, squinted at the signature, then tossed the papers on the desk. "Why do you bother?" he asked.

"Bother with what?" Anton asked.

Kropotkin tapped the orders with a stubby index finger. "Comrade Stalin signed these orders. You can do whatever the hell you want. You don't need my permission."

"It is a courtesy," said Anton.

Kropotkin sat forward, resting his forearms on the desk. He stared at Pekkala. "The Emerald Eye. I heard you were dead."

"You are not the only one who heard that."

"I also heard that you could not be bought, but here you are working for *them*." He jerked his chin towards Anton.

"I have not been bought," Pekkala told him.

"Bribed, then. Or threatened. It doesn't matter. One way or another, you are working for them now."

The words cut into him, but Pekkala chose not to reply.

Kropotkin turned his attention to Anton. "You look familiar. You were one of the Cheka guards, weren't you?"

"Perhaps," Anton replied.

"There is no *perhaps*. I don't forget faces, and I saw you at the tavern the whole time you were here. How many times did I see Cheka men come to fetch you when you were too drunk to walk? And judging from your face, either you are perpetually bruised or you didn't waste any time going back to your old habits. Now you come here to my office and talk to me about *courtesy*? You gentlemen can go to hell. How is that for courtesy?"

"What's got you all steamed up?" demanded Anton.

"You want to know? Fine, I'll tell you. This was a nice, quiet place until your lot brought the Romanovs here. Since then, nothing's ever been the same. You know what people think of when you say the word 'Sverdlovsk'?" He made a gun with his thumb and index finger and set it against his temple. "Death. Execution. Murder. Take your pick. None of it's good. And every time things start to settle down, one of you people drops in and stirs things up again. Nobody wants you here, but I can't kick you out." He jerked his chin towards the door. "So just do your work and then leave us alone."

Pekkala took the grenade from the deep pocket inside his coat and set it on the desk.

Kropotkin stared at it. "What's that? A gift?"

"Someone pitched it through our window last night," Pekkala answered, "but forgot to pull the pin."

"It's German," added Anton.

Kropotkin picked up the grenade. "Actually, it's Austrian. The German stick grenades had belt clips on the cylinder here." He tapped at the gray soup can which contained the explosives. "The Austrian ones didn't."

"You were in the war?" Pekkala asked.

"Yes," replied Kropotkin, "and you learn these things when enough of them get thrown at you."

"We were hoping you might know where it came from."

"The Whites used these," replied Kropotkin. "Most of the men who attacked Sverdlovsk had been in the Austrian Army before they came over to our side. Many of them were still using Austrian equipment."

"You think it might be someone who was with the Whites?" asked Pekkala.

Kropotkin shook his head. "The man who threw this was not with the Whites."

"So you know who might have thrown this?"

Kropotkin's eyes narrowed. "Oh, I know exactly who threw this at you. There's only one man insane enough to throw one of these at you who is also stupid enough not to have pulled the cord when he threw it. His name is Nekrasov. He was one of the militiamen who guarded the Romanovs before the Cheka came in and threw him out. I expect he's still holding a grudge. As soon as the lights went on again in the Ipatiev house, he must have guessed that you people were back."

"But why would he bother to throw it?"

"Best ask him that yourselves." Kropotkin snatched up a pencil, scrawled an address on a notepad, tore off the sheet, and held it out. "This is where you'll find him."

Anton removed the paper from his hand.

"Don't take it the wrong way," laughed Kropotkin. "He tries to kill everybody. He just stinks at it. If Nekrasov hasn't thrown at least one bomb at you by the time you leave, you might as well have stayed at home."

"At least I'm not the only one they hate around here," said Anton, when he and Pekkala were back out in the street. "Do you want me to come with you to see Nekrasov?"

"I'll handle it," said Pekkala. "You look as if you could use some sleep."

Anton nodded, his eyes narrowed against the morning sunlight. "I won't argue with that."

The door opened a crack. From the darkness inside the house, a man peered out at Pekkala. "What do you want?"

"Nekrasov?"

The door swung wide, revealing a man with wavy gray hair and two days' worth of stubble on his chin. "Who wants to know?"

"My name is Pekkala," he replied. Then he punched Nekrasov in the jaw.

When Nekrasov woke up, he was slumped in a wheelbarrow with his arms tied to the wheel behind his back.

Pekkala was sitting on a dark green wooden crate with rope handles. The crate had been stamped with the double-headed Habsburg eagle of the Austro-Hungarian Army. Under that, in yellow letters, were the words GRANATEN and ACHTUNG-EXPLOSIVEN.

Nekrasov lived in a small, thatched-roof cottage with a white picket fence at the front. Inside, the ceiling was so low that Pekkala had to stoop, weaving among dried sprigs of sage, rosemary, and basil, tied with strands of grass and dangling from the beams. As his hand brushed them aside, the smell of the spices drifted softly through the air.

With his hands hooked under Nekrasov's armpits, Pekkala had dragged the man through a room with an old-fashioned bench set against the wall—the kind once used as beds in these single-story houses. Neatly folded on the bench was a blue blanket, along with a dirty red pillow, revealing that the bench was still being used for its original purpose. Next to the bench, Pekkala had found the box of grenades. Seventeen of the original thirty were still inside, each one wrapped in brown wax paper. When he opened the lid of the box, the marzipan smell of the explosives wafted up into his face.

It had rained in the night and now the sun was burning off the moisture. While waiting for Nekrasov to regain consciousness, Pekkala had made himself a cheese sandwich in the man's kitchen. Now he was eating the sandwich for his breakfast.

Nekrasov's eyes fluttered open. Blearily, he looked around, until he caught sight of Pekkala. "What did you say your name was?"

"Pekkala," he replied, as he finished his mouthful.

Nekrasov struggled briefly, against the ropes, then sagged and glared at Pekkala. "You could at least have tied me to a chair."

"A wheelbarrow is just as good."

"I see you have discovered my grenades."

"They weren't hard to find."

"The Whites left them behind. How did you track me down so quickly?"

"The police chief told me about you."

"Kropotkin!" Nekrasov leaned over the side of the wheelbarrow and spat. "He owes me money."

Pekkala held up the grenade. "Would you mind telling me why you threw this through the window last night?"

"Because you people make me sick."

"Which people are you talking about?"

"The Cheka. The GPU. The OGPU. Whatever you call yourselves now."

"I am none of those things," said Pekkala.

"Who else would go into that house? Besides, I saw one of your men go into the tavern last night. I recognized him. He's one of the Cheka bastards who was guarding the Romanovs when they disappeared. You damned Commissar, at least have the decency to tell me the truth."

"I am no Commissar. I am an investigator. I have been engaged by the Bureau of Special Operations."

Nekrasov barked out a laugh. "What was their name last week? And what will it be next week? You're all the same. You just keep changing the words around until they don't mean anything anymore."

Pekkala nodded with resignation. "I have enjoyed our little chat," he said. Then he got up and turned toward the door.

"Where are you going?" called Nekrasov. "You can't just leave me here."

"I'm sure someone else will come by. Eventually. It doesn't look like you receive a lot of visitors, and to judge from what Kropotkin had to say about you, even those who do come are unlikely to set you free anytime soon."

"I don't care. They can go to hell and so can you!"

"You and Kropotkin share a similar vocabulary."

"Kropotkin!" Nekrasov spat again. "He's the one you want to investigate. The Whites treated him well when they came into town. They didn't rough him up like they did everybody else. And when the Reds came back, they made him the chief of police. He's playing both sides, if you ask me, and a man who plays both sides will do anything."

In the open doorway, Pekkala squinted up into the sky. "It looks as if it's going to be a hot day."

"I don't care," replied Nekrasov.

"It's not you I'm thinking of," said Pekkala. "It's those grenades." He nodded at the crate.

"What do you mean?" asked Nekrasov, staring at the ACHTUNG-EXPLOSIVEN lettering.

"That case is dated 1916. Those grenades are thirteen years old. A soldier like yourself must know that dynamite becomes very unstable if it is not stored correctly."

"I stored them! I kept them right beside my bed!"

"But before that."

"I found them in the woods." His voice seemed to grow smaller.

Once more Pekkala stared up at the mare's-tailed blue sky. "Well, good-bye." He turned to leave.

"Go to hell!"

"As you said."

Pekkala started walking.

"Wait!" Nekrasov shouted. "All right. I'm sorry I threw a grenade at you."

"If I had a ruble for every time I'd heard that"—Pekkala paused and turned—"I would only have one ruble."

"Well, what more do you want?"

"You could answer some questions."

"Questions about what?"

Pekkala returned. He sat down again on the crate. "Is it true you were one of the militiamen who guarded the Ipatiev house?"

"Yes, and the only one who's left alive, too."

"What happened to the others?"

"There were twelve of us. When the Whites came, we were ordered to hold a bridge on the outskirts of the town. We tipped over a cart to block the way and took cover behind it. But that didn't stop the Whites. They rolled up an Austrian mountain howitzer. Then they fired two rounds at us on a flat trajectory at a range of less than one hundred meters. At that range, you don't even *hear* the gun go off. The first round killed half the people I was with. The second round hit the cart dead center. I don't remember that. All I know is when I woke up, I was lying in the ditch by the side of the road. I was naked except for my boots and one sleeve of my shirt. Everything else had been torn off my body by the blast. One of the cart wheels was hanging from a tree branch on the other side of the road. There were bodies everywhere. They were on fire. The Whites had left me for dead and gone through. I was the only survivor of the men they sent to hold that damn bridge."

"Nekrasov, I understand why you would hate the Whites, but I don't see what you have against the Cheka. After all, the only thing they did was replace you as guards for the Romanovs."

"All? That's all they did?" Again he struggled to free himself, but the bonds were tight and he gave up. "The Cheka humiliated us! They said we were stealing from the Tsar."

"Were you stealing?"

"It was only little stuff," he protested. "There were nuns from the convent in town. They brought food in baskets, and the Tsar gave them books as presents in return. We swiped a few potatoes. You can go ask the nuns, if there're any of them left. They're closing down the convent. Canceling *God*! What do you think of that?"

"Was that all you took? A few potatoes?"

"I don't know!" Nekrasov's face had turned red. "Sometimes a fountain pen might disappear. Sometimes a deck of fancy playing cards. Little stuff, I'm telling you! Nobody starved. Nobody even went to bed hungry. We were told to make them feel like they were prisoners. We weren't allowed to talk to them. Not even to look at them, if we could help it. What mattered was that the

Romanovs were safe. Nobody escaped. Nobody broke in. We were to hold them until the Tsar could be put on trial, and that is exactly what we were doing."

"And what about the rest of the family?"

"I don't know. Nobody said anything about putting them on trial. And for certain nobody said anything about *killing* them! Then these Cheka men come in and make a big fuss over a few stolen potatoes. They throw us out and then what happens? There's no trial! Instead, the whole family gets shot. Then, when those Cheka guards have finished blasting away at unarmed women and children, they get out of town as fast as their legs will carry them and leave us to fight off thirty thousand Whites who've got cannons and"—his foot lashed out at the crate—"enough grenades that they can afford to leave cases of them just lying in the woods. And that's why I hate them. Because we did our job and they didn't."

Pekkala went to the front of the wheelbarrow and untied Nekrasov's arms from the wheel.

Nekrasov did not get up. He only lay there, massaging his wrists where the rope had dug into his skin. "In a town this size," he explained, "a man's life can boil down to a single moment. One thing he said or did. That's all he is remembered by. And nobody thinks about us holding our ground on that bridge until they blew us to pieces with a howitzer. All we're remembered for is a couple of stolen potatoes."

With the toe of his boot, Pekkala lifted up the lid of the crate. He replaced the unexploded bomb inside it. "Why didn't you pull the pin?"

"I was drunk," replied Nekrasov.

"No, you weren't. I searched this house while you were out and there isn't a thimbleful of alcohol in here. You weren't drunk, Nekrasov." Pekkala held a hand out to Nekrasov and helped him to his feet. "There must be another reason."

"I'm nuts."

"I don't believe that, either."

Nekrasov sighed. "Maybe I'm just not the type to butcher a person in their sleep."

"And what about the Tsar?"

"I killed people in the war, but that was different. An unarmed man? Women? Children? The same goes for the men who were with me. If shooting the Romanovs is what needed to be done, it's just as well the Cheka took our place."

"So you think the Cheka murdered the Tsar?"

Nekrasov shrugged. "Who else would have done it?"

WHEN PEKKALA RETURNED TO THE IPATIEV HOUSE, HE FOUND ANTON sitting on the back step of the house, a slab of stone worn by the countless footsteps of those who had lived and worked here before the house became frozen in time. He was eating something out of a frying pan, scooping up its contents with a wooden mixing spoon.

Kirov appeared in the kitchen doorway, the sleeves rolled up on his shirt. "Did you find the old militiaman?" he asked.

"Yes," replied Pekkala.

"Have you placed him under arrest?"

"No."

"Why not?" asked Kirov. "He tried to kill us last night!"

"If he had wanted to kill us, we would already be dead."

"All the same, I think you should have arrested him," the Commissar insisted. "It's the principle of the thing!"

Anton laughed. "Just what the world needs more of. A boy, a gun, and principles."

"Did he confess to killing the Tsar?" Kirov demanded.

"No."

"There's a surprise," mumbled Anton.

"It's not the Romanovs he hated," said Pekkala. "It's you and your friends in the Cheka."

"Well, he can get in line like everybody else," said Anton. "The Militia. The Whites. The Romanovs. That police chief, Kropotkin. Even those nuns at the convent hated us."

"In fact," continued Pekkala, "he's convinced that the Cheka were responsible for the death of the Romanovs."

Kirov whistled through his teeth. "The Cheka think the militia killed the Tsar. The militia think the Cheka did it. And Mayakovsky thinks they survived!"

"Well," said Pekkala, "at least we can rule out survival."

"What about the Cheka?" Anton asked. "Do you mean you actually believe we might have had something to do with it?"

Pekkala shrugged.

Anton wagged the wooden spoon at him. "Are you placing me under suspicion?"

Sensing that another fight was about to break out between the brothers, Kirov tried to change the subject. "Don't you have something else to say?" he asked Anton.

"I already apologized," replied Anton, shoveling up another mouthful from the pan.

"A public apology! That's what we agreed."

Anton groaned. He set the frying pan down on the cobblestones and let the spoon fall with a clatter onto the blackened surface of the pan. "I apologize for calling you a cook. You are a chef. A mighty *chef*."

"There," said Kirov. "Was that so difficult?"

Anton sucked at his teeth and said nothing.

"What did you make?" Pekkala was peering into the frying pan.

"Chicken with gooseberry sauce!" announced Kirov.

"Where did you find the ingredients for that?" asked Pekkala.

"Our new friend, Mayakovsky," replied Kirov.

"Make that our only friend," Anton corrected.

"He says he can get his hands on anything we want," said Kirov.

Anton looked over his shoulder at Kirov. "Wait a minute. How did you pay for this? I'm the one holding on to our cash."

"You didn't wonder about that while you were eating it, did you?" Kirov demanded. "Let's just say we only have enough fuel coupons to drive most of the way back to Moscow."

"Damn it!" shouted Anton. "Why don't we just raid Mayakovsky's house and take whatever we need?"

"We could," agreed Pekkala, "but I think he knows more than he's told us so far. Sooner or later, he'll come back with more information."

"We don't have time for sooner or later," Anton snapped.

"Rushing through an investigation," Pekkala said as he bent down and streaked one finger through the sauce in the pan, "is like rushing through a meal..." He tasted the sauce. His eyes closed. "That's very good," he muttered. "And besides, with your help, things will go much more quickly."

"I'm already helping," said Anton.

"How exactly," asked Pekkala, "except with eating the food?"

"I'll help," Kirov volunteered cheerfully.

"You stick to being a cook," Anton grumbled.

"The more people we can talk to," Pekkala pointed out, "the faster this will go."

Kirov jabbed Anton in the spine with the toe of his boot. "Do you want to go back to steaming open letters?"

"All right!" Anton moaned angrily. "What do you want me to do?"

After assigning each of them a section of the town, Pekkala explained that he needed them to go door-to-door and learn what they could about the night the Romanovs disappeared.

Anton scowled. "We can't do that! Officially, the Romanovs

were executed by order of the government. If word gets out that we're looking for whoever killed the Tsar and his family—"

"You don't have to tell them that. Just say there have been some new developments. You don't have to explain what those are, and most people will be too concerned with the questions you are asking them to think about questions of their own. Ask if they saw any strangers in town around the time the Romanovs disappeared. Ask if any bodies have been found since then. If someone from out of town buried a murder victim in a hurry, it's unlikely to have stayed hidden from the locals."

"It's been a long time since that night," grumbled Anton. "If they've kept their secrets this long, what makes you think they'll tell us any now?"

"Secrets grow heavy," Pekkala answered. "In time, the weight of them becomes too much to carry. Talk to people who work out of doors—postmen, foresters, farmers. If anything was going on in the days leading up to the disappearances, they are more likely to know than those who stayed inside. Or you could go to the tavern . . ."

"The tavern?" Anton brightened.

Kirov rolled his eyes. "All of a sudden, he is willing to help."

"People are more likely to tell you their secrets there than any other place," said Pekkala. "Just make sure you stay sober so you can listen to what they are saying."

"Of course," said Anton. "What do you take me for?"

Pekkala didn't answer. He was staring at the frying pan. "Is there any left?" he asked.

"A bit." Anton handed him the pan.

Pekkala sat down beside his brother on the stone step. There was no chicken left, but by working the wooden spoon around the edges of the pan, he gathered up some of the sauce and a single jade green gooseberry which his brother had been too full to eat. The still-warm, buttery sauce, flecked with chopped parsley and thickened with fried bread crumbs, crunched between his teeth. He tasted the sweetness of onion and the earthiness of simmered carrots. Then he let the gooseberry rest on his tongue, and slowly pressed it against the roof of his mouth until the firm round edges gave way, almost like a sigh, spilling warm, sharp-tasting juice into his mouth. Saliva welled up from under his tongue, and he sighed, recalling winters in his cabin in the Krasnagolyana forest when his only food for days on end had been boiled potatoes and salt. He remembered the silence of those nights, a stillness so complete that he could hear the faint hiss which he could only detect when there were no other noises. Often, in the forest, he had heard it: there were times in the winter months when it seemed almost deafening to him. When he was a child, his father had explained that it was the noise of his blood moving through his body. That silence, more than any barbed-wire fence, had been his prison in Siberia. Even though Pekkala's body had left that prison behind, his mind had remained trapped inside it. Only now, as these tastes formed unfamiliar arcs across his senses, did he slowly feel himself emerging from his years as a convict.

Following his arrest at the Vainikkala railway station, Pekkala was transported to the Butyrka prison in Petrograd. The Webley and his copy of the Kalevala *were handed over to the authorities. He was told to sign a huge book containing thousands of pages. The book had a steel plate covering everything except the space for him to write his name. From there, guards brought him to a room where he was made to strip and his clothes were taken away.*

Alone, Pekkala paced nervously around the small room. The walls were painted brown up to chest height. Above that, to the high ceiling, everything was white. The light in the room came from a single bulb above the door, covered with a wire cage. The room contained no bed or chair or any other furniture, so when Pekkala grew tired of pacing, he sat on the floor with his back against the wall, his knees drawn up to his bare chest. Every few minutes, a peephole in the door scraped open and Pekkala saw a pair of eyes looking in at him.

It was while he waited naked in the cell that prison guards, searching his clothes, discovered the emerald eye beneath the lapel of his coat.

Over the weeks that followed, in those few times when his head was clear enough to think straight, Pekkala would ask himself why he had not thrown away the badge which revealed his identity. Perhaps it was just vanity. Perhaps he imagined he would one day return to serve in his former capacity. Perhaps it was because the badge had become a part of him and he could no more be separated from it than he could be parted from his liver or his kidneys or his heart. But there was another possibility for why he had held on to the badge, and it was that part of him had not wanted to escape. Part of him knew his fate had become so entwined with that of the Tsar that even his freedom could not sever the bond.

As soon as the Butyrka prison staff realized they had captured the Emerald Eye, Pekkala was separated from the other prisoners and brought to a place known as the Chimney.

They led him to the cell and shoved him inside. Pekkala tumbled down one step into a space the size of a small closet. The door clicked shut. He tried to stand, but the ceiling was too low. Black-painted walls sloped above him, lower at the back and curving to a point just above the door. The space was so narrow that he could not lie down, nor could he stand except hunched over. A bright bulb glared down from a wire mesh cage, so close to his face that he could feel its heat. A wave of claustrophobia washed over him. His jaw locked open and he gagged.

After only a few minutes, he could not take it anymore and banged on the door, asking to be released.

The peephole slid back. "The prisoner must be silent," said a voice.

"Please," Pekkala said. "I can't breathe in here."

The peephole clanged shut again.

Before long, his back spasmed from bending over. He let himself slide down the wall, pressing his knees against the door. This helped for a few minutes, but then his knees cramped. He soon discovered that there was no position in which he could get comfortable. There was no air. Heat from the lightbulb pulsed against the back of his head and sweat poured down his face.

Pekkala fully expected to die. Before that, he knew, he would be tortured. Having reached this inevitable conclusion, he was filled with a curious sensation of lightness, as if his spirit had already begun a slow migration from his body.

He was ready for it to begin.

The three men spread out through the town.

Kirov took the houses on the main street. He made sure he had pages in his notebook. He sharpened two pencils. He combed his hair and even brushed his teeth.

Anton caught up with him as he was shaving, using the mirror of the Emka so that he could see what he was doing.

"Where are you going?" asked Kirov.

"To the tavern," replied Anton. "That's where people tell their secrets. Why dig them out of their houses when they can come to me there?"

Pekkala decided to follow up on Nekrasov's story about the militia stealing from the baskets of food delivered by the sisters of the Sverdlovsk convent. He wondered if the nuns had actually seen the Romanovs during their captivity. Perhaps they'd even spoken to the family. If that was true, they would have been the only people outside the militia or the Cheka to do so.

His route to the convent took him around the edge of town. Determined to question as many people as he could along the way, he stopped at several houses. No one came to the door. The owners were home. They simply refused to answer. He could see one old couple, sitting in chairs in a darkened room, blinking at each other while the sound of his fist on their door echoed about the house. The old couple did not move. Their brittle fingers, draped over the armrests of their chairs, hung down like pale creeper vines.

Finally, a door opened.

A wiry man, his pocked face covered by an unkempt white beard, asked Pekkala if he'd come to buy some blood.

"Blood?" asked Pekkala.

"From the pig," replied the man.

Now Pekkala could hear a gurgling squeal, coming from somewhere behind the house. It rose and fell like breathing.

"You have to cut their throats," the man explained. "They have to bleed to death or the meat doesn't taste right. Sometimes it takes a while. I drain the blood into buckets. I thought that's what you wanted."

Pekkala explained why he was there.

The man didn't seem surprised. "I knew you'd come looking for the truth sooner or later."

"What truth is that?"

"That the Romanovs weren't all killed the way the papers said they were. I saw one of them the night after they were supposed to have been executed."

"Who did you see?" Pekkala felt a tightness in his chest, hoping this might lead him to Alexei.

"One of the daughters," the man answered.

Pekkala felt his heart sink. Like Mayakovsky, this old man had convinced himself of something Pekkala knew to be false. He could not understand it.

"You don't believe me, do you?" asked the man.

"I don't think you are lying," said Pekkala.

"It's all right. The Whites didn't believe me, either. One of their officers came to my house, right after they chased the Reds out of town. I told him what I'd seen and he said straight up that I must have been dreaming. He told me not to mention it to anyone, unless I wanted to end up in trouble. And when I heard him threaten me like that, I was more certain than ever that I'd seen one of the daughters after all."

"Where was she when you saw her?" asked Pekkala.

"Down at the railroad yard in Perm. That's the next stop after Sverdlovsk on the Trans-Siberian. I used to be a coupler down there."

"A coupler?"

The man made two fists and fitted his knuckles together. "A coupler makes sure the right cars are joined to the right engines. Otherwise a load of goods which has come all the way from Moscow will find itself going back the way it came instead of heading out to Vladivostok. The night after the Romanovs disappeared, I was coupling up carriages on a train bound for the east. We were trying to clear out the railyard before the Whites arrived. Trains were coming through at all hours, not on the usual schedule. Night trains are mostly all freight, but this one had a passenger car—the only one on the train. There were black curtains pulled across the windows and the carriage had a guard at each end with a rifle and a bayonet. That's where I saw her."

"You went inside the train?"

"Are you kidding? Those bastards with the long knives would have skewered me!"

"But you said there were curtains over the windows. How did you see her?"

"I was walking down on the tracks beside the carriage, checking the wheels like we're supposed to do, and one of the guards jumps down into the gravel. He points his gun at me and asks me what I'm doing. So I tell him I'm a coupler, and he yells at me to get lost. He didn't know what a coupler was either, so I says to him, 'Fine, I'll get lost and when the engine pulls out, you'll be left standing here on the siding. If you want to leave when the rest of the train does,' I tell him, 'you'd better let me do my job.' "

"And did he?"

"He got right back on the train and then I hear him yelling at somebody else who'd come to ask what all the fuss was about. You see, whoever was in that carriage, they didn't want anybody getting off and they didn't want anybody getting on. But as I was walking back to couple up the car, one of the curtains moved aside"—he made the motion of parting the curtain—"and I saw the face of a woman looking down at me."

"And you recognized her?"

"Of course I did! It was Olga, the eldest daughter. All scowly like she is in the pictures. And she looks me right in the eye and then the curtain closes up again."

"You are sure about it being Olga?"

"Oh, yes." The man nodded. "There could be no mistake."

A woman walked around the side of the house, holding a long knife in one hand and a bucket of blood in the other. Behind her came a child wearing a dandelion yellow dress and no shoes. With her tiny chin, big inquisitive eyes, and nose no bigger than the knuckle of Pekkala's little finger, the child looked more doll than human. The woman set the bucket down. "Here it is," she said. Steam was rising off the blood.

"He hasn't come for that," said the man.

The woman grunted. "I carried that all the way around."

"Now you can carry it all the way back," the man told her.

"Are you sure you don't want it?" insisted the woman. "It's very nutritious. Look at my daughter here. She's the picture of health and she drinks it."

The child smiled up at Pekkala, one hand knotted in her mother's dress.

"No, thank you," said Pekkala. He looked at the blood, rocking from side to side in the bucket.

"He came to hear my story," said the man. "About the princess on the train."

"There's more to that," the woman said. "Did you tell him about the young girl they found in the woods?"

"I didn't tell him," said the man, irritated that his wife was trying to upstage him, "because I didn't see it for myself."

The woman paid no attention to her husband. She laid the knife on top of the bucket. Blood had dried black on the blade. "There was a girl seen wandering in the forest, over by Chelyabinsk. She was hurt. She had a bandage on her head. Like this." With fingers trailing like weeds in a stream, she traced a path across her mouse-gray hair.

"How old was she? What did she look like?"

"Well, she wasn't a child. But she wasn't an adult, either. She had brown hair. Some foresters tried to talk to her, but she ran away. Then she went to the house of some people, but they handed that girl right over to the Cheka. That's the last anyone saw of her. It was one of the middle daughters. Tatiana. Maybe Maria. She had escaped from the Reds, but they caught up with her again. She was almost free. It's so sad. So terribly sad."

There was a look in her face which Pekkala had seen many times before. The woman's eyes grew bright as she spoke of the tragedy. As she repeated the words "terribly sad," her cheeks flushed with a pleasure that seemed almost sexual.

"How did you learn about this?"

"A woman from Chelyabinsk. She used to buy from us. She fell in love with an officer of the Whites. When the Whites left, so did she. Are you sure you don't want some of this?" The woman pointed once more at the bucket.

As Pekkala walked away, he turned once and looked back.

The parents were gone, but the child in the yellow dress remained standing on the doorstep.

Pekkala waved.

The child waved back, then giggled and ran behind the house.

In that moment, some half-formed menace spread like wings behind Pekkala's eyes, as if that child was not really a child. As if something was trying to warn him in a language empty of words.

THE CONVENT WAS AN AUSTERE WHITE BUILDING AT THE TOP OF A steep hill on the outskirts of town. Lining the road, poplar trees rustled their leaves in a breeze he could not feel. As he climbed the hill, he shed his heavy black coat and carried it under his arm. Sweat dripped into his eyes, and he wiped it away with the sleeve of his shirt. His heart thumped angrily against his ribs.

Tall black iron railings ringed the convent. In the courtyard, pale, sand-colored gravel simmered in the afternoon sun. Outside the front steps, a crew was loading crates into a truck.

The gates were open and Pekkala walked through, his feet crunching over the gravel. Climbing the convent steps, he had to stand aside as two men carried out a small piano.

More boxes filled the front hall.

It looked as if the entire building was being emptied.

Pekkala wondered if he had arrived too late. He paused, sweat cooling on his face.

"Have you come for the piano?" asked a woman's voice.

Pekkala looked around. At first he could not see anyone.

The woman cleared her throat.

Pekkala glanced up. He saw a nun, wearing a blue and white habit, standing on the balcony which overlooked the hall. The nun's face was picture-framed in the starched white cloth of her bonnet.

"You have arrived too late," she told him. "The piano just left." She spoke of it as if the piano had walked out on its own.

"No." Pekkala shook his head. "I am not here for the piano."

"Ah." The nun made her way down the staircase. "Then what is it you've come to steal from us today?"

While Pekkala assured her that he had not come to rob the convent, the nun busied herself with inspecting the splintery crates, rapping on them with her knuckles as if to test the soundness of the wood. At first, he obtained nothing more than her name, Sister Ania; even this she seemed to grudge him. She picked up a checklist, stared at it, and put it down again. Then she wandered away, leaving Pekkala to follow her while he continued with his explanation.

"Pekkala," repeated Sister Ania. "What kind of name is that?"

"I am from Finland, but I have been gone a long time."

"I have never been to Finland, but that name sounds familiar to me."

"There was another name by which I was a little better known."

The nun, who had gone into a small sitting room and was in the process of shutting the door in Pekkala's face, suddenly paused. "So you have changed your name. I hear it's all the rage these days. Taking after Comrade Stalin, I see."

"Or you, perhaps, Sister Ania."

"And what is this other name of yours?" she asked.

Pekkala turned up his lapel. "The Emerald Eye," he said.

Slowly, the door opened again. The harshness had vanished from her face. "Well," she said, "it is a comfort to know that in this day and age, one's prayers are sometimes answered after all."

Pekkala and the nun sat on flimsy chairs in a room bare except for some framed photographs on the walls. All were portraits of nuns. The pictures had been colored in by hand, and the cheeks of the nuns were balls of pink, their lips clumsily traced.

Only the blue of the habits had been correctly drawn. The artist had attempted to fill in the eyes, but instead of adding life to the picture, he had succeeded only in making them look afraid.

"We are being temporarily shut down," explained Sister Ania.

"Temporarily?"

"Our beliefs, at this moment in time, are no longer in accord with the governing body, according to the Central Office of the Ural Soviet. The surprise is not that they are doing this to us, Inspector. What astonishes me is that it took them this long to get round to it." Sister Ania sat straight-backed in her chair, her hands in her lap. She looked poised but uncomfortable. "The other sisters have all been dismissed. I am to stay on as caretaker of this empty building. Most of our belongings are to be placed in storage. Where, I don't know. How long, I don't know. And why, I don't know either. Either we should be shut down or we should not be shut down. Instead, we are being held in a kind of suspended animation, like insects trapped in amber. But something tells me you have not come to investigate this particular injustice."

"I regret that I have not."

"Then I am guessing this has something to do with the Romanovs."

"That is correct."

"Of course it is. After all, what else would bring you to this backwater?"

"To tell you the truth, I am compelled by circumstance—"

"We are all compelled by circumstance," interrupted Sister Ania. "I believe I can save you the trouble of wearing me down with your interrogation techniques."

"Sister Ania, that is not what I . . ."

Her hand rose from her lap, then settled slowly back again. "I have waited a long time to tell what I know to someone I feel I can trust. He spoke of you, you know, in those few moments when we were able to talk. 'If only the Emerald Eye were here,' he would say."

Pekkala felt a weight settle on him, like chains draped around his neck. "Did he really believe I could have helped him, under arrest and surrounded by armed guards?"

"Oh, no," replied Sister Ania. "But I think his world just made more sense when you were in it."

"I should have stayed," muttered Pekkala, more to himself than to the nun.

"And why didn't you?"

"He ordered me to leave."

"Then you should have no regrets."

Pekkala nodded, the chains so heavy on his shoulders that he could barely draw breath into his lungs.

"When the Tsar spoke of you, I realized that he had created in the Emerald Eye an image of himself as he would have wished to be but never could."

"And how is that?" asked Pekkala.

"A man who had no need of things which he himself had found he could not live without."

"Yes," agreed Pekkala. "I believe there is some truth to that."

Sister Ania sighed heavily. "Anyway, what does it matter now, except to old believers like ourselves? He is gone now, and you will hear many stories in this town about the night the Romanovs disappeared."

"I have heard some of them already."

"There are almost as many versions as there are people in Sverdlovsk. I cannot vouch for all of them, but what I can tell you is that the Romanovs had reason to believe they would be rescued."

"Rescued? Do you mean by the Whites?"

"No. The Tsar knew that if the Whites came close enough

to this town, the Reds would simply execute him and his family. This rescue was to take place before then. A plan had been worked out."

"May I ask how you knew about it?"

"I brought them messages."

"And you had written them?"

"Oh, no. I only delivered the messages."

"Then who did they come from?"

"A former officer in the army of the Tsar asked me if I could get a message through to the Romanovs. This was in the early days of their captivity at the Ipatiev house, when the militia were still guarding them. The officer told me that a group of loyal soldiers were prepared to storm the house and transport the whole family to safety."

"And you agreed?"

She nodded sharply. "I did."

"So I can assume that your loyalties were also with the Tsar."

"Let us say that this eviction notice from the Ural Soviet does not come as a complete surprise. I offered to deliver the messages myself, so that no one else in the convent need know about them."

"How were they delivered?"

"Rolled up and hidden inside corks which were used to plug bottles of milk."

"How did the Tsar reply?" asked Pekkala. "Were his messages also hidden in corks?"

"No, it was not possible to remove the messages without damaging the corks. The Tsar came up with his own method. It was quite ingenious. He used books. They were given to me as gifts, but I passed them along to the officer."

"And these books contained messages?"

"None that the militia guards could find. I wasn't even sure myself how the messages were getting through. There were no pieces of paper tucked inside or notes written into the margins. It was only after the Romanovs disappeared that the officer explained how the messages had been hidden."

"And how was it done?"

"The Tsar used a pin"—she pinched the air in front of her—"making tiny holes beneath letters to spell out words. He always began on page ten."

"And did the officer ever speak to you about these messages?"

"Oh, yes. He even offered to take me away with him when the Romanovs were rescued. But he never got the chance."

"Why not?"

"At first, the Tsar wrote back that he was willing to be rescued, but only if the whole family could be brought away. Alexei was ill. The Tsar worried that the boy might be too weak to make an extended journey. He was anxious to avoid any bloodshed, even among the militia who were guarding him."

"What happened to change his mind?"

"Shortly after the local militia were replaced by the Cheka security detachment, the Tsar sent a message ordering the officer not to attempt a rescue."

"Why would the Tsar do that," asked Pekkala, "when it was his only chance of escape?"

"That I cannot tell you," Sister Ania said. "The officer said it would be too dangerous for me to know, since he could no longer guarantee my safety."

"Did you ever see this officer again?"

"Oh, yes," she replied. "We are still friends, he and I."

"Sister Ania, it is important that I speak to this man, whoever he is."

She looked at him carefully. "If that officer were here beside me now, he would say I had already told you too much."

"I am not here to find a man who tried to save the Tsar," said Pekkala. "I am here to find the one who put a bullet in his chest."

Her lips twitched. "So it is true what the papers said." It was not a question.

"Yes," said Pekkala. "The Tsar is dead."

She sighed heavily. "There are many who believed that he survived."

"It is possible, however, that one of the children has survived."

Sister Ania's eyes widened. "Possible? What does that mean? Please, Inspector—is one of them alive or not?"

"That is what I am investigating, Sister Ania. It is why I am speaking to you now."

"Which one?" she insisted. "Which child?"

"Alexei."

She struggled to remain composed. "That poor boy . . . He had already endured so much."

"Yes."

Suddenly she leaned towards him. "And what do you believe, Inspector Pekkala?"

"My investigation is not yet complete."

"No!" She slapped one hand against her knee. "What do *you* believe? Do you think he is alive or not?"

"I think he might be, yes." His voice barely rose above a whisper. "And if there is any chance that the Tsarevich is alive, I think your officer might help me to locate him."

"You will find him at the police station," said Sister Ania, without hesitation.

"He is under arrest?"

"On the contrary," she said. "He is in charge of the place. His name is Officer Kropotkin."

"Kropotkin. This will not be my first conversation with the police chief."

"That is just as well," she replied. "He does not make a good first impression."

Sister Ania walked Pekkala back towards the entrance.

As Pekkala passed by the crates filled with the belongings of the convent, he wondered in what dark warehouse they would be locked away and, if they ever saw the light of day again, what would be remembered of their owners and what convenient lies would be admitted.

Before they stepped from the cool shade of the building into the glare of the gravel courtyard, Sister Ania rested her hand on his shoulder. "If the Tsarevich is alive, promise me you will see to it that no harm comes to him, Inspector. He has suffered enough for crimes he did not commit."

"I give you my word," Pekkala answered.

They walked out into the sun.

"Do you believe in miracles, Inspector Pekkala?"

"It is not in my nature."

"Then maybe it is time you started."

Propped against the convent wall was an old bicycle, its leather seat cracked and the black paint covered by a film of dust. The wooden handles showed a burnish of hard use, and the treads on the tires had been worn down almost smooth. In spite of its age, the old machine possessed a certain dignity, as those things do which have accompanied a person on the journey of their lives.

Pekkala looked beyond the iron gates at the long walk down into Sverdlovsk. A fierce blue sky beat down upon the road. The dappling shadows of the poplar trees seemed to offer no comfort at all.

He stared at the bicycle, imagining the cool breeze he would feel upon his face as he freewheeled down the hill, instead of drearily trudging through the heat.

Sister Ania followed his gaze. "Take it," she told him. "Otherwise, those men will carry it away. By the time it is released from storage that bicycle will be an antique, if it isn't one already. If it will do you any good at all, please take it now and do not say another word about it."

Pekkala straddled the bicycle, the old leather seat not as comfortable as he would have liked.

"Well," said Sister Ania, smiling slightly, "let's see how you handle it. I don't want to be responsible for you breaking your neck."

He rode around in a circle on the gravel path. It had been years since he'd last ridden a bicycle and the front wheel wobbled as he struggled to stay upright.

"Perhaps I have made a mistake," she said.

"Not at all," he reassured her as he came to an uncertain halt beside her.

She reached out to him.

Pekkala took her small pink hand in his.

Her touch shocked Pekkala like a jolt of electricity. It had been years since he'd last held the hand of a woman.

"We need you," she told him. "Don't ever leave us again."

Pekkala opened his mouth, but no sound came out. He was too overwhelmed to speak.

Sister Ania squeezed his hand, then let go. Turning, she walked back into the convent.

Far below, at the base of the hill, the road forked left and right. The right fork led into town. The left fork passed along the side of a weed-choked pond and on into a pale green sea of barley fields.

As soon as Pekkala cleared the gates, the road sloped sharply downwards. From then on, gravity propelled him and there was no need for him to pedal. His eyes began to water. The wind in his ears, like the roaring of a gas flame, was all that he could hear. Suddenly, catching himself completely by surprise, Pekkala laughed.

When the bicycle was going so fast that he felt the back wheel begin to shudder, he reached out with his fingers, closed them around the bare metal of the brake levers, and gave them a light squeeze. But the bike did not slow down. Pekkala glanced down in time to see the old rubber brake pads coming apart in chunks as they connected with the wheel rim.

With no idea why, Pekkala was still laughing. He could not help himself.

He gave the brakes a tighter squeeze and the bicycle slowed momentarily. Then both pads flew off completely. He looked behind at the rear brakes and only then did he notice that the cable was missing, rendering them useless.

He roared with laughter and the wind poured into his mouth.

The wheels were buzzing now.

Pekkala struggled to stay on the bike as the trees went by in a blur, a swishing sound as each one passed.

By the time he reached the bottom of the hill, he was holding on for his life. He banked left, gripping the wood handles as tightly as he could. The road leveled out. He straightened the handlebars. Everything seemed to be working. Pekkala had just allowed himself a moment of silent self-congratulation when he heard a loud *crack* from somewhere behind him. The rear tire had exploded. Out of control, he veered to the left and blew through the tall grass which grew at the side of the road. For a brief moment, he had the sensation of flying, as if the free-spinning wheels might carry him up into the sky. A second later, garlanded with buttercups, daisies, and purple-flowered tangles of vetch, Pekkala pitched forward over the handlebars and into the pond.

For a second, he lay there, facedown. The trees he had passed on his way down the hill still flickered behind his closed eyes.

Then, planting his feet in the mud, Pekkala stood. Pond weeds clung to his coat like green confetti. A bloom of stirred-up silt spread out around him.

As he made his way back to dry ground, pulling at the bicycle and exhausted by the weight of water in his clothes, an image of his childhood returned—of himself and Anton, dragging sleds behind them and struggling under the burden of their winter clothes. They used to sled down a steep hill near their house. The hill was used only in summer, when woodsmen dragged timber out of the forest, rolling the logs downhill to a river where they could be floated to the sawmill in town. In winter, he and Anton had the hill all to themselves. It was back before things changed between them—before the crematory oven, before Anton left to join the Finnish Regiment. Since then, the gap had only widened. Pekkala wondered, as the breath grew hot in his lungs, if they could ever return to the way things were before. Not without a miracle, he told himself. Maybe Sister Ania is right. Maybe it is time to start believing.

"IS IT RAINING?" OFFICER KROPOTKIN WAS STILL SEATED AT HIS DESK, as if he had not moved since they'd last spoken. He turned around in his chair and looked out through his window at the blue sky.

"No," replied Pekkala. "It is not raining."

Kropotkin turned back to Pekkala. "Then why are you dripping on my floor?"

"I have been in the duck pond."

"Leaving no stone unturned, are you?"

Instinctively, Pekkala brought out his notebook. He opened it. A trickle of water poured out onto the floor. "I have a few questions," he said.

As Pekkala gave the details of his conversation with Sister Ania, Kropotkin's face became redder and redder until finally he leaped up from his chair and shouted, "*Enough!* If all the brides of Christ are as talkative as Sister Ania, then I hope for His sake that Jesus has gone deaf in His old age! What kind of trouble has she gotten me into?"

"None."

"And what is it you want to know from me?"

"Why did the Tsar inform you that he no longer wanted to escape?"

"That isn't what he said. He simply ordered me not to attempt a rescue."

"Why did you think he did that?"

"He may have heard about what happened to his brother, the Grand Duke Mikhail, who was being held under guard in another part of the country."

"He was shot while trying to escape, wasn't he?"

"Not exactly." Kropotkin shook his head. "Apparently Mikhail had been communicating with a group who claimed they were still loyal to the Tsar. Mikhail followed their instructions and, only a few weeks before the Tsar was executed, he gave his guards the slip. What he didn't realize was that the men who had promised to save him were actually members of the Cheka. They had set him up. As soon as he escaped, they gunned him down." Kropotkin shrugged. "After that, maybe the Tsar no longer trusted us, and who can blame him? But I would gladly have given up my life to rescue him. If it had worked, who knows? This country might be a different place today."

"I have spoken to a number of people who believe that more than one of the Tsar's children survived."

"What you are hearing," said Kropotkin, "is the collective guilt of this town. Even if it were possible to believe that the Tsar and the Tsarina were guilty of the crimes held against them by the politicians in Moscow, no one in their right mind could be persuaded that those children deserved to die. At worst, they might have been spoiled. They might have been sheltered from the world. But that was not their doing, and it does not amount to a crime. There are those who despised the Tsar long before he arrived in Sverdlovsk, but people will always despise someone who has more than they do, and it is easier to hate something at a distance. But when the Tsar arrived with his family, they were forced to see him as another human being. To kill a family who stand unarmed before you requires something more than hate. It is why, in the stories they have told you, the children were allowed to go free."

"So you do not believe anyone survived?"

"If they had," replied Kropotkin, "I think we would have heard from them by now. Of course, there is one other possibility."

"And what is that?"

"That the Tsar had received another offer of escape."

"But the only messages getting through to the Tsar from outside came from you."

"I don't mean from outside. I mean from inside the Ipatiev house."

"You mean the Cheka?"

"Maybe they planned to kill him while he was trying to escape, just like they did with the Grand Duke Mikhail."

Pekkala shook his head. "The Tsar was not killed while trying to escape."

"Then perhaps someone in the Cheka guards really did intend to rescue him."

"To me," said Pekkala, "that seems almost impossible."

"Do you really find it so incredible that someone would go to such lengths to keep the Tsar alive?" asked Kropotkin. "After all, your own survival is nothing short of miraculous."

"Yours as well," added Pekkala. "The Communists must have suspected you of collaborating with the Whites. And yet they still made you their chief of police in Sverdlovsk."

"The Reds needed someone who could keep the peace," explained Kropotkin. "At the time, they couldn't afford to be picky. Since then, they have not seen fit to get rid of me. But that day will come. The only way to have a future in this country is to have no past. That is a luxury neither you nor I possess, and sooner or later we will pay the price for it."

"What will you do when they decide that they no longer need you, Kropotkin?"

Kropotkin shrugged. "My line of work might change, but the things I care about, the things for which I am prepared to risk my life, will not."

"To the people running this country, that makes you a dangerous man."

"Not half as dangerous as you, Inspector Pekkala. I am a man of flesh and blood. I can be made to disappear without a trace. But getting rid of you"—Kropotkin smiled—"now that would take some doing."

"You talk as if I'm bulletproof," said Pekkala, "which, I can assure you, I am not."

"Not you," replied Kropotkin, aiming a finger at Pekkala, "but that."

Pekkala realized Kropotkin was pointing at the emerald eye badge, visible now since the soaked lapel of his coat had been turned up. "Even though your life can be snuffed out in an instant, the Emerald Eye is already the stuff of legend. It cannot simply be dismissed out of hand, and the truth is, they do not want to dismiss it. They need you, Pekkala. They need your legendary incorruptibility—just as the Tsar did before them. Most legends have the luxury of being dead, but as long as you remain alive, you are as dangerous to them as you are valuable. The sooner you are gone, the safer they will feel."

"Then they will not have long to wait," Pekkala told him. "As soon as this case has been solved, I am leaving the country forever."

Kropotkin sat back in his chair. He tapped the end of a pencil against his thumbnail. "I hope that is true, but what they have in you, they will not want to lose. They will do everything they can to keep you here, where they can still control your fate. If they succeed, everything you have worked for will be lost and you and I will find ourselves on opposite sides in this war."

"I have no wish to become your enemy," said Pekkala.

Kropotkin nodded. "Then, for both our sakes, let us hope that when the time comes you will make the right choice."

Days went by, while Pekkala lingered in his cell, waiting for the interrogations to begin.

Food was delivered once a day through a sliding panel just beneath the peephole. He received a bowl of salty cabbage soup and a mug of tea. Both the bowl and the mug were made of such soft metal that he could crumple them in his fist as if they had been made of clay.

After the food was taken away, two guards escorted him to a toilet. One guard stood in front and one behind. Only the guard behind him spoke. "If you step to the left. If you step to the right." The guard did not finish his sentences. He did not have to. Instead, he reached from behind and tapped the cold metal barrel of a gun against Pekkala's cheek.

The guard in front started walking and Pekkala felt a gentle push from the guard behind.

Thick gray carpet covered the prison floors. The guards' boots were soled with felt. Except for the quiet commands issued by the guards, the silence at Butyrka was complete.

They led him down a windowless corridor, lined with doors, to a room with a hole in the middle of the floor and a bucket of water set beside it.

Minutes later, he was on his way down the hall again, bare feet padding on the carpet. He stumbled back into his cell.

He couldn't sleep. All he could do was slump into a kind of semiconsciousness. His knees, crunched against the door, grew permanently numb. He lost all feeling in his feet.

He had not been prepared for the waiting. It grated on his nerves until his whole mind had frayed like the tatters of a flag left flapping in a hurricane.

With no glimpse of the outside world, he soon lost track of how long he had been in the prison.

Using his thumbnail, Pekkala made a small groove in the wall to show when the food came. He noticed other scratches on the walls, similar to his own, which also seemed to have been made with a fingernail. There were several different sets, one with over a hundred marks. The sight of that filled him with dread. He knew he could not last a hundred days in this cell.

On what he imagined was his twenty-first day at Butyrka, the guards escorted Pekkala to a different room, in which there were two chairs, separated by a small metal-topped desk.

He had been naked since his first hour at the prison, but now one of the guards handed him a set of beige-colored pajamas made from thin, musty-smelling cotton. The bottoms had drawstrings at the ankles but not at the waist. From then on, one of Pekkala's hands was constantly occupied with holding up his trousers.

The guards left, closing the door behind them.

A minute later, an officer entered the room, carrying a small briefcase. He was of medium height, with a pocked and freckled face, yellowy-green eyes, and a tangle of thick black hair. Although his uniform fitted him, he did not seem at ease in it, and Pekkala guessed he had not been wearing it for long.

The officer opened the briefcase. From it, he removed Pekkala's Webley, which he had been carrying at the time of his arrest at Vainikkala. The man held up the gun, examining it carefully. His thumb accidentally touched the button for loading the Webley and the barrel of the gun folded forward suddenly, exposing the chambers of the cylinder. The officer was startled and almost dropped the gun.

Pekkala had to stop himself from lunging forward to catch it, to keep the Webley from falling to the floor.

The officer caught the gun just in time. Hurriedly, he replaced it in the briefcase. The next thing he removed was the emerald eye. With the badge resting on his fingertips, the man tilted it back and forth so that the gemstone caught the light. "Your enemies call you the monster of the Tsar." The man replaced the badge inside the case. "But you do not look like a monster to me." Lastly, he removed Pekkala's book. He flipped through it, staring without comprehension at the words of the Kalevala. *Then he dropped that, too, back where he had found it.*

He cleared his throat several times before he spoke again. "Did you know that Finland has declared its independence from Russia?"

Pekkala had not known. The news shocked him. He wondered how his father, such a loyal supporter of the Tsar, must be feeling.

"As you see," continued the officer, "from these things which we have found in your possession, we know exactly who you are, Inspector Pekkala." He spoke in a voice so quiet that it seemed almost timid.

"Georgia," replied Pekkala.

"Excuse me?"

"Georgia," Pekkala repeated. "Your accent."

"Ah, yes, I am from Tiflis."

Now Pekkala remembered. "Dzhugashvili," he said. "Josef Dzhugashvili. You were responsible for a bank robbery in 1907 which left over forty people dead." He could hardly believe that a man he had once hunted as a criminal was now sitting before him, on the other side of an interrogator's table.

"That is correct," said Dzhugashvili, "except that now my name is Josef Stalin and I am no longer a robber of banks. Now I am chief advisor to the People's Commissariat."

"And you are here to give me some advice?"

"I am. Yes. Advice which I hope you will take. A detective with your experience could be very useful to us. Many of your former comrades have agreed to work with the new government. This is, of course, after they have informed us of the details of their work." He studied Pekkala for a moment. Then he held up one stubby finger, like a man checking the direction of the wind. "But I think you are not going to be one of those people."

"I am not," agreed Pekkala.

"This much I was told to expect," Stalin said. "Then you understand that things must go another way."

THAT EVENING, WHEN PEKKALA RETURNED TO THE IPATIEV HOUSE, HE found Kirov boiling potatoes in the kitchen. The windows wept with condensation.

Pekkala sat down at the table, folded his arms, and lowered his head until his forehead was resting on his wrists. "No deals with Mayakovsky today?"

"The old son of a bitch is crafty," replied Kirov. "He gives us enough to whet our appetites, then lets us go hungry while his prices go through the roof."

"I expect he'll start charging more for information, too."

"I was talking about information," replied Kirov, "but I know how to deal with types like that."

"Oh, yes?"

Kirov nodded. "You give them a present."

"But why?"

"Because they're not expecting it. People like Mayakovsky don't have friends and don't need friends. They don't get presents very often and when they do, it throws them completely off balance."

"You're smarter than you look," grunted Pekkala.

"That's how I can get away with being smart." Kirov sighed. "But I wasn't smart enough to scrounge up more than a few potatoes in town today."

"Did you learn anything when you were there?" asked Pekkala.

"Only that this whole town has gone mad." With a wooden spoon, Kirov stirred the potatoes in the pot of boiling water. "Almost everyone I talked to swore they'd seen one of the Romanovs alive. Never the whole family together. Just one of them. You'd think the Tsar and his wife and his children had all run off in different directions that night, and yet somehow they ended up at the bottom of that mine shaft."

Pekkala lifted his head. "Except one."

"Still," said Kirov, "I don't believe Alexei has survived."

"Why do you say that?"

"Even if the killer had let him go free, how long do you think he would have survived on the run in the middle of a revolution? A hemophiliac? That boy might as well be made of porcelain. Alexei didn't stand a chance."

"Why Alexei is not among the dead I can't even begin to guess," said Pekkala, "but as long as he is missing, the search for him has to continue. In the meantime, I think the Tsar believed he could escape from Sverdlovsk, only not without help. What I don't know yet is who he thought was going to help him, and how he ended up dead. He may have been tricked, or the rescue attempt could have failed. Maybe the Cheka guards killed the Romanovs when they realized they were under attack. That could be why the dead guards were found in the basement. Perhaps the man who came to rescue the Tsar panicked and threw the bodies down the mine shaft, rather than leave them to be discovered in the Ipatiev house."

"That way," Kirov speculated, "the Reds would assume that the Tsar and his family were still alive. They'd waste their time looking for the Romanovs and not just for whoever tried to rescue them." With a handkerchief wrapped around the pot handle, he emptied the milky-colored water down the drain. A cloud of steam swirled up around him. He set the pot on the table, then sat down opposite Pekkala. "But what do I know? I'm just here as an observer."

"Kirov," said Pekkala, "you will make a fine detective someday."

"You wouldn't say that if you knew how little I'd turned up. All I got was a stack of photographs."

"Photographs?"

"Some old lady gave them to me. Said they were from Katamidze's studio. Said Katamidze gave them to her as a gift, but after Katamidze disappeared, she was afraid she'd get into trouble for holding on to them."

"Where are they?"

"They're in the front room. I was going to throw them in the fire, seeing as we are running out of wood to burn—"

Before Kirov had finished his sentence, Pekkala dashed out of the room.

"They're mostly landscapes, nothing important," called Kirov. "You won't find the Tsar in any of them!"

A moment later Pekkala returned. A sheaf of photographs was clutched in his fist. There were about two dozen of them, their ends curled up and torn. A haze of fingerprints stained the images. Most were pictures of the town. The church with its onion dome spire. The main street, with the Ipatiev house in the distance and a blurred, ghostly image of a horse and cart crossing in front of the camera's view. There was a pond, with the same church in the distance. On the other side of the water, a woman in a long skirt and headscarf stooped to gather something in the weeds. A few of the photos were of the nuns whose images he had seen on the walls of the convent. On these, it looked as if Katamidze had been trying to color them but had given up halfway through the process.

"These must be his rejects," muttered Pekkala. He sat back and rubbed his tired eyes.

"I told you they weren't important," said Kirov.

Each man speared a potato and began to eat, puffing their cheeks with the heat.

Anton stumbled in, his breath a fog of pickled beets and Lake Baikal sprat. These fish, dried and shriveled to the shape of crumpled cigars, hung threaded on wires above the bar, their tiny bones like musical notes under the hard, translucent flesh. If a customer wanted a fish, he simply reached up and twisted the body, snapping off its head, which remained on the wire. Men with no money would then pick off the head and eat it, chewing the metallic-tasting cartilage until nothing remained.

Anton tossed a notebook on the table. "It's all in there," he said.

Pekkala picked up the notebook and flipped through it. "These pages are blank."

"You must be a detective, after all," said Anton.

"You call this help?" asked Pekkala, struggling to contain his anger.

Anton sat down at the table. He spotted the photographs and picked them up. "Ooh, pictures."

"They belonged to Katamidze," explained Kirov.

"Any naked ones?" asked Anton.

Kirov shook his head.

"I bet Mayakovsky has them. He seems to have everything else."

"I told you not to drink," said Pekkala.

Anton dropped the stack of photos. "You *told* me?" he asked. Then he slammed his hand down on the table. "You mean you *ordered* me! You can't go to a tavern and not drink! I did my job, just like you told me to, so you can just lay off me, Inspector." He hawked out the last word as if it were a chunk of fat. "The tavern is where people tell their secrets! That's what you said."

"But you have to be sober to hear them!" Pekkala snatched the wooden apple which lay on the table and threw it at his brother.

Anton's hand shot up. The apple slapped into his palm and he closed his fingers around it. He gave his brother a triumphant look.

"Did you offer to rescue the Tsar?" asked Pekkala.

The gloating look sheared off his face. "What?"

"You heard me," replied Pekkala. "When you were guarding the Romanovs, did you offer to let him and his family escape?"

Anton laughed. "Have you completely lost your mind? What possible reason would I have for helping them? There was a time when all I wanted was a place among the Finnish Regiment, but you stole that from me. I had to make some different plans, which did not include the Tsar."

"You could have rejoined the Regiment!" said Pekkala. "They didn't kick you out for good."

"I was going to come back, until I found out you were on your way to Petrograd to take my place. Did you honestly expect me to endure that humiliation? Why didn't you stay home and take over the family business the way our father planned for you to do?"

"The way he planned?" repeated Pekkala. "Don't you realize he was the one who sent me to take your place in the Regiment?"

Anton blinked. "He sent you?"

"After we received the telegram that you had been suspended. We didn't know that it was only temporary."

"But why?" Anton stammered. "Why didn't you tell me back then?"

"Because I couldn't find you. You had disappeared."

For a long time, nobody spoke.

Anton seemed rooted to the spot, too stunned to move. "I swear I didn't know," he murmured.

"It doesn't matter anymore," Pekkala told him. "It's too late now."

"Yes," Anton replied, speaking like a man in a trance. "It is too late." Then he walked out into the courtyard.

"Perhaps," said Kirov, after a moment, "one of the other Cheka guards made an offer to the Tsar. Your brother might not have known anything about it."

"You mean he was too drunk to know," Pekkala said.

Both men looked out at Anton, who stood slumped against the wall, one arm held up against the stone for balance. A bright arc of piss splashed down onto the ground. Then he walked out of the courtyard, into the street, and was gone.

"He's going straight back to the tavern," said Kirov.

"Perhaps," Pekkala agreed.

"They'll beat him up all over again."

"He doesn't seem to care."

"At the Bureau," said Kirov, "when they assigned me to the case, I was told his drinking might be a problem."

"He's not as drunk as he wants us to believe."

"What do you mean?"

"Did you see the way he caught the apple?"

"You were testing his reflexes?"

Pekkala nodded. "If he had been really drunk, he would never have reacted that quickly."

"Why would he pretend to be drunk?"

"Because he's hiding something," said Pekkala, "but whether it has to do with this investigation or if it is something from our past, or both, I do not know."

"Are you saying we can't trust him anymore?" asked Kirov.

"We never could," Pekkala answered.

"There is something we would like to know," said Stalin. "Eventually you will tell us. The only variable in this equation is what remains of you, physically and spiritually, by the time you have answered the question."

Pekkala felt almost relieved that the process had begun. Anything was better than the agony of standing hunched inside that chimney of a cell. It was the curve of the ceiling which terrified him most, as if the room were slowly caving in. Every time he thought of it, fresh sweat beaded on his face.

"Fortunately," continued Stalin, "we only have one question for you."

Pekkala waited.

"Would you like a cigarette?" Stalin asked. From his trouser pocket, he removed a red and gold box with the word MARKOV *on the cover.*

Pekkala recognized them as the brand which Vassileyev used to smoke.

"The former director of the Okhrana was kind enough to leave behind a considerable supply in his office," explained Stalin.

"Where is he now?"

"He is dead," said Stalin matter-of-factly. "Do you know what he did? When he knew we were coming to arrest him, he filled his artificial leg with explosives. Then, in the police van on the way to this prison, Vassileyev set off the bomb. The axle of the van ended up on the roof of a two-story building." Stalin laughed softly. "Explosives in a wooden leg! I can't deny he had a sense of humor."

He held out the box of cigarettes, awkwardly rotating his wrist so that the white sticks faced Pekkala.

Pekkala shook his head.

Stalin snapped the box shut. "In the days ahead, I ask you to remember that my first offer to you was one of friendship."

"I won't forget," said Pekkala.

"Of course you won't. That famous memory of yours would not allow it. That is why I am confident that you will be able to answer my question."

"What do you want to know?"

"Where are the Tsar's reserves of gold?"

"I have no idea."

Stalin breathed out quietly, his lips slightly pursed, like someone learning to whistle. "Then it must be wrong, what I have heard."

"What did you hear?" With each passing minute, that strange lightness which was the certainty of death filled more and more of Pekkala's body. By the time they get around to killing me, he thought, there will be nothing left to feel the pain.

"I heard that the Tsar trusted you," said Stalin.

"With some things."

Stalin smiled faintly. "Pity," he said.

Two weeks later, Pekkala was dragged out of his cell and returned to the interrogation room. He had to be carried, because he could no longer walk. The tops of his toes were burned raw on the carpet as the guards hauled him along, each with one of Pekkala's arms hooked over his shoulder.

Released by the guards, Pekkala walked the last few paces to his chair in the interrogation room. Trembling like a man with a high fever, he sat down and tried to keep his balance. His feet were swollen to twice their normal size, the nails blackened from blood which had congealed beneath them. He could not lift his hands above his shoulders. He could no longer breathe through his nose. Every few breaths, he would cough violently, his knees drawn up towards his chest. Blue flashes arced across his vision, accompanied by pain like a spike driven into his skull.

Stalin was there. "Now would you like a cigarette?" He asked it in that same, half-timid voice.

Pekkala opened his mouth to speak, but started coughing again. He managed only to shake his head. "I don't know where the gold is. I am telling you the truth."

"Yes," replied Stalin. "I am now convinced of that. What I would like to know instead is this: Who did he trust with the task of removing the gold?"

Pekkala did not answer.

"You do know the answer to this," Stalin told him.

Pekkala remained silent. Dread came loping like a black dog down the tunnels of his mind.

"When this is over," said Stalin, "and you reflect on what will happen to you now, you may regret that perfect memory of yours."

Later that evening, Pekkala sat in the front room, with his back against the wall, legs stretched out across the bare floorboards. The *Kalevala* lay on his lap.

Kirov came in, carrying a pile of wood for the fire. He dumped it with a clatter on the hearth.

"No sign of Anton?" asked Pekkala.

"No sign," replied Kirov, slapping the wood dust off his palms. He nodded towards the *Kalevala*. "Why don't you read me some of your book?"

"Unless you speak Finnish, you wouldn't understand."

"Read some anyway."

"I doubt you will find this on your list of texts approved by the Communist Party."

"If you won't tell, then I promise that neither will I."

Pekkala shrugged. "Very well." He opened the book and began to read, the Finnish words rolling like thunder in his throat and cracking off the roof of his mouth like the snap of lightning in the air. Although he read from this book all the time, he rarely spoke its text out loud, and it had been years since he'd had the chance to speak his native tongue. Even his brother had abandoned it. As he read now, it sounded both distant and familiar, like a memory borrowed from another person's life.

After a minute, he stopped and looked up at Kirov.

"Your language," Kirov said, "sounds like someone prying nails out of wood."

"I'll try to find some way to take that as a compliment."

"What did it mean?"

Pekkala's gaze returned to the book. He stared at the words and slowly they began to change, speaking to him in the language Kirov could understand. He told Kirov the story of the wanderer Väinämöinen and his attempts to persuade the goddess Pohjola to come down from the rainbow where she lived and join him in his travels. Before she would agree, Pohjola gave Väinämöinen impossible tasks to perform, such as tying an egg into a knot, splitting a horsehair with a dull knife, and scraping birch bark from a stone. While performing the final task, which was to make a ship out of wood shavings, Väinämöinen gashed his knee with an axe. The only thing which would stop the bleeding was a spell called the Source of Iron, and Väinämöinen set out to find someone who knew the magic words.

"Are they all as strange as that?"

"They are strange until you understand them," replied Pekkala, "and then it is as if you've known them all your life."

"Did you ever read that story to Alexei?" asked Kirov.

"I read him some, but not that one. To hear of a spell like that would have given him hope where there was none." As he spoke these words, Pekkala could not help wondering if his own hopes for finding Alexei alive were as hollow as a spell to stop the boy's bleeding.

EARLY THE NEXT MORNING, SOMEONE KNOCKED ON THE FRONT DOOR. "Mayakovsky!" groaned Kirov, rubbing the sleep out of his eyes. "I hope he's brought more than potatoes."

"That's not Mayakovsky," Pekkala said. "He always comes through the courtyard." He got up and stepped over Anton, who had returned sometime that night.

Opening the door, he found Kropotkin waiting on the other side. The police chief wore his blue service tunic, but had left all the buttons undone. His uniform cap was nowhere in sight and his hands remained tucked in his pockets. His straight combed hair and squared-off jaw gave him the appearance of a boxer dog.

Kropotkin was the most slovenly-looking policeman Pekkala had ever seen. The Tsar would have fired him on the spot, thought Pekkala, for daring to appear like that.

"A call came in for you last night," said Kropotkin.

"Who from?"

"The asylum at Vodovenko. Katamidze says he has remembered something you asked him about. A name."

Pekkala's heart slammed in his chest. "I will leave immediately."

"I already told your Cheka man," he said. "I met him at the tavern last night. I gave him the message, but I thought he might be too drunk to understand me. I thought I'd better come by this morning, just to be sure you got the news."

"I'm glad you did," said Pekkala.

Kropotkin rattled the change in his pockets. "Look, Pekkala, I know we didn't get off to a good start, but if there is anything I can do to help you, you know where to find me."

Pekkala thanked him and closed the door.

Anton was still asleep, wrapped in a blanket.

Pekkala took one corner of the blanket and heaved it upwards.

Anton rolled out onto the floor cursing. "What's going on?"

"Katamidze! The telephone call from Vodovenko! Why didn't you tell us last night?"

Anton struggled upright, bleary-eyed. "I was going to tell you in the morning." Just above the velvet curtains, bolts of sunlight slanted through the windows, illuminating dust which spiraled slowly through the air. "But I guess it is the morning, so I'm telling you now."

"We should have been on the road hours ago." Pekkala grabbed Anton's clothes off the floor and threw them in his face. "Get dressed. We're leaving now."

Kirov appeared out of the kitchen. "Fried army meat for breakfast!" he announced.

Pekkala pushed past him and out into the courtyard.

Kirov watched him go, the smile fading from his face. "What's going on?" Then he turned to Anton and asked again, "What's the matter?"

Anton was pulling on his boots. "Get in the car," he said.

Ten minutes later, they were on the road.

Driving south to Vodovenko, they passed through the village of the temporary lie. The barrier was down over the road but they found the guardhouse locked and unmanned.

After moving the barricade, they continued on and soon found themselves on the main street. The place was deserted, as if the population had abruptly fled, leaving behind shops whose windows brimmed with bread, meat, and fruit. But when Pekkala got out of the car to have a closer look, he realized that everything behind the glass was made of wax.

They stopped at the little railway station and looked off down the empty tracks, which trailed out to the horizon. A broom stood propped against one of the support columns of the station house roof.

None of them spoke. The emptiness of the place seemed to command their silence.

Pekkala thought back to the faces he had seen when they passed through before. He remembered the fear hidden behind the masks of their smiles.

They got in the car and drove on.

Later that day, when they pulled into the courtyard at Vodovenko, the red-haired attendant came out to meet them.

"You're too late," he said.

Pekkala climbed out of the car, his hip joints sore from sitting cramped inside the Emka. "What do you mean we are late?"

"Not late." The attendant shook his head. "Too late."

"What happened?"

"We're not sure. A suicide, we think."

The three men did not bother to sign in and the attendant did not ask for their weapons. They hurried through the armored door and down the corridors until they came to a room whose floor and walls up to chest height were plated with white tiles, like those inside a shower. Four large lights hung down from the ceiling. It was the mortuary.

Katamidze's body lay on a metal-topped table, half covered with a cotton blanket. The photographer's lips and eyelids and the tip of his nose had turned a mottled blue, but the rest of his skin looked as pale as the tiles on the walls. His feet, which were facing the door, stuck out from under the blanket. Attached by wire to the big toe of his right foot was a metal disk on which a number had been stamped. The nails had turned a yellow color, like the scales of a dead fish.

Anton leaned against the wall by the door, his eyes fixed on the floor.

Kirov followed behind Pekkala, too curious to be appalled.

"Poison," said Pekkala.

"Yes," agreed the attendant.

"Cyanide?"

"Lye," said the attendant.

Gently, Pekkala set his hand on Katamidze's face and lifted one of the eyelids. The whites of the dead man's eyes had turned red from burst blood vessels. Examining the area around the eyes, Pekkala noticed a faint blush extending from the cheekbone up to the line of the forehead. He traced his fingers down the side of the man's neck, probing the flesh. When he reached Katamidze's larynx he traced his finger over fragile horseshoe-shaped bone. It gave under gentle pressure, indicating that it had been crushed. "Whoever killed him," he said, "held on to his throat until he was sure Katamidze would not survive, but it was not strangulation that killed him. Where was he found?"

"In his cell," replied the attendant.

Pekkala jerked his head towards the door. "Show me," he said.

The attendant led them to Katamidze's cell.

"Where do you use lye in this building?" asked Pekkala, striding ahead.

"In the gardens sometimes." The attendant's legs were shorter than Pekkala's. He was struggling to keep up with Pekkala. "We use it to clear out the drainpipes a couple of times a year."

"Was he dead when you found him?"

"Almost. I mean he died before we had a chance to unlock him."

"Did he say anything?"

"No. I mean . . ."

"What do you mean?" demanded Pekkala.

The attendant became flustered. "For God's sake, his insides were burned out. Whatever he tried to say, the poor bastard was too far gone for us to understand. Here. This is the place."

An orderly was mopping out the room. The air was thick with the smell of bleach, mingled with a reek of vomit and the piercing bitterness of lye. The cell had no windows, only a metal cot which folded up into the wall. There was no other furniture. A chain bolted into the wall hung down to the center of the cot. An iron cuff dangled from the chain.

Pekkala lifted the chain, then let it fall again. The metal links rattled against the wall. "He was locked to this?"

Anton's breathing had grown shallow. Suddenly, he left the room; his hurried footsteps faded away down the corridor.

The attendant watched him go. "Some people have no stomach for a place like this," he said.

Kirov remained where he was, peering over Pekkala's shoulder.

"All inmates are locked to their bunks after lights-out," the attendant explained. "During the day, the beds are folded up and the cuffs are released."

"What happens to the prisoners then?"

The orderly continued swabbing the floor as if the men were not there.

"Prisoners are allowed out for fifteen minutes a day. The rest of the time, they sit on the floor, or they walk around their cells."

"So you think he drank the lye before you chained him up for the night?"

The attendant nodded. "Yes. That's the only possibility."

Pekkala brought his face close to the attendant's. "You know damned well this was no suicide."

The orderly's mop came to a sudden halt. From the twisted gray strands, sudsy water sluiced across the floor.

"Out," said the attendant.

The orderly dropped his mop and scurried out of the room.

"Somebody gripped Katamidze's neck," Pekkala said.

"He scratched at himself. He was out of his mind."

"There were other marks. Pressure marks. Somebody had him by the throat. His esophagus was damaged."

"The lye . . ."

"Something had been pushed down there, probably a funnel of some sort. Then the lye was emptied into his stomach."

The attendant had begun to sweat. He set his hand against his forehead and looked down at the floor. "Look, Inspector, in the end, does it really matter if he killed himself or not?"

"Of course it matters!" shouted Pekkala.

"What I mean is," explained the attendant, "this is a house of madmen. Fights break out. Feuds go on which have no end and no beginning. These men have been removed from the world so that they can no longer be a danger to society, but that does not stop them from being a danger to each other. There is only so much we can do—"

"Why did you try to persuade me it was suicide?"

"A suicide"—the attendant's hand flowed outwards, as if to ease the words out of his mouth—"requires only an internal investigation. But a murder needs a full-blown inquiry. Inspector, you know what that means. Men who are innocent, who are only trying to do a difficult job, will find themselves condemned as criminals. If there was any way that we could keep this quiet—"

"Were any intruders reported in the building?"

"Our security is designed to keep people in, not to keep them out."

"So you are saying that anyone could walk in here and gain access to the inmates?"

"They'd have to get past me first," the attendant replied, "or whoever else was on duty."

"And is the front desk ever unattended?"

"Not officially."

"What does that mean?" Pekkala snapped.

"It means that sometimes we have to answer the call of nature, if you know what I mean. Or we step out for a cigarette. Or we go to the cafeteria to grab a bowl of soup. If no one's at the desk, all a person has to do is ring the buzzer and we come and get them."

"But if no one was here, they could get hold of a key."

The attendant shrugged. "Not officially."

"In other words, yes."

"There is a whole cabinet of entrance keys. Everyone who works in the asylum has one. They pick up the key when they arrive and they drop it off again when they leave. Each person's key hangs on a peg with a number which corresponds to that person."

"And is the cabinet locked?"

"Officially . . ."

"Don't."

"It should be, but sometimes it isn't. But look, it's like I said, this place is meant to keep people inside. An inmate trying to escape has to get out of his cell, which is locked, and through this door, which is also locked. People don't break into asylums."

"Do you know of anyone here who might have hated Katamidze enough to kill him?"

"Inspector, the inmates in this place do not need a reason for killing. That's why they are in Vodovenko. And if you are telling me he was strangled, why go to the trouble of pouring lye down his throat?"

"To make it look like the work of a madman," Pekkala answered, "so that no one would suspect a person from outside the asylum."

"Wouldn't it be simpler to believe that it actually was someone in here?"

Pekkala thought of Occam's razor. "It might be simpler, but it wouldn't be the truth. He had something to tell us, and somebody got to him first."

Pekkala went out into the corridor.

The attendant followed him. He caught Pekkala's sleeve. "Why would someone from outside break into this place and kill a wretch like Katamidze?"

"He knew a name."

"Just a name? He died for that?"

"He would not be the first," said Pekkala. Then he started walking for the door.

On Pekkala's seventy-fifth day in the Butyrka prison, two guards strapped him to a plank. They tilted him so that his feet were above the level of his head and threw a wet towel over his face. Then one of the guards poured water onto the towel until he could not breathe and his mind became convinced that he was drowning.

He did not know how long this went on.

He had fallen into a place inside his mind which he had not known existed until that moment. With everything they had done to him until then, his conscious mind had balanced the information they were looking for against the pain they were causing him. His task became to keep the scales from tipping. But as he drowned beneath the towel, the scales disappeared completely and something unconscious took over. A terrible blackness, tinged with dusty red, spread out like a cloud through his brain and he no longer knew who he was, or what he cared about. Nothing mattered except staying alive.

When they removed the towel from his face, he spoke the name they had been asking. He had not intended to say it. The name almost seemed to speak itself.

Pekkala was returned to his cell immediately.

When the cell door closed, Pekkala wept. He held his hand over his mouth to stop the noise. Despair opened like a chasm before him. Tears ran over his knuckles. When the crying stopped, he realized he was going to die.

The following day, when the guards arrived, he allowed himself to be guided past the corridor of chimney cells until they reached an empty room. The floor was wet. The space could not have been more than a few yards wide and long, but it seemed so vast after living in the chimney that Pekkala's first reaction was to press himself up against the wall, as if he had been led to the edge of a cliff.

The guard handed Pekkala a piece of bread, then shut the door.

Pekkala took a bite of the bread and spat it out again. The bread gets worse and worse, he thought.

Then water started spraying out of a hole in the wall.

Pekkala screamed, dropped to the floor, and curled up in a ball.

The water kept spraying.

It was warm.

After a while, he raised his head. All he could see was the water spraying down on him. The piece of bread bubbled in his hand, and then he realized it was soap. He rubbed it all over his face.

Water sluiced over his body and ran away black with dirt, down a hole in the corner of the room. Pekkala climbed to his knees and stayed under the stream of water, chin against his chest, hands resting on his thighs. The falling water thundered in his ears.

Eventually, there was a squeaking sound and the water shut off.

Dressed in his soaked pajamas, Pekkala stumbled into the hall. In spite of the shower, dried blood crusted around his nostrils. Its metallic taste lingered in the back of his mouth.

"Hands behind your back," the guard told him.

"Step to the left, step to the right," said Pekkala.

"Shut up," said the guard.

Pekkala and the two guards walked down a corridor until they came to a heavy iron door studded with rivets. The door was opened. A smell of damp air wafted into Pekkala's face. Then the two guards hauled him down a long spiral staircase lit by bulbs in metal cages.

The basement, thought Pekkala. They are taking me down to the basement. Now they are going to shoot me. He felt glad that he would not have to go back into the chimney. His soul had all but vanished now. His body felt like a small and leaky boat, almost sunk beneath the waves.

"Are you sure?" Kirov asked, as he steered the Emka through the gates of Vodovenko.

"They are calling it a suicide," said Pekkala. "But that's not what it was."

"We should get out of Sverdlovsk," Anton warned. "We should leave now. We shouldn't even go back to collect our stuff."

"No," replied Pekkala. "We will proceed with the investigation. We are getting closer now. The killer can't be far away."

"But shouldn't we at least find a more secure location than the Ipatiev house?" asked Kirov.

"We need him to think we are vulnerable," Pekkala answered. "If whoever killed the Romanovs knows we are closing in on him, then he knows he can no longer hide. It will be only a matter of time before he comes looking for us."

It was morning.

Pekkala sat by the water pump on an upturned bucket, the Webley resting by his foot. A hand-sized mirror, made of polished steel, was propped in the crook of the pump handle. Pekkala was shaving, a dingy froth of soap upon his face and the blade rustling faintly as it carved across the contours of his chin.

He'd slept only a couple of hours. After their return from Vodovenko, the three men had agreed to stand watch in turns throughout the night and every night from then on until the investigation was complete.

Suddenly, a face peeked around the corner of the courtyard wall.

Pekkala reached for the gun.

The face ducked out of sight. "It's only me!" called a voice from behind the wall. "Your old friend, Mayakovsky."

Pekkala set the gun back down. "What do you want?" he asked.

Cautiously, Mayakovsky stepped back into the courtyard. In his arms, the old man carried a basket made from woven bulrush stalks. "I bring gifts! These are some things which Kirov has requested." Mayakovsky looked at the gun. "You are a little jumpy today, Inspector Pekkala."

"I have reason to be jumpy."

"Shaving, I see. Yes. Good for the nerves. Yes." Mayakovsky gave a nervous laugh. "Occam would be pleased."

"What?" asked Pekkala.

"Occam's razor." He pointed at the blade in Pekkala's hand. "The simplest explanation that fits the facts . . ."

". . . is usually right," said Pekkala. He wondered where Mayakovsky had bartered for that piece of knowledge. "What brings you here?"

"Ah, well, you might say it is Occam who brings me here, Inspector Pekkala."

Pekkala scraped the razor down the length of his throat, then whipped the soap off the blade and pressed the cutting edge to his skin.

Mayakovsky placed the basket on the doorstep and sat down

beside it. "My father was a handyman for the Ipatiev family. I used to wait here for him when I was a child, as he finished up his work for the day. I swore that someday I would buy this place. In the end, of course, the house could not be bought. And who would have wanted it anyway, after the things that happened here?"

"The house you have seems big enough," said Pekkala.

"Oh, yes!" answered Mayakovsky. "I have a different bedroom for every day of the week. But it is not this house." He patted the stone on which he sat. "Not the one I swore I would own."

"Then the only thing driving you is greed."

"Do you think I would have been happier if I had bought the Ipatiev house?"

"No. Greed does not rest until it has been satisfied, and greed is never satisfied."

Mayakovsky nodded. "Precisely."

Pekkala glanced up from his shaving mirror. "All right, Mayakovsky, what are you driving at?"

"Since I do not own this house," explained the old man, "the dream of owning it persists. I have come to realize that the dream of owning it is now worth more to me than the house itself. I tried to pretend otherwise. How can a man admit that his whole life has been spent searching for something he does not actually want?"

Slowly, Pekkala lowered the razor from his face. "He can admit it, if he faces the truth."

"Yes," agreed Mayakovsky, "if, like Occam's razor, he can understand where the facts are pointing him."

"I pity you, Mayakovsky."

"Save some pity for yourself, Inspector." Mayakovsky's forged smile flickered on and off, as if it were attached to some faulty electrical current. "You also seem to be in search of a thing you do not really want."

"And what is it you think I'm looking for?" asked Pekkala.

"The Tsar's treasure!" spat Mayakovsky. Until now, the old

man had been choosing his words carefully, but now they sounded like an accusation.

"What do you know about that?" Pekkala wiped the soap from his blade onto a dish towel laid across his knee.

"I know that the Tsar had hidden it so well that no one could find it. Not that they didn't try. I saw them. The carriage shed in this courtyard was filled with the trunks the Romanovs brought with them. Beautiful trunks. The kind with curved wooden railings and brass locks, each trunk numbered and named. Well, the militia searched them and stole a few things, but they didn't really know what they were looking for—just a bunch of books and fancy clothes. Those Cheka boys must have figured out that even if the valuables themselves weren't in the trunks, they might discover a clue as to where they could find them. Every night, those Cheka guards sneaked out and searched those trunks, but they never found anything."

"What makes you think that, Mayakovsky?"

"Because if they had found it, Inspector Pekkala, they would have no use for you. Why else would they have kept you alive?"

"Mayakovsky," said Pekkala, "I am here to investigate the possibility that the execution of the Romanovs was not fully carried out."

Mayakovsky nodded sarcastically. "More than a decade after they vanished. Do the wheels of bureaucracy in Moscow really turn as slowly as that? The Romanovs are a footnote in history. Whether they are alive or dead no longer matters."

"It matters to me."

"That is because you are also a footnote in history—a ghost searching for other ghosts."

"I may be a ghost," said Pekkala, "but I am not searching for that gold."

"Then your emerald eye is blind, Inspector, because you are being used by someone who is. You said it yourself—greed is never satisfied. The difference between us, Inspector, is that I have faced the facts and you have not."

"I will decide that for myself, Mayakovsky."

As if prompted by some invisible signal, both men rose to their feet.

"Katamidze is dead," Pekkala said. "I thought you should know."

"People don't last long in Vodovenko."

"He knew who murdered the Tsar. He may have been the only one who could have told me the name of the killer."

"I may be able to help you," said Mayakovsky.

"How?"

"There is someone Katamidze knew, someone he might have spoken to before he disappeared from Sverdlovsk."

"Who?" asked Pekkala. "For God's sake, Mayakovsky, if you know anything at all . . ."

Mayakovsky held up his hand. "I will talk to this person," he said. "I must go about this carefully."

"When can you let me know?"

"I will see to it at once." The old man's voice was calm and reassuring. "I may have an answer for you later today."

"I expect it will come at a price. You must know by now that we don't have much to give you."

Mayakovsky tilted his head. "There is one thing I've had my eye on, so to speak."

"And what is that?"

He nodded towards Pekkala's black coat, which hung from a nail on the wall. Just visible under the lapel was the oval of the emerald eye.

Pekkala breathed out through his teeth. "You drive a hard bargain."

Mayakovsky smiled. "If I did anything less, I would have no respect for myself."

"What about your basket?"

"Keep it, Inspector. Think of it as a down payment on that badge of yours."

WHEN PEKKALA HAD FINISHED SHAVING, HE WIPED THE LAST FLECKS of soap from his face, carefully folded the razor, and put it in his pocket. He walked into the kitchen and was surprised to find Anton sitting there with his feet up on the table, reading a copy of *Pravda*. "Look what I bought," he said, without looking up.

"That paper is a week old," said Pekkala.

"Even week-old news is news in a place like this." Anton folded the paper and slapped it down on the table.

"Mayakovsky was here," said Pekkala, handing over the basket.

Anton removed a loaf of dark rye bread and gnawed off a piece. "And what did our little house troll want for this?" he asked with his mouth full.

"He says he might know someone who spoke to Katamidze on the night the Romanovs were killed. He might be able to get us a name."

"Let's hope," mumbled Anton, "that he's more help to us than last time."

With the contents of the basket—a small partridge, a bottle of milk, some salted butter, and half a dozen eggs—Kirov put together a meal. He chopped up the partridge, tore the bread into crumbs, and mixed them together in a cracked bowl which he found under the sink. Then he kneaded in some butter and the yolks of several eggs. He stoked the stove until the iron plate on top seemed to ripple from the heat. He shaped the mixture into oval cakes and fried them.

Afterwards, the three men sat around the stove, letting the fire die down while they ate with their hands and only their handkerchiefs for plates, scalding their fingers on the hot, buttery cakes.

Pekkala ate as slowly as he could, letting each thread of the taste weave its way through his brain as the cakes dissolved in his mouth.

"My family owned a tavern," Kirov said, "in a town called Torjuk on the Moscow-Petrograd road. In the old days, with horse carriages passing through all the time, the place was very busy. There were small rooms upstairs for guests, and downstairs the windows were made from pieces of stained glass held together with strips of lead. It smelled of food and smoke. I remember people coming in half frozen from their carriage rides, stamping the snow off their boots and sitting down at the big tables. Coats would pile up by the door in heaps taller than I was. It was always busy in there, and the chef, whose name was Pojarski, had to be ready to cook meals for people whenever they came in, day or night. In winter, when things got quiet and the stove cooled down, Pojarski would sleep on the top of it. But when the Nikolaevsky railroad began running between the two cities, it didn't pass through Torjuk. The road almost closed down, there were so few carriages traveling on it. But my family kept the tavern open. During the week, Pojarski cooked for the guests, if there were any, but on Sundays he would prepare a meal for me and my parents after we came back from church. This is what he used to cook for me. He seasoned it with vodka and sage and called it a Pojarski cutlet. I looked forward to it all week. What you are eating now is the reason I wanted to become a chef."

"You went to church?" Anton had wolfed down his food. Now he was wiping the grease from his hands onto his handkerchief. "Not exactly good credentials for a Commissar."

"Everyone went to church in Torjuk," replied Kirov. "There were thirty-seven chapels in the town."

"That's all gone now," said Anton.

"Be quiet and eat," whispered Pekkala.

Later that day, Pekkala was on his hands and knees, scraping the ashes from the fireplace. He had opened the curtains. Beams of sunlight fell in crooked pillars across the scuffed wood floor.

When he paused to wipe sweat from his face, he saw Mayakovsky emerge from his house.

Mayakovsky picked up a cardboard box lying on the doorstep. He opened it, smiled, and glanced towards the Ipatiev house. Then, carrying the box, he walked across the street. This time, he did not go around to the back of the house but came straight to the front door. The sharp, dry clacks of the brass horseshoe knocker echoed through the house.

Before Pekkala could get to his feet, Kirov came out of the kitchen and opened the door.

"Kirov!" said Mayakovsky. "My good friend, Kirov!"

"Well, hello, Mayakovsky."

"I knew there was something special between us."

"I'm glad you think so," replied Kirov.

Pekkala rested on his knees, his hands mottled gray with ash, enjoying Kirov's attempts to be polite.

"We understand each other," Mayakovsky continued, "and I won't forget it. Thank you!"

"You're very welcome, Mayakovsky. I'm glad we're getting on so well."

The door closed. Kirov stood in the doorway to the front room, arms folded, a bemused look on his face. "There goes another one who's lost his mind. Just like everyone else in this town."

"He was thanking you for the present you left on his doorstep."

"I didn't give him anything," Kirov said.

"You didn't?" Pekkala looked out through the windows. "But I thought you said you were going to give him a present. To throw him off balance."

"I was, but I never got around to it."

Halfway across the road, the box still in his hands, Mayakovsky paused and turned.

His eyes locked with Pekkala's.

A burn of adrenaline seared across Pekkala's stomach. "Oh, Christ," he whispered.

The smile faltered on Mayakovsky's face. Then he disappeared. Where he had stood, for a fraction of a second, was a pink cloud of mist. The windows rippled like water. Then a wall of fire blew into the house. The shock wave picked up Pekkala and threw him to the opposite side of the room. He hit the wall. His eyes filled with dust. Metallic-reeking smoke poured into his lungs. He could not breathe. He felt sharp pain in his chest. All around him, fragments of glass were bouncing off the walls, skimming across the floor, flickering like diamonds in the air.

The next thing Pekkala knew, Kirov was dragging him out of the room. The front door had been blown open. Out in the street the cobblestones were scattered with debris. Whole tree branches lay in the road, the leaves curled into burned black fists.

When they reached the kitchen, Anton was there.

The two men lifted Pekkala up onto the table.

Pekkala tried to sit up, but Anton held him down.

A wet cloth smeared across his face.

Anton was saying something, but he couldn't hear a thing.

Then Kropotkin was there, his mop of blond hair sticking out from under a police cap.

Finally, like a radio whose volume was slowly being turned up, Pekkala's hearing began to return. He pushed aside the wet cloth, now soaked in blood, heaved himself off the table, and staggered down the hallway towards the road. His face itched. He scratched at his cheeks; his fingers came away with tiny pieces of glass embedded in them.

"You have to lie down," Kirov insisted, following him.

Pekkala ignored him. He reached the street and stopped.

Where Mayakovsky had been standing, there was only a black circle on the stones. Above, in the shattered branches of the trees, hung shreds of the old man's clothing.

Kirov seized him by the arm. "We should go inside." His voice was gentle and persistent.

Pekkala stared at the scorched leaves, at the broken glass and shattered masonry. His toe nudged against something. He looked down and saw what looked like the broken handle of a white pottery jug. He picked it up. The surface was hard and slippery. A moment went by before he realized that it was a piece of Mayakovsky's jaw.

"Let's go," Kirov said.

Pekkala looked at Kirov as if he could not recall who he was. Then he let himself be led back inside the house.

Kirov spent the next half hour picking shards of glass from Pekkala's face with a needle-nose pliers. They glittered in their tiny nests of blood.

Kropotkin stood in the corner of the room, glancing nervously in Pekkala's direction. "Is he well enough to talk yet?" the police chief asked.

"I can talk," Pekkala replied.

"Good," Kropotkin said. "Listen to me. I have offered you a police guard until we can get this cleared up, but this Cheka man"—he pointed at Anton—"says it's not necessary."

"We don't know who planted that bomb," said Anton.

"Well, it wasn't me, if that's what you're insinuating." Kropotkin's face grew red.

"I told them we should never have come back," said Anton.

"He's right." Kirov's voice cut in. "We won't need a guard."

"And why not?" demanded Kropotkin.

"Because we are leaving first thing in the morning. We'll head to Moscow and make our report. Then, if they'll let us, we'll return, this time with a company of soldiers."

"That will take too long." Pekkala stood up. "We haven't found what we are looking for."

Kirov rested his hands on Pekkala's shoulders. "No. What we were looking for found us instead. You warned us this might happen, and it did."

"We weren't prepared enough," said Pekkala. "We'll take more precautions next time." He walked to the front room. Sunlight glimmered off pieces of broken glass, making the floor look as if it was scattered with patches of fire. The neat pile of ashes he had been collecting had blown across the floor like the shadow of a tornado. The wallpaper was ripped as if by the claws of a giant cat. He walked over to something embedded in the wall. As he wrenched it from the plaster, he realized it was the bowl of Kirov's pipe. The force of the blast had driven it like a nail into the wall.

Pekkala turned to find Anton standing in the doorway.

"Please," his brother pleaded. "We have to leave."

"I can't," replied Pekkala. "It's too late now."

In the middle of the night, he woke from a sleep in which he could not breathe.

Kirov was leaning over him, a hand over Pekkala's mouth and nose. He pressed a finger to his lips.

Pekkala nodded.

Slowly, Kirov removed his hand.

Pekkala sat up and gasped in a breath.

"There's someone in the house," Kirov whispered.

Anton was on his feet. He had already drawn his gun. He stood in the doorway to the hall, peering into the shadows. "In the basement," he told Pekkala and Kirov.

Pekkala felt a tremor run through him at the thought of something alive down there in the dried blood and the dust. He drew the Webley from its holster.

Pekkala moved sideways as he descended to the basement, his bare feet gripping the wooden steps, which creaked as his weight settled on them.

Behind him, Kirov carried one of the lanterns.

"Don't light that until I tell you," whispered Pekkala. Reaching the bottom of the stairs, Pekkala could hear nothing except the rasp of breathing from Anton and Kirov. Then, unmistakably, he caught the sound of someone crying. It was coming from the room in which the murders had taken place.

Now that his eyes were adjusting to the darkness in front of him, Pekkala could see the door was open.

The crying continued, muffled, almost as if it was coming from inside the walls.

Pekkala sucked in the musty air. Moving to the doorway of the old storage room, he peered inside and could make out the stripes of the wallpaper, but it was almost too dark to see anything else. The broken plaster looked like a sheet of dirty snow upon the floor.

The sound came again, and now he glimpsed a shape in the room's far corner. It was a person, huddled and facing the wall.

Anton stood beside Pekkala. His eyes were shining in the dark.

Pekkala nodded and the two brothers rushed across the room, feet kicking up the debris.

The figure turned. It was a man, on his knees. His crying rose to a terrible wail.

"Shoot him!" shouted Anton.

"No! Please, no!" The man cowered at Pekkala's feet.

Anton pressed the gun against his head.

Pekkala knocked it aside and grabbed the stranger by the collar of his coat. "The lantern!" he shouted to Kirov.

A match flared. A moment later, the soft glow of the lantern spread across the walls.

Pekkala yanked the man off his knees, forcing him onto his back.

The lantern swung in Kirov's grip. Shadows pitched and rolled across the bullet-spattered walls.

The man held his clawed hands over his face, as if the light would burn away his skin.

"Who are you?" demanded Pekkala.

"Move your damn hands!" shouted Kirov.

Slowly, his fingers slid away. The man's eyes were tightly shut, his face unnaturally pale in the lamplight. He had a broad forehead and a solid chin. A dark mustache and a close-cropped beard covered the lower part of his face.

Pekkala pushed Kirov's arm aside, so that the lantern was no longer in the man's face.

At last, the man's eyes flickered open. "Pekkala," he murmured.

"My God," whispered Pekkala. "It's Alexei."

"How can you be sure?" hissed Kirov.

He had walked with Pekkala out into the courtyard, while the man remained behind, guarded by Anton.

"It's him," Pekkala said. "I know."

Kirov took Pekkala by the arm and shook him. "The last time you saw Alexei was more than ten years ago. I'm asking you again—how can you be sure?"

"I spent years with the Romanovs. That's why the Bureau of Special Operations brought me here, so I could identify them whether they were alive or dead. And I'm telling you that is

Alexei. He has his father's chin, his father's forehead. Even if you've only seen pictures of the family, there's no mistaking that he is a Romanov!"

Reluctantly, Kirov released his grip. "I think it's the same person I saw looking in the window that night."

"And you told me he looked like the Tsar."

"All right," Kirov said, "but even if it is Alexei, what the hell is he doing here?"

"That's exactly what I'm going to find out."

Kirov nodded, satisfied. "If we agree, then I say we leave as soon as possible. Until we can get him to Moscow, none of us are safe in this house."

"Anton will remain on watch," said Pekkala. "He almost opened fire down there in the basement. I don't want him in the room while we are questioning Alexei."

They brought Alexei into the kitchen. Alexei sat on one side of the table, Kirov and Pekkala on the other.

Anton stood outside in the courtyard. He seemed relieved not to be part of the interrogation. After what happened to Mayakovsky, all Anton seemed to care about was getting out of town.

It was the middle of the night.

A lantern rested on the table. Its apricot-colored flame burned steadily, warming the room.

Wind moaned around the piece of cardboard which had been taped over the broken kitchen window.

Alexei looked sickly and disheveled. He had aged beyond his years. His shoulders hunched and he scratched nervously at his arms as he spoke. "They told me you were gone, Pekkala, but I never believed it. When I heard you had turned up in Sverdlovsk, I had to see for myself if it was true."

"You heard?" asked Kirov. "Who told you?"

"And who are you to speak to me that way?" replied Alexei, flaring.

"I am Commissar Kirov, and as soon as I am satisfied that you are who you say you are, we can begin a civil conversation. Until then, you can answer the questions."

"There are still people in this town who consider the Romanovs their friends," said Alexei.

Kropotkin, thought Pekkala. The police chief must have known all along where Alexei was hiding.

"Excellency—" began Pekkala.

"Don't call him that," snapped Kirov. It was the first time he had raised his voice to Pekkala.

"He's right," said Alexei. "Just call me by my name." With the heel of his palm, he wiped the tears out of his eyes.

"We found your parents, Alexei," Pekkala told him, his face haggard and serious. "Your sisters, too. As you probably know by now, you are the only one who survived."

Alexei nodded. "That is what I was told."

"By whom?" demanded Kirov.

"Let him talk!" ordered Pekkala.

"By the people who looked after me," Alexei told them.

"Start at the beginning," Pekkala urged him gently. "What happened on the night you were taken from this house?"

"We were down in the basement," said Alexei. "A man had come to take a photograph of us. We were used to it. Many had been taken since our confinement in Tsarskoye Selo and after that in Tobolsk. He was just about to take his photo when a man in an army uniform burst into the room and started shooting."

"Did you know him?" asked Pekkala.

"No," replied Alexei. "The guards were always changing, and there had been so many since our family was placed under arrest. The photographer had set up two bright lights. They were shining in our faces. I could barely see the man and there was only a second before he began shooting. After that, the room filled with smoke. My father shouted. I could hear my sisters screaming. I must have fainted. The next thing I remember, the man was carrying me up the stairs. I struggled, but he gripped me so tightly that I could barely move. He carried me out into the courtyard and made me climb into the front seat of a truck. He said that if I tried to get away I would end up like the rest. I was too terrified to disobey. Several times he went back into the house, and each time he came out he was carrying one of my family. I could see the way their heads hung down, the way their arms were dangling. I knew they were dead. Then he loaded them into the truck."

"What happened after that?"

"He climbed in behind the wheel and we drove away."

"In which direction?"

"I don't know where we went. It was the first time I had been outside that house in many weeks. There was thick forest on either side of the road and it was very dark. We stopped outside a house. The people inside were waiting. They came around to my side of the truck. The driver told me to get out and as soon as my feet touched the ground, the truck drove away into the night. I never saw the man again. I never knew his name."

Pekkala sat back in his chair. The muscles in his neck, which had bunched like a fist beneath his skin, slowly began to unclench. He now felt sure this was indeed Alexei Romanov. In spite of the years which had passed since he'd last seen the prince, there was no mistaking the physical resemblance. It was as if the Tsar's own face shimmered out of Alexei, through his cheeks, through his chin, through his eyes.

But Kirov was not yet convinced. "And these people who looked after you?" he insisted. "Who were they?"

Alexei's words came quickly now. He seemed anxious to explain all he could. "It was an elderly couple. The man's name was Semyon and the old woman was Trina. I never knew their last names. All they would say was that they were friends and that my life had been spared because I was innocent. They fed me and clothed me. I was ill. I stayed with them for many months."

It did not surprise Pekkala to hear this. In the eyes of the Russian people, Alexei had never shared the guilt heaped on his parents. The aloofness of the sisters and of their mother had only worked against them in the judgment of public opinion. Even at the height of the Revolution, with Lenin calling for rivers of blood to be spilled, Alexei had been spared the brunt of his rage. Pekkala had always believed that if mercy had been shown to anyone, it would have been towards Alexei.

"Did you try to escape?" Kirov asked.

Alexei laughed softly. "Where was there for me to go? The countryside was crawling with Bolsheviks. We'd seen that on the journey to Sverdlovsk. Eventually, I was smuggled aboard a train on the Trans-Siberian Railroad. I ended up in China and after that, Japan. I have traveled all over the world on my way back to this place."

Pekkala remembered what his brother had said about people having sighted Alexei in strange corners of the planet. Now he wondered how many of those sightings had been real. "Why did you come back to this country?" he asked. "You are not safe here."

"I knew it was dangerous," replied Alexei, "but there was only one country where I felt that I belonged. I have been here for several years now. If people believe you are dead, they stop looking for you. And even if they think they recognize you, they persuade themselves their eyes are playing tricks on them. The safest thing for me to do is not to try to look like someone else. There are only a few who know who I really am. When I heard you were here, I knew you were looking for me. And I knew that if it really was you, I could not stand by and let you search for something you might never find. I remember the things you did for my family."

"The situation is more dangerous than you imagine," Pekkala

said. "The man who killed your family knows we are looking for him, and we have reason to believe he is close by. Stalin has promised you amnesty, and I believe that his offer is genuine, but we must get you to Moscow as quickly as possible. As soon as this has been done, Alexei, I will continue the search for this man who murdered your parents and your sisters, but for now my only concern is for your safety." Pekkala rose and he and Kirov left the room.

They stood outside with Anton.

"What do you think?" Pekkala asked them. "We must all be in agreement before we can proceed."

Kirov spoke first. "The only way I could know if he is who he says he is would be if I had seen him before. Since I haven't, I need to rely on your judgment."

"And do you?" asked Pekkala.

"Yes," replied Kirov earnestly. "I do."

Pekkala turned to his brother. "Well? What do you think?"

"I don't care who he is or who he says he is," Anton replied. "We need to get out of here. If he wants to come with us to Moscow, then let him. If he doesn't, I say we leave him behind."

"Then it is settled," said Pekkala. "We'll leave for Moscow first thing in the morning."

Anton and Kirov remained in the courtyard, while Pekkala returned to the kitchen.

He sat down at the table.

"I have good news, Alexei. We'll be leaving for Moscow . . ."

Before he could continue, however, Alexei reached across the table and gripped Pekkala's hand. "That man outside. I don't trust him. You have to keep him away from me."

"That man is my brother. Someone died here today. My brother's still in shock. The strain of these past days has proved too much. Don't judge him for the way he is now. Once we are on our way to Moscow, you'll see a different side of him."

"I owe you my life," Alexei said. "I owe you everything."

Hearing those words, the guilt of abandoning the family rose up and overwhelmed Pekkala. He turned his head away and tears spilled down his cheeks.

LATER THAT NIGHT, AS PEKKALA STOOD WATCH, SITTING IN THE darkness of the kitchen with the Webley laid out on the table, Alexei came in to see him.

"I couldn't sleep," he said, taking a seat at the opposite side of the table.

Pekkala was silent. There were so many questions he wanted to ask—about the places the young man had been, about the people who had helped him, and the plans he had for the future. But for now, those would have to wait. Although Alexei seemed strong on the outside, Pekkala could only guess at how deeply his mind had been scarred by the events he had witnessed, or how much his hemophilia had caused him to suffer. To haul such memories too swiftly to the surface would be like bringing up a deep-sea diver without giving him the chance to adjust to the pressure of a world above the waves.

"Since we last met," Alexei said, "my life has not been easy."

"I do not doubt it, Excellency, but you have good reason to be optimistic about the future."

"Do you really believe that, Pekkala? Can I trust these people you are taking me to see?"

"I trust that you're worth more to them alive than dead."

"And if they allow me to live," said Alexei, "what then?"

"That is up to you."

"I doubt that, Pekkala. My life has never been my own to do with as I please."

"For now, I do not think we have a choice," Pekkala replied, "except to go to Moscow and accept the terms we have been offered."

"Perhaps there is another way," said Alexei.

"Whatever it is, I will do my best to help."

"All I would like is a chance at a normal life."

"Sometimes, I think your father would gladly have given up all of his power and his riches to have had precisely that."

"I need some chance at independence. Otherwise, I will be like an animal in a zoo, a curiosity, relying on the kindness of strangers."

"I agree," said Pekkala, "but what kind of independence do you mean?"

"My father hid some of his wealth."

"Yes, although I don't know how much or where."

"Surely that isn't true. My father trusted you with everything."

"There was an officer named Kolchak—"

"Yes," interrupted Alexei. His voice sounded suddenly impatient. "I know about Kolchak. I know he helped my father hide the gold, but he would never have taken the risk of not informing someone else of its whereabouts."

"That is also what they said when I was a prisoner in Butyrka, but even they believed me, eventually."

"That's because you held out, Pekkala! They couldn't break you."

"Excellency," said Pekkala, "they did break me."

As they went downstairs to the basement of the prison, Pekkala's fingertips brushed against black-painted walls made from uneven slabs of rock. They entered a space with a very low ceiling which dripped with condensation. The dark earth felt soft as cinnamon powder beneath his feet.

When the guards released Pekkala, he dropped to his knees in the dirt.

By the light of a caged bulb, he saw someone cowering in the corner. The figure barely looked human, more like some pale and unknown crea-

ture fished up from the bowels of the earth. The man was naked, legs straight out in front, hands covering his face. His head had been shaved and he was covered with bruises.

As Pekkala looked around, he realized that others stood hidden in the shadows. All wore the Cheka uniform of olive brown tunics and blue trousers tucked into knee-length boots.

One of the men began to speak.

Pekkala instantly recognized Stalin's voice.

"Maxim Platonovich Kolchak . . ."

Kolchak? thought Pekkala. Then, as he stared at the creature, he began to see the cavalry officer's face beneath the mask of bruises.

"You," Stalin continued, "have been found guilty of counterrevolutionary activity, theft of government property, and abuse of rank and privileges. You are hereby condemned to death. You no longer exist."

Kolchak raised his head. As his eyes locked with Pekkala's, the creature tried to smile. "Hello, Pekkala," he said. "I want you to know I have given them nothing. Tell His Excellency . . ."

The roar of gunshots was deafening in the cramped space of the room.

Pekkala pressed his hands against his ears. Concussion waves passed through his body.

When the fusillade had stopped, Stalin stepped forward and fired point-blank into Kolchak's forehead.

Then Pekkala was dragged to his feet and frog-marched back up the stairs.

By the time Pekkala arrived in the interrogation room, Stalin was already there. As before, the briefcase lay on the table, a box of Markov cigarettes beside it.

"It's just as Kolchak told you," said Stalin. "We knew all along that the Tsar had given him the task of removing the gold to a secure location, but Kolchak gave us absolutely nothing. It is almost incredible, considering what we put him through." He opened up the red box of Markovs, but this time he did not offer one to Pekkala.

"But how long had Kolchak been here?" Pekkala asked.

Stalin picked a fleck of tobacco off his tongue. "Since long before we got our hands on you, Inspector."

"Then why did you want his name from me? Everything you did"—he tried to stop his voice from cracking—"it served no purpose at all."

"It depends on how you look at it," replied Stalin. "You see, it is useful for us to know the point at which men like yourself can be broken. And it is equally important to know that there are others, men like Kolchak, who cannot be broken at all. Personally, what gives me the greatest satisfaction is that now you know what kind of man you are." He tapped the ash off his cigarette onto the floor. "The kind who can be broken."

Pekkala stared in disbelief at Stalin, whose face appeared and disappeared in cobras of tobacco smoke. "Go ahead," he whispered.

"Excuse me?"

"Go ahead. Shoot me."

"Oh, no." Stalin drummed his fingers on the briefcase which contained the relics of Pekkala's life. "That would simply be a waste. Someday we may need the Emerald Eye again. Until then, we will send you to a place where we can find you if we need you."

Six hours later, Pekkala climbed aboard a train bound for Siberia.

Alexei stared in disbelief. "Considering all that my family has done for you, this is how you choose to repay us?"

"I am sorry, Excellency," said Pekkala. "I am telling you the truth. We are in danger here."

"I see no danger," said Alexei, rising to his feet. "All I see is a man I once thought I could count on, no matter what."

Just before sunrise, Kirov wandered into the kitchen. The imprint of a tunic button, with its hammer and sickle design, was molded into his cheek where he had slept upon it. "I should have taken over from you hours ago," he said. "Why did you let me sleep?"

Pekkala barely seemed to notice Kirov. He stared at the Webley, lying on the table in front of him.

"When do we leave for Moscow?" Kirov asked.

"We don't," replied Pekkala. He explained what had happened in the night.

"If he won't go willingly," said Kirov, "I have the authority to arrest him. We'll take him to Moscow in handcuffs if we have to."

"No," said Pekkala. "He has been living in fear for so long now that he has forgotten how it is to live any other way. He has fastened onto the idea of his father's gold as the only way he can protect himself. There's no point trying to force him into changing his mind. I just need time to reason with him."

"We need to leave now," protested Kirov. "It's for his own good."

"Putting a man in handcuffs and telling him you're doing him a favor is not going to convince him. He must go willingly or he might do something rash. He might try to escape, in which case he could get hurt, and with his hemophilia, any injury might prove life-threatening. He might even try to hurt himself. Even if we did get him to Moscow, he might refuse to accept the amnesty, in which case they would execute him just to save themselves the embarrassment."

Kirov sighed. "Too bad we can't uproot the whole city of Moscow and bring it here. Then we wouldn't have to worry about transporting him."

Pekkala stood abruptly. "That's not a bad idea," he said, and dashed out into the courtyard.

Kirov went to the doorway, bewildered. "What's not a bad idea?"

Pekkala grabbed the bicycle leaning up against the wall. Tendrils of dried pond weed still clung to the spokes.

"What did I say?" Kirov asked.

"If we can't bring him to Moscow, we can bring Moscow to him. I'll be back in one hour," Pekkala said, mounting the bicycle.

"Remember, that thing doesn't have any brakes," Kirov warned, "and the back tire is flat, as well!"

Pekkala wobbled out into the street, on his way to Kropotkin's office. His plan was to put in a call to the Bureau of Special Operations in Moscow and instruct them to send out a platoon of guards to ensure the safety of the Tsarevich. Even if the guards left at once, he estimated that it would take several days for them to arrive. In the meantime, they would keep Alexei hidden in the Ipatiev house with as many police as Kropotkin could spare stationed outside. Pekkala would use the days between now and then to give the Tsarevich a chance to talk, and for Pekkala to regain his trust. By the time the escort arrived from Moscow, Alexei would be ready to go with them.

Pekkala pedaled as fast as he could. Without brakes, when he came to corners, he dragged his toes over the cobblestones in an attempt to slow down. Racing down narrow side streets, his senses filled with the tar-like smell of laundry soap, of ashes scraped from stove gratings and smoky tea brewed up in samovars lingering in the damp morning air. In picket-fenced gardens, he glimpsed bony stands of white birch, their coin-shaped leaves flickering silver to green and back to silver like sequins on a woman's party dress.

He was so preoccupied that he did not notice the narrow road ended in a T. There was no chance to take the corner, or even to slow down, and there, spreading out in front of him as he emerged from the side street, was the familiar sapphire blue expanse of the duck pond.

Pekkala leaned hard on the handlebars. Jamming one heel into the ground, he skidded to a halt in a cloud of dust, barely an arm's length from the water.

When the dust settled, Pekkala saw a woman, standing among

the reeds on the opposite bank of the pond. She held a large basket, which was filled with gray teardrop-shaped husks. She wore a red headscarf, a dark blue shirt rolled up to the elbows, and a brown ankle-length dress whose hem was slick with mud. The woman stared at him. She had an oval face with eyebrows darker than her streaked blond hair.

"My bicycle," explained Pekkala. "No brakes."

She nodded without sympathy.

There was something familiar about the woman, but Pekkala could not place her. So much for perfect memory, he thought. "Excuse me," he asked her, "but do I know you?"

"I don't know you," replied the woman. She went back to picking through the reeds.

Yellow monarch butterflies flew around her, their bobbing movements like those of paper cutouts dangled from pieces of thread.

"What are you gathering?"

"Milkweed," the woman answered.

"What for?"

"They pack it into life jackets. I get good money for this." She held up one of the gray husks and crushed it in her fist. Feathery white seeds, light as a puff of smoke, drifted out across the water.

In that instant, he remembered her. "Katamidze!" he shouted.

Her face turned red. "What about him?"

"The photograph." In the box of reject pictures, Pekkala had seen her just as she was now, by the side of this pond, that silver cloud like the ghostly blur of a face in the moment it was captured on film.

"That was a long time ago, and he said they were purely artistic."

"Well, it certainly had a—" He thought about the pink splotched cheeks of the nuns. "A certain quality."

"It wasn't my idea to pose naked."

Pekkala breathed in sharply. "Naked?"

"That old man Mayakovsky bought the pictures, every one of them. Then he started selling them off to the soldiers. Reds when they were here, Whites when they marched in. Mayakovsky didn't care, as long as they paid. Maybe you bought one."

"No." Pekkala tried to reassure her. "I only heard about them."

She hugged the basket to her chest. "Well, I guess everyone has heard about them."

"You were standing right there." Pekkala pointed at her. "Right there where you are now."

"Oh, that picture." She lowered the basket again. "I remember now. He said he wasn't happy with it."

"How well did you know Katamidze?"

"I knew him," she began, "but not the way people say I did. He's gone, you know. He doesn't live here anymore. He lost his mind. That night he went to photograph the Tsar. He said he saw them slaughtered right before his eyes. I found him hiding in his attic, talking some gibberish about how he'd come face-to-face with the Devil."

"Have you told this to anyone else?"

"When the Whites were here, they came to my house. But by then Mayakovsky had sold them some pictures. I never told them I'd seen Katamidze that night, and they never asked me about it. All they wanted to know was where they could get some more photos."

"What happened to Katamidze after you found him in the attic?"

"He was in a bad state. I told him I would send for a doctor. But before I could do anything to help him, he ran out of the house. He never came back. A couple of years later, I heard that he had ended up in prison."

"This person he came face-to-face with . . ."

"Katamidze said he was a beast on two legs."

"But a name. Did Katamidze hear a name?"

"He said that when the Tsar saw this man, he called out a word. Then they got into an argument, but Katamidze didn't know what it was about."

"What word did the Tsar call out?"

"Nothing that made any sense. Rodek. Or Godek. Or something."

Pekkala felt suddenly cold. "Grodek?"

"That's it," said the woman, "and then the shooting started."

A suffocating weight bore upon Pekkala. With his pulse thumping in his neck, he rode back to the Ipatiev house, arriving in the courtyard just as Anton carried out a handful of dishes to wash at the pump. He had taken off his tunic. The sleeves of his shirt were rolled up and his suspenders stretched across his shoulders.

As Anton cranked the squeaky iron pump handle, a gush of water spilled out on the cobblestones, bright as mercury in the night. He sat on an upturned bucket and began to scrub the dishes with an old brush, its bristles splayed out like the petals of a sunflower. He glanced up just in time to see his brother bearing down on him. But it was too late. Pekkala towered over Anton, his face contorted with anger.

"What's the matter with you?" Anton asked.

"Grodek," snarled Pekkala.

Anton's face turned suddenly pale. "What?"

Pekkala lunged at him, grabbing Anton by his shirt collar. "Why didn't you tell me it was Grodek who murdered the Tsar?"

The dish slipped from Anton's hands. It shattered on the stones. "I don't know what you're talking about."

"You send me to look for a murderer and all the while you know exactly who it is. I don't care how much you hate me, you still owe me an explanation."

For a moment, Anton's face remained a mask of surprise. He seemed about to deny everything. Then, suddenly, he faltered. With the mention of that name, a scaffolding of lies collapsed inside him. The mask he had been wearing fell away. In its place was only fear and resignation. "I told you we should have left."

"That is not an answer!" Pekkala shook his brother.

Anton did not resist. "I'm sorry," he mumbled.

"Sorry?" Pekkala let go of his brother and stood back. "Anton, what have you done?"

Wearily, the older man shook his head. "I would never have dragged you into this if I had known about our father sending you to join the Finnish Regiment. All this time I thought it was you who made that choice. I have spent years hating you for something that wasn't your fault. I wish I could go back and change things. But I can't."

"I thought Grodek was in prison. He was supposed to be in there for life."

Anton stared down at the cobblestones. All his energy seemed to have gone out of him. "When the Petrograd police barracks were stormed, back in 1917, the rioters burnt all the records. Nobody knew who was in jail for what, so when they took over the prison later that same day, they decided to release all the prisoners. As soon as Grodek got out, he joined the Revolutionary Guard. Eventually, he was recruited by the Cheka. When he heard that a group of Cheka were being assigned to guard the Romanovs, he volunteered for the job. I only found out who he was when we arrived here in Sverdlovsk. I had never met him before then."

"And you didn't think to tell me this?"

"I didn't tell you because I didn't think you would agree to help with the investigation if you knew Grodek was out. The only way the Bureau would let me hold on to my promotion was if I persuaded you to investigate the case."

"And is it true? Did Grodek offer the Tsar a chance to escape when he was stationed at the Ipatiev house?"

"Yes. In exchange for the Tsar's gold reserves. Grodek swore that he would free the family if the Tsar would lead him to where they were hidden. The Tsar agreed. It was all worked out."

"And you were helping him, weren't you?"

Anton nodded. "Grodek needed someone to create a diversion while he led the family out of the house and drove them away in one of our trucks."

"And what were you supposed to get in exchange?"

"Half of everything."

"And what was this diversion?"

"Grodek and I told the other guards that we were going to the tavern. We'd been going every night, so nobody thought it was unusual. I broke into the police chief's office and put in the call to the Ipatiev house. I said I was from the garrison at Kungur, just on the other side of the Ural Mountains. I said that the Whites had bypassed Kungur and were heading for Sverdlovsk. I told them to send all available men to set up a roadblock. Then I would join the other guards at that roadblock, saying that I had just come from the tavern. I'd tell them that Grodek was too drunk to come with me. Then I'd make sure we stayed at the roadblock as long as possible, so that Grodek would have time to free the Romanovs."

"If that was the plan, then why bring Katamidze into it?"

"We knew that at least two guards would be left behind to watch the Romanovs while the others were setting up the roadblock. The Tsar was afraid that his family might be hurt while the guards who stayed behind were being overpowered. He refused to agree to the rescue until Grodek came up with the idea of having a photographer sent over. That way, he could make sure they were all gathered safely in the basement until the guards had been disposed of."

"But wouldn't the guards think it was suspicious that Katamidze arrived after dark?"

"No. The times were crazy. We received orders at all hours of the day and night. Commands issued by Moscow sometimes took six hours to reach here. By that time, it could be the middle of the night for us, but if the order said it had to be carried out immediately, that was what we had to do."

"So Grodek planned to kill two of your own men as part of this rescue?"

Slowly, Anton raised his head. "Have you forgotten what you trained him to do? Grodek set up a Revolutionary cell with the sole purpose of assassinating the Tsar. And then, when those people learned to trust Grodek with their lives, he betrayed every last one of them. They all died because of Grodek, even the woman he loved. What were two more lives after that?"

"More than two," said Pekkala. "Because he never intended to free the Tsar, did he?"

"The Tsar had told Grodek that the treasure was hidden nearby. He said he could lead Grodek to it that same night. Grodek's plan was to accompany the Tsar to the hiding place, get the gold, and then kill him and the Tsarina. We discussed letting the children go free. Grodek promised he wouldn't kill them unless he had to. Afterwards, he would say that the Tsar and the Tsarina had been shot while trying to escape. But that's not what happened. It all went wrong."

"What did happen?"

"They got into an argument. Grodek said that when he went down to the basement, the Tsar started taunting him, saying that the treasure was right there in front of him, that the Romanovs themselves were the treasure. Grodek thought the man had gone out of his mind. When he realized that the Tsar was never going to lead him to the gold, he snapped. He started shooting."

"Why did he spare Alexei?"

"He knew he had to get rid of the bodies, so that it would look as if the Romanovs had escaped. Grodek wanted a hostage, in case he ran into White Army detachments and his escape route was blocked. Listen, brother, I will tell you everything I know, but right now we are still in danger."

"I know about the danger," said Pekkala.

Suddenly, Anton's eyes widened.

Pekkala swung around just in time to see Alexei's boot crash into the side of Anton's head. Anton's eyes fluttered. His mouth locked open, teeth bared, as the pain drilled through his skull. Then he slumped back, unconscious. Blood dripped from his head, seeping into cracks between the stones.

Alexei kicked Anton again. This time Pekkala held him back.

"What the hell is going on?" Kirov demanded, appearing out of the dusk.

"That is the man who helped to kill my family!" Alexei stabbed a finger at Anton. "He just confessed to it! This is the murderer you have been looking for."

"Is it true?" Kirov asked Pekkala.

"Grodek killed the Tsar. My brother helped him."

"But I thought you said Grodek was in prison for life!"

"He was released during the Revolution. I never knew about it until Anton told me." Pekkala turned to Alexei. "I am now almost certain that Grodek is the one who killed the photographer Katamidze, and Mayakovsky too. He may have let you live that night he killed the others in your family, but if he feels that we are near to catching him, he won't feel safe again until all of us are dead. Including you, Alexei."

"If you want me to be safe," said Alexei, "then you can start by killing him." He gestured at Anton, sprawled and bleeding on the cobblestones.

"No," replied Pekkala. "This is not the time for vengeance."

"The vengeance would be yours as well," Alexei urged. "He has been working against you all along. If you won't kill him, then let me do it. And afterwards you can take me to my father's gold. Then I will gladly go with you to Moscow. Otherwise, I will take my chances here."

Pekkala thought back to the boy he had once known, his gentle nature torn away, and of the rage which had taken its place. "What happened to you, Alexei?"

"What's happened is that you betrayed me, Pekkala! You are no better than your brother. My family might still be alive if it wasn't for you."

Pekkala felt as if a hand was closing on his throat. "Whatever you choose to believe about me, I came here to find you and to help you if I could. We are all victims of the Revolution. Some of us have suffered from it, and others have suffered for it, but in one way or another all of us have suffered. No amount of gold will ever change that."

A strange look came over Alexei's face.

It was a moment before Pekkala understood what it was. He had pitied the Tsarevich long before the fortunes of his family had turned. But now, Pekkala realized, Alexei was pitying him.

Alexei stared down at Anton, who lay spread-eagled in a puddle of his own diluted blood. Then he pushed past Kirov and stormed inside the house.

Pekkala sat down heavily upon the ground, as if his legs had collapsed underneath him.

Kirov knelt down beside Anton. "We need to get him to a doctor," he said.

WHILE KIROV STAYED BEHIND TO GUARD ALEXEI, PEKKALA LIFTED Anton into the backseat of the Emka and drove to the police station. Kropotkin climbed in and the three traveled to the clinic of a man named Bulygin, who was the only doctor in town.

On the way, Pekkala told Kropotkin that Alexei was now at the Ipatiev house.

"Thank God," Kropotkin kept repeating.

Pekkala also explained about Grodek and requested that Kropotkin put in a call to the Bureau of Special Operations, requesting an armed escort for the Tsarevich's return to Moscow. "In the meantime," said Pekkala, "I'll need as many of your police as you can spare to stand guard outside the house."

"I'll see to it as soon as we have dropped off your brother at Bulygin's."

"No one is to know the Tsarevich is inside, not even the policemen guarding the house." If news got out about Alexei, Pekkala knew that the Ipatiev place would be mobbed. Even those who wished him well would pose a threat. He remembered the disaster which had taken place at the Khodynka field in Moscow on the day of the Tsar's coronation in 1896. Crowds which had gathered to witness the occasion rushed towards tables of food which had been provided for them. Hundreds of people lost their lives in the stampede. Under the circumstances, especially with a bomb maker like Grodek still at large, the situation could be even worse.

Bulygin was a bald man with an emotionless face and a small mouth which barely moved when he spoke. Anton was still unconscious when Bulygin laid him out on an operating table and shone a light into each of his eyes. "He has a concussion, but I see nothing life-threatening. Let me keep him here for observation. He should be conscious again in a matter of hours, but if his condition changes for the worse, I will let you know immediately."

Returning to the Ipatiev house, Pekkala dropped Kropotkin off at the police station.

"I have seen your brother take a lot of beatings," Kropotkin told him. "One more won't do him any harm. I'll keep an eye out for this man Grodek. In the meantime, let me know if you need any more help."

Arriving at the Ipatiev house, Pekkala found Kirov sitting at the kitchen table. He was staring at Pekkala's copy of the *Kalevala.*

"How is your brother?" asked Kirov.

"He should be fine. Where is Alexei?"

Kirov jerked his head towards the stairs. "Up on the second floor. Just sitting there. He isn't very talkative."

"When did you start reading Finnish?"

"I'm just looking at the illustrations."

"Troops are on their way from Moscow. I'll go and explain things to Alexei."

"You need a new copy of this book," Kirov called to Pekkala as he walked out of the room.

"What's wrong with that one?"

"It's full of holes."

Pekkala grunted and walked on.

He was halfway up the stairs when he stopped. Then he turned and ran back downstairs. "What do you mean it's full of holes?"

Kirov held up a page. Light through the kitchen window glinted through tiny puncture marks scattered across the page. "See?"

"Give me the book." Trembling, Pekkala held out his hand.

Kirov slapped it shut and handed it over. "Your language has too many vowels," he complained.

Pekkala took a lantern from the kitchen shelf and ran down to the basement. There, in the darkness at the bottom of the stairs, he lit the lamp and set it down before him.

The nun had told him about the Tsar's method for smuggling messages out past the guards, using a pin to mark out letters on the pages. Now Pekkala thought back to that day at his cottage, when the Tsar had returned the book. At the time, he had thought the Tsar was just rambling, but now, as he held up the pages one by one, he could see tiny pinholes marked beneath different letters. Pekkala took out his notebook and began to assemble the words.

It took only a few minutes for him to decipher the message. When he had finished, he ran back up the stairs, taking the book and lantern with him. He dashed through the hall and up to the second floor.

Alexei was sitting in a chair by the window in an otherwise empty room.

"Alexei," said Pekkala, as he tried to catch his breath.

Alexei turned. Nestled in his hands was a Russian army revolver.

"Where did you get that?"

"Do you think I would go about unarmed?"

"Please put it down," said Pekkala.

"It appears I have run out of options."

"I know where it is," said Pekkala. Seeing Alexei alone like this, Pekkala wondered if the Tsarevich was contemplating suicide.

"Where what is?"

"The treasure. You were right. Your father did tell me."

Alexei narrowed his eyes. "You mean you lied to me?"

"He left a message in this book. The message was hidden. I didn't realize it was there until now."

Slowly, Alexei rose to his feet. He put the gun in his pocket. "Well, where is it?"

"Close. I will take you straight to it."

"Just tell me," said Alexei. "That's all I need."

"It's important that I take you there myself. I will explain on the way."

"All right," said Alexei, "but let's not waste any more time."

"We will go at once," said Pekkala.

They met Kirov at the bottom of the stairs.

Pekkala explained what they were doing.

"It was in the book all along?" asked Kirov.

"I never would have found it if you hadn't spotted the holes."

Kirov looked bewildered. "And you say it is close by?"

Pekkala nodded.

"I'll get the car ready," said Kirov.

"No," Alexei told him. "Pekkala is the only one I trust. I promise that as soon as we get back, I will drive with you to Moscow."

"Are you sure about this?" asked Kirov.

"Yes," replied Pekkala. "Someone should stay here in case the doctor calls about Anton. We'll be back in an hour or so." He handed the book to Kirov. "Look after this," he said.

"WHY WON'T YOU TELL ME WHERE WE ARE GOING?" ASKED ALEXEI, as the Emka raced beyond the outskirts of Sverdlovsk.

"I will when we get there," replied Pekkala.

Alexei smiled. "All right, Pekkala. You just lead the way. I have waited a long time for this. I can wait a few minutes more. Of course, you will not go away empty-handed. There will be something in it for you, too."

"You can keep it, Excellency," Pekkala replied. "As far as I'm concerned, your father's treasure stands for everything that got him killed."

Alexei held up his hands and laughed. "Whatever you say, Pekkala!"

The Emka turned off the Moscow Highway, and headed down a potholed dirt track, tires splashing through muddy water. A minute later, Pekkala swung the car off the dirt track and into a field of tall grass. The clearing was surrounded by dense woods. At the far end, a crooked chimney rose from a dilapidated building. The Emka rolled across the field. At last, they came to a stop and Pekkala cut the engine. "We're here," he said. "We'll need to walk the last—"

"But that's the old mine over there," said Alexei. "That's where the bodies were dumped."

Pekkala left the car. "Come with me," he said.

Alexei got out and slammed the Emka's door. "This is no joke, Pekkala! You promised me that gold."

Pekkala walked to the edge of the mine shaft and stared down into the darkness. "The treasure is not gold."

"What?" Alexei stood back from the mouth of the pit, unwilling to get near the edge.

"It's diamonds," said Pekkala, "and rubies and pearls. The Tsar had them sewn into specially made clothes. I couldn't tell from the message how much there is or who was wearing them. Probably your parents and your elder sisters. Obviously, with your sickness, he would not have expected you to carry such an extra weight, and the less you knew about it, the safer you would be. I am telling you this now, Alexei, because I did not want to upset you. The bodies are still here. That is where we'll find the treasure."

"Gems?" Alexei appeared to be in shock.

"Yes," replied Pekkala, "more than most people could even imagine."

Alexei nodded. "All right, Pekkala, I believe you. But I'm afraid to go down in that mine."

"I understand," said Pekkala. "I'll go by myself." He brought out the towing rope, and fastened one end to the bumper of the Emka. Then he threw the heavy coil into the darkness. The rope shushed through the air as it uncoiled. Far below, there was a slap as it struck the ground. Then he fetched Anton's flashlight from the glove compartment and the leather satchel he had brought with him from the forest of Krasnagolyana. "I'll put the treasure in here," he explained. "I may need to send parts of it up to you separately. I'm not sure I can climb this rope and carry it all at the same time." He turned on the flashlight, unsure if it would even work. As light splashed down into the mine shaft, Pekkala sighed with relief that Kirov had remembered to replace the batteries.

Standing at the edge of the pit, Pekkala hesitated. Fear spread like wings inside his chest. He closed his eyes and breathed out slowly.

"What's the matter?" asked Alexei.

"You'll need to lift the rope from the ground. Otherwise, it will drag against the edge of the mine shaft and I won't be able to get a grip on it as I go over the side. Once I'm on the way down, I can handle it myself."

Alexei took up the rope. "Like this?" he asked.

"The rope is still too low."

Alexei closed the gap between them, his hands tight on the rough brown hemp, lifting it as he moved.

"You'll have to come closer," said Pekkala, "just until I can get my feet against the wall of the mine shaft. Then I'll be fine."

Now they were only an arm's length apart, their hands almost touching.

Pekkala glanced into Alexei's face. "Almost there," he said.

Alexei smiled. His face had turned red from the effort of lifting the heavy rope. "I won't forget this," he promised.

Just as Pekkala was ready to lower himself over the side, he noticed the jagged white line of an old scar on Alexei's forehead. He stared at it in confusion. A wound like that would probably have killed a hemophiliac. And then, like a ghostly image sliding over the features of Alexei, Pekkala glimpsed a different person. He was transported back many years, to a frigid day in Petrograd. He was on a bridge, overlooking the Neva River. Standing before him was Grodek, his face filled with terror at the thought of jumping from the bridge. As Grodek tried to dash past, Pekkala brought the barrel of the Webley down on his head. Grodek sprawled on the slush-covered ground, his forehead gashed by the front sight of the pistol. It was that same wound, the purple centipede crawling up into his hairline, which he had refused to cover up with bandages throughout the trial. The scar had faded so that it was almost invisible. Only now, as the skin around it flushed from exertion, did the old wound reappear.

"Grodek," whispered Pekkala.

"It's too late, Pekkala. You should have listened to your friends. But you wanted too much to believe."

"What have you done with him?" stammered Pekkala. "What have you done with Alexei?"

"The same thing I did to the others," Grodek replied. Then he let go of the rope.

Still attached to the bumper, the hemp cord snapped down. The shock almost tore it from Pekkala's hands. He staggered backwards, desperate to keep his balance. But he was already too far out over the mine shaft. He toppled backwards. With the rope still in his grasp, he slid down, palms burning, kicking with his feet at the walls of the mine shaft, air rushing past him. Then his foot caught against a lip of stone. He clenched his hands around the rope. The skin of his palms had torn open, cauterized by the heat of holding on, but his grip held. With a jarring twist of his spine, everything stopped. Pekkala swung out and then back, his body slamming against the stone. He struggled to catch his breath. Wheezing, he lifted his knee, trying to gain a secure foothold. Just when he thought he had done this, his shoe came off. As he began to fall again, the weight of his body tore into his shoulder blades. He cried out in pain. His hands felt as if they had been held against a flame. This time he let go of the rope. He tumbled into the darkness, legs kicking. Then the blackness took shape, rushing up to meet him. He landed heavily, the wind knocked out of his lungs. Unable to breathe, he rolled, hands clawing in the dirt, mouth open and gasping for the air that would not come. As his consciousness faded, he curled over, forehead touching the ground, and in that arching of his body, his lungs released. He sucked in a mouthful of air filled with the stench of decay.

Grodek's face appeared over the mouth of the pit. "Are you there, Pekkala?"

Pekkala groaned. He took another breath.

"Pekkala!"

"Where is Alexei?"

"Long gone," Grodek answered. "Don't worry, Pekkala. There is nothing you could have done. I kept him alive in case I needed a hostage. When I was dumping the bodies, he got out of the truck and tried to run away. I warned him to stop or I'd fire, but Alexei kept running. That's why I had to shoot. He died the same night as the rest of his family. He is buried at the edge of this field. I had no choice."

"No choice?" shouted Pekkala. "None of them deserved to die!"

"Neither did Maria Balka," answered Grodek. "But I do not blame you, Pekkala. I have never considered you my enemy. From that day on the bridge to this, you and I have been on paths which were not of our own making. Whether we chose them or not, our paths have now converged. You have your brother to thank for that. He is the one who contacted me after that lunatic photographer decided to speak up. I would never have allowed him to live except the Tsar insisted upon it. And when Stalin chose to put you on the case, I thought we'd have a chance of locating that gold after all. If I'd only known it wasn't gold we were looking for, I might have found it sooner."

"You won't get what you came for," said Pekkala. "I know you're too afraid to come down here."

"You're right," Grodek said. "Instead, you will gather up the gems, put them in that leather bag, and tie it to the end of the rope. Then all I have to do is haul them up."

"Why would I do that for you?"

"Because if you do, I will get in that car and drive away and you will never see me again. But if you don't, I will go back into town and finish off the job I started on your brother. I'll take care of that Commissar as well. I don't want to do it, Pekkala. I know you think the blood of the Romanovs is on your hands, but the truth is that they brought it on themselves. It is the same with your brother. He has brought this on himself. Even so, he does not deserve to die. He believed you when you told him that you could not find the Tsar's treasure. But I knew you'd get your hands on it eventually, and I was right. In the meantime, I had to keep threatening him. When he came back from the tavern black and blue, it was because I'd been knocking his head against the wall. When I came up with the idea of impersonating Alexei, he told me he couldn't go through with it. I said I'd kill you if he mentioned my name. He knew I'd do it, too, so he kept his mouth shut. When you found out for yourself that I was here, he was going to warn you. That's why I had to shut him up. He saved your life, Pekkala. The least you can do is save his."

"If I gave you the jewels," shouted Pekkala, "then what? You would leave me here to rot?"

"They'll find you. When we're not back in an hour, that Commissar will go looking for that message in the book. He'll have you out of here before nightfall, but only if you hurry. Five minutes, Pekkala. That is all I'm giving you. If I don't have those gems by then, I will leave you here to die among the bodies of your masters. With your brother and Kirov dead, there'll be no one in Sverdlovsk to find you. By the time they figure it out, you'll be just another body in the dark."

"How do I know you'll keep your word?"

"You don't," replied Grodek, "but if you hand me those jewels, I will have what I came for and I won't hang around here any longer than necessary. Now hurry! Time is running out."

Pekkala knew he had no choice except to follow Grodek's instructions.

After groping around on the floor, he eventually found his satchel. He opened the flap, brought out his flashlight, and turned it on.

The mummified and broken faces of the Romanovs loomed out of the dark. They lay as he had left them. Among their rotted clothing, buttons of metal and bone reflected the light.

On his knees before the corpse of the Tsar, Pekkala grabbed the dead man's tunic in his hands and pulled apart the cloth. It tore easily, sending up a faint cloud of dust as the threads ripped away. Beneath the tunic, Pekkala found a waistcoat made of heavy white cotton, like sailcloth. It looked to him like the kind of protective vest worn by fencers. It was ridged with many rows of stitching. The vest had been fastened with string ties instead of buttons. The knots were tightly done, so he pulled at the strings until they broke. Then, as gently as he could, he laid the Tsar facedown, tore away the tunic, and removed the vest, sliding it up over the skeletal arms. The vest was heavy. He threw it to one side.

"Three minutes, Pekkala!" Grodek called down.

As quickly as he could, Pekkala removed the other vests. They were all of the same construction, each one tailor-made to fit the body of the one who wore it. When the last of them had been removed, Pekkala turned away from the half-naked corpses, their papery flesh shrunk tight across the bones and framed by shreds of decayed clothing.

"One minute, Pekkala!"

He stuffed the vests into the satchel, but only half of them would fit. "You'll have to throw the satchel down again. There's more than I can send up in one bag."

"Tie it to the rope!"

Soon the leather satchel lifted jerkily into the air, scraping against the walls as it rose to the surface.

He heard Grodek laughing.

A moment later, the empty satchel slapped into the dirt, trailing the snake of hemp rope.

Pekkala packed in the remainder of the vests and they were also lifted to the surface.

Far in the distance he heard a gunshot, the sound like a dry twig snapping. It was coming from above ground. Then someone shouted. Anton was calling his name.

Pekkala struggled to his feet.

Now he could hear Grodek's voice, and Kirov's too, their shouting interspersed with blasts of gunfire. He squinted up into the patch of light which marked the entrance to the tunnel. There was a scream, and suddenly the light flickered. Pekkala saw what looked like a huge black bird. It was a man, falling. He barely had time to step back before the body slammed into the ground.

Pekkala rushed to where the man lay on his face. He could not tell who it was. Turning over the body, he realized it was Anton. His body had been horribly broken by the fall. Anton's eyes blinked open. He coughed up blood and gasped. Then he raised one hand and took hold of Pekkala's arm. Pekkala held on to him, while Anton's grip became weaker. In those last moments, as his brother's life unspooled into darkness, Pekkala's thoughts drifted back to when he and Anton were children, sledding on the woodcutter's hill. It seemed to Pekkala that he could even hear their laughter, and the whispering of the sleds as they raced over the frozen ground. Finally, Anton's breath trailed out in a sigh. His fingers slipped away. And the image which had been so clear in Pekkala's mind only a moment before dissolved into particles of gray, spreading farther and farther apart until finally the picture was lost and he knew that his brother was dead.

Pekkala's whole body went numb. The pain in his rope-burned hands and from his knees and his shoulders and his back all merged into a ringing emptiness inside him. His heart seemed to be slowing down, like a pendulum swinging to a stop. He felt his whole life circle back towards its source, to that intersecting point at which a person either dies or must begin again. He closed his eyes and, in the blind man's black, Pekkala felt death spread its arms around him.

Then he heard a whispering in the air. The rope slapped down beside him. "Hold on," Kirov called to him. "I'll get you out."

Once more, Pekkala closed his hands around the gritty hemp. The pain returned, but he forced himself to ignore it. Above, he heard an engine fire up and then he felt himself lifted off the ground. As his feet left the earth, he glanced down at his brother, laid out beside the bodies of the Romanovs, as if he had been with them all along. Then the black walls of the mine shaft closed over them.

A minute later, Kirov dragged him onto level ground.

The first thing Pekkala saw was Grodek. He lay on his stomach, hands cuffed behind his back, the fingers curled like the claws of a dead bird. Blood soaked through the cloth of his shirt.

"You have to stop him," gasped Grodek. "He says he's going to kill me."

Across the field, half buried in the tall grass, stood another car. Its windshield had been shattered by bullets. Steam billowed from the punctured radiator, and the shiny black sides showed silver scabs where bullets had gone through the metal.

Kirov set his foot on Grodek's back and ground his heel into the bullet wound in his shoulder.

Grodek shrieked with pain.

Kirov's face showed no emotion.

"How did you find me?" asked Pekkala.

"As soon as your brother woke up," replied Kirov, "he borrowed the doctor's car and came to find me. He told me about Grodek. At first, neither of us knew where you had gone. Then I remembered the book. I deciphered the message. We came here as quickly as we could. When we got to the field, I tried to keep Grodek pinned down while Anton came around the side, but Grodek spotted him and opened fire. Anton was wounded. Grodek threw him into the pit." Now Kirov hauled Grodek to his feet, lifting him by the cuffs. "And now it is time to settle the accounts."

Grodek cried out as his arms were bent back.

"I hear you are afraid of heights," said Kirov, as he hauled Grodek towards the mine shaft.

Kirov held him over the edge.

Grodek writhed and begged.

All Kirov had to do was let go.

He was about to cross a line from which there was no turning back. Already, Kirov seemed to be a different man from the Junior Commissar Pekkala had met in the forest, lifetimes ago. Pekkala felt helpless to prevent what was about to happen. Part of him wanted it, knowing that if Kirov did not cross that line today, the time would surely come when he would have no choice. But Pekkala realized that he could not stand by and let it happen. He called out to Kirov, ordering him to stop, knowing it might already be too late.

For a moment Kirov seemed confused, like a man snapping out of hypnosis. Then he leaned back, fist clenched around the handcuff chain, pulling Grodek away from the precipice.

Grodek dropped to his knees, sobbing.

Pekkala walked over to the vests. They lay in a heap, the white cotton looking stained and brittle in the daylight. He lifted one of them and held it up, feeling the weight drag at his arm. The rotten cloth tore open and a stream of diamonds poured out on the ground, sparkling like water in the sunlight.

One week later, Pekkala was in Moscow.

He sat in a wood-paneled room whose tall windows, framed

by crimson velvet curtains, looked out onto Red Square. An eighteenth-century Thomas Lister grandfather clock, which had once stood in the Catherine Palace, patiently marked time in the corner of the room.

The desk in front of him was bare except for an empty wooden pipe holder.

He did not know how long he had been waiting. Now and then he glanced at the large double doors. Outside, he heard soldiers marching in the square.

A dream he'd had the night before still echoed in his head. He was in Sverdlovsk, on that bicycle, flying downhill without brakes, heading straight for the duck pond again. Just as before, he had ended up in the water, soaked and covered in weeds. When he rose from the pond, he saw a person standing in the rushes on the other side. It was Anton. His heart jumped when he saw his brother. Pekkala tried to move but found that he could not. He called, but Anton did not seem to hear. Then Anton turned and walked away and the bulrushes closed up around him. Pekkala stood there for a long time—at least it seemed so in his dream—thinking of the day when he would cross that pond. Like Anton, he would stand on that far shore, looking back where he had come from, without pain or anger or sadness, and then he, too, would disappear into the world that lay beyond the water.

Suddenly a door opened in the wall behind the desk. It was shaped so much like one of the panels that Pekkala had not even noticed it was there.

The man who walked into the room wore a plain brownish-green wool suit, whose jacket had been fashioned in a military cut so that its short stand-up collar closed across his throat. His dark hair, streaked with gray above his ears and temples, had been combed straight back on his head and a thick mustache bunched under his nose. When he smiled, his eyes closed shut like those of a contented cat. "Pekkala," he said.

Pekkala rose to his feet. "Comrade Stalin."

Stalin sat down opposite him. "Sit," he said.

Pekkala returned to his chair.

For a moment, the two men regarded each other in silence.

The ticking of the clock seemed to grow louder.

"I told you we would meet again, Pekkala."

"The setting is more pleasant than before."

Stalin sat back and looked around the room, as if he had never really noticed it before. "It's all more pleasant now."

"You asked to see me."

Stalin nodded. "As you requested, credit for the return of the Tsar's jewels to the Soviet people has been given to Lieutenant Kirov. Actually"—Stalin scratched at his chin—"it is Major Kirov now."

"Thank you for letting me know," said Pekkala.

"You are free to go now," said Stalin, "unless, of course, you might consider staying on."

"Stay on? No, I am bound for Paris. I have a meeting which is long overdue."

"Ah," he said. "Ilya, isn't it?"

"Yes." It made Pekkala nervous to hear him say her name.

"I have some information about her." Stalin was watching him closely, as if they were playing cards. "Permit me to share it with you."

"Information?" asked Pekkala. "What information?" He thought, *Please don't let her be hurt, or sick. Or worse. Anything but that.*

Stalin opened a drawer on his side of the desk. The dry wood squeaked as he pulled. He withdrew a photograph. For a moment, he studied it, leaving Pekkala to stare at the back of the picture and wonder what on earth this was about.

"What is it?" demanded Pekkala. "Is she all right?"

"Oh, yes," replied Stalin. He laid the picture down, placed a finger on top of it, and slid the photograph towards Pekkala.

Pekkala snatched it up. It was Ilya. He recognized her instantly. She was sitting at a small café table. Behind her, printed on the awning of the café, he saw the words *Les Deux Magots*. She was smiling. He could see her strong white teeth. Now, reluctantly, Pekkala's gaze shifted to the man who was sitting beside her. He was thin, with dark hair combed straight back. He wore a jacket and tie and the stub of a cigarette was pinched between his thumb and second finger. He held the cigarette in the Russian manner, with the burning end balanced over his palm as if to catch the falling ash. Like Ilya, the man was also smiling. Both of them were watching something just to the left of the camera. On the other side of the table was an object which at first Pekkala almost failed to recognize, since it had been so long since he had seen one. It was a baby carriage, its hood pulled up to shelter the infant from the sun.

Pekkala realized he wasn't breathing. He had to force himself to fill his lungs.

Stalin rested his fist against his lips. Quietly, he cleared his throat, as if to remind Pekkala that he was not alone in the room.

"How did you get this?" asked Pekkala, his voice gone suddenly hoarse.

"We know the whereabouts of every Russian émigré in Paris."

"Is she in danger?"

"No," Stalin assured him. "Nor will she be. I promise you that."

Pekkala stared at the baby carriage. He wondered if the child had her eyes.

"You must not blame her," Stalin told him. "She waited, Pekkala. She waited a very long time. Over ten years. But a person cannot wait forever, can they?"

"No," admitted Pekkala.

"As you see"—Stalin gestured towards the picture—"Ilya is

happy now. She has a family. She is a teacher, of Russian, of course, at the prestigious Ecole Stanislas. No one would dare to say she does not love you still, Pekkala, but she has tried to put the past behind her. That is something all of us must do at some point in our lives."

Slowly, Pekkala raised his head, until he was looking Stalin in the eye. "Why did you show this to me?" he asked.

Stalin's lips twitched. "Would you rather have arrived in Paris, ready to start a new life, only to find that it was once more out of reach?"

"Out of reach?" Pekkala felt dizzy. His mind seemed to rush from one end of his skull to the other, like fish trapped in a net.

"You could still go to her, of course." Stalin shrugged. "I have her address if you want it. One look at you and whatever peace of mind she might have won for herself in these past years would be gone forever. And let us say, for the sake of argument, that you might persuade her to leave the man she married. Let us say that she even leaves behind her child—"

"Stop," said Pekkala.

"You are not that kind of man, Pekkala. You are not the monster that your enemies once believed you to be. If you were, you would never have been such a formidable opponent for people like myself. Monsters are easy to defeat. With such people, it is only a question of blood and time, since their only weapon is fear. But you—you won the hearts of the people and the respect of your enemies. I do not believe you understand how rare a thing that is, and those whose hearts you won are out there still." Stalin brushed his hand towards the window, and out across the pale blue autumn sky. "They know how difficult your job can be, and how few of those who walk your path can do what must be done and still hold on to their humanity. They have not forgotten you. And I don't believe you have forgotten them."

"No," whispered Pekkala, "I have not forgotten."

"What I am trying to tell you, Pekkala, is that you still have a place here if you want it."

Until that moment, the thought of staying on had not occurred to him. But now the plans he'd made held no meaning. Pekkala realized that his last gesture of affection for the woman he'd once thought would be his wife must be to let her believe he was dead.

"More than a place," continued Stalin. "Here, you will have a purpose. I realize how dangerous your work can be. I know the risks you take, and I cannot promise that the odds of your survival will improve. But we need someone like you . . ." Suddenly Stalin seemed to falter, as if even he could not fathom why Pekkala would continue to shoulder such a burden.

In that moment, Pekkala thought of his father, of the dignity and patience he had learned from that old man.

"The job . . ." Stalin grasped for words.

"Matters," said Pekkala.

"Yes." Stalin breathed out. "It matters. To them." Once more, he gestured towards the window, as if to take in the vastness of the country with a single sweep of his hand. Then he brought his hand in and his palm thumped hard against his chest. "To *me*." Now Stalin's confidence returned, and all confusion vanished, as if a shadow had been lifted from his face. "You might be interested to know," he continued, "that I have spoken to Major Kirov. He made a couple of requests."

"What did he want?"

Stalin grunted. "The first thing he wanted was my pipe."

Pekkala glanced at the empty pipe holder on the desk.

"It was such a strange thing to ask for that I actually gave it to him." Stalin shook his head, still puzzled. "It was a good one. English briar wood."

"What was his other request?"

"He asked to work with you again, if the opportunity ever presented itself. I hear he is a decent cook," said Stalin.

"A chef," replied Pekkala.

Stalin thumped the desk. "Even better! This is a big country, filled with terrible food, and someone like that would be good to have along."

Pekkala's face was still unreadable.

"So." Stalin sat back in his chair and touched the tips of his fingers together. "Would the Emerald Eye consider an assistant?"

For a long time, Pekkala sat there in silence, staring into space.

"I need an answer, Pekkala."

Slowly, Pekkala stood. "Very well," he said. "I will return to work at once."

Now Stalin rose to his feet. He reached across the desk and shook Pekkala's hand. "And what should I tell Major Kirov?"

"Tell him," said Pekkala, "that two eyes are better than one."

ACKNOWLEDGMENTS

The author would like to thank the following, in alphabetical order, for their help and encouragement in the writing of this book: Loyale Coles, Randall Klein, Brian McLendon, Bill McMann, Steve Messina, Kate Miciak, Nita Taublib, and all the others who make up the extraordinary team at Bantam Dell and The Random House Publishing Group.

WHAT REALLY HAPPENED TO THE ROMANOVS?

Note on Dates

On February 1, 1918, Russia switched from the Julian to the Gregorian calendar, which was in use elsewhere in the world. The Julian system was twelve days behind the Gregorian system until March 1900, after which it was thirteen days behind. For the sake of accuracy, the dates I have listed are what the Russians themselves would have used, being from the Julian calendar until the time the switch was made and thereafter from the Gregorian calendar.

FEBRUARY 1917

Conditions for Russian soldiers on the battlefront against the German and Austro-Hungarian armies have reached the breaking point. Demonstrations and workers' strikes spread through most Russian cities, including Moscow and Petrograd.

MARCH 2, 1917

Nicholas II abdicates, naming his brother Mikhail as the heir to the Russian throne and passing over his own son, Alexei, whom he believes to be too young and frail to withstand the strain of leading the country.

MARCH 3, 1917

Mikhail, believing the situation to be already too far gone, refuses to accept the throne.

MARCH 4, 1917

Nicholas II and his family are placed under house arrest at the Tsarskoye Selo estate outside Petrograd. A plan is worked out to transport the family into exile in Britain. After a wave of public protest, the British government rescinds the offer.

MAY–JUNE 1917

Protests and strikes continue. Food and fuel shortages lead to widespread looting.

JUNE 16, 1917

The Russian Army launches an all-out assault on the Austro-Hungarian front. This attack turns into a major defeat for the Russians.

AUGUST 1, 1917

With conditions worsening in Petrograd, the provisional government decides to move the Romanov family, along with their personal doctors, nurses, and private tutors for the children, to the Siberian city of Tobolsk. By August 6, the family is living in a mansion belonging to the former governor of Tobolsk.

NOVEMBER 20, 1917

Russia begins surrender talks with Germany.

DECEMBER 16, 1917

The Revolutionary Government orders the restructuring of the army. All officers are to be elected democratically and the military ranking system is abolished.

FEBRUARY 23, 1918

Pravda, the Communist Party newspaper, demands stricter conditions of confinement for the Romanovs. The Romanov family is placed on army rations and told that they will be moved to an even more remote location—the town of Ekaterinburg, east of the Ural mountains.

APRIL 20, 1918

Policed by Red Guards under the command of Commissar Yakovlev, the Romanovs and a few members of their household staff arrive by train in

Ekaterinburg. At the station they are met by a large and hostile crowd, who demand that the Romanovs be killed. The Romanovs are interned in the house of a local merchant named Ipatiev. A tall stockade fence is built around the house, and the windows on the upper floors are whitewashed to prevent anyone from seeing in or out. Guards for the Ipatiev house are recruited from among local factory workers in Ekaterinburg.

MAY 22, 1918

The Czechoslovakian Legion, having joined forces with the many disparate anti-Bolshevik groups known as the White Army, refuses an order by the Revolutionary Government to lay down its arms. Many of these soldiers are deserters from the Austro-Hungarian army who chose to fight with the Russians during the First World War. Unable to return to their own country, they march almost the entire length of Russia, to Vladivostok. From there, they are to be transported halfway around the world to France, to join the fighting on the Western Front on the side of their French, British, and American allies. The White Army numbers more than 30,000 men, an unstoppable force, which begins to make its way east, following the path of the Trans-Siberian Railroad.

JUNE 12, 1918

Mikhail, the brother of the Tsar, is being held prisoner in the city of Perm. Lodging at the Hotel Korolev, renamed "Hotel No. 1" by the Bolsheviks, he and his valet, Nicholas Johnson, are permitted to wander the streets as long as they do not leave the city. On this night, Grand Duke Mikhail and Johnson are ordered out of their rooms by a Cheka death squad under the command of Ivan Kolpaschikov, taken to a wooded area known as Malaya Yazovaya, and shot. The Bolsheviks do not announce his death, reporting instead that he has been rescued by White Russian officers. In the coming months, "sightings" of the Grand Duke will pour in from all corners of the world. His body and the body of Nicholas Johnson have never been found.

JULY 4, 1918

The local guards are dismissed after they are accused of stealing from the Romanovs. Their place is taken by Cheka officer Yurovsky and a contingent of "Latvians" who are in fact mostly Hungarians, Germans, and Austrians. From now on, the only guards allowed inside the Ipatiev house belong to the Cheka. Guards are posted all over the house, even outside the bathrooms. The Romanovs live on the second floor. They are permitted to do their own cooking, relying on a diet of army rations and donations from the nuns of the Novotikvinsky Convent in Ekaterinburg.

JULY 16, 1918

With the White Army approaching the region of Ekaterinburg, Commissar Yurovsky receives a telegram ordering that the Romanovs be put to death, rather than risk having them be rescued by the White Army. This telegram was presumably sent by Lenin, although its origin is still unclear.

Yurovsky immediately orders his guards to hand in their issue Nagant revolvers. He then loads the weapons, returns them to their owners, and notifies them that the Romanovs are to be shot that night. Two of the Latvians refuse to shoot women and children in cold blood.

Yurovsky details one guard for every member of the Romanov family and their entourage, so that each man will be responsible for a single execution. The total number of guards is eleven, which corresponds to the number of people in the Romanov family, plus the Tsarina's lady-in-waiting, Anna Demidova; a cook named Kharitonov; their physician Dr. Botkin; and a footman named Trupp, who are also to be shot.

JULY 17, 1918

At midnight Yurovsky wakes the Romanov family and orders them to get dressed. He tells them that there is disorder in the town. Approximately one hour later, the entourage is led down to the basement, which Yurovsky has chosen as the place of execution.

When the Romanovs reach the basement, the Tsarina Alexandra requests chairs, and three are brought in. The Tsarina sits in one of them, Alexei in another, and the Tsar himself in the third.

A truck that has been ordered for the purpose of transporting the dead after the executions does not show up until almost 2 A.M. When the truck arrives, Yurovsky and the guards descend to the basement and enter the room where the Romanovs have been waiting. It is so crowded that some of the guards are forced to remain standing in the doorway. Yurovsky informs the Tsar that he is to be executed.

According to Yurovsky, the Tsar's reply is "What?" He then turns to speak to his son, Alexei. At this moment, Yurovsky shoots him in the head.

The guards then begin firing. Although Yurovsky has planned for an orderly sequence of events, the scene rapidly deteriorates. The women are screaming. Bullets ricochet off the walls and, it appears, off the women themselves. One guard is shot in the hand.

Having failed to kill the women, the guards then try to finish them off with bayonets, but are unsuccessful. Finally, the women are each shot in the head.

The last to die is Alexei, who is still sitting in his chair. Yurovsky shoots him several times at point-blank range.

The bodies are brought up into the courtyard of the Ipatiev house, carried on improvised stretchers made from blankets laid across harness beams removed from horse carriages. The dead are loaded into a truck and covered with a blanket.

At this point Yurovsky realizes that the guards have robbed the Romanovs of the valuables they were carrying in their pockets. He orders the items returned. Under threat of execution, the guards return the objects to Yurovsky. The truck drives towards an abandoned mine which has been chosen as the burial site for the Romanovs and their entourage. Before reaching its destination, however, the truck encounters a group of about twenty-five civilians who have been detailed by another member of the Cheka as a burial crew. The civilians are angry because they were expecting to execute the Romanovs themselves. They unload the bodies from the truck and immediately begin robbing the dead. Yurovsky threatens to shoot them unless they stop.

Yurovsky then realizes that no one in the group, including himself, knows exactly where the mine shaft is located. Nor has anyone thought to provide digging equipment for the burials.

Yurovsky loads the bodies back onto the truck and searches for another burial site. By dawn he has located another abandoned mine near the village of Koptyaki, which is about three hours' walking distance from Ekaterinburg.

The bodies of the Romanovs are unloaded once again from the truck. They are stripped and a fire is prepared for burning the clothes prior to hiding the bodies in the mine. As the bodies are being undressed, Yurovsky discovers that the Romanovs are wearing waistcoats into which hundreds of diamonds have been sewn, which explains why the bullets failed to kill the Romanov women. The valuables are hidden and later transported to Moscow. After the clothing is burned, Yurovsky orders the bodies to be thrown into the mine shaft and then attempts to collapse the mine with hand grenades. The effort is only partially successful and Yurovsky realizes that he will have to re-inter the bodies somewhere else.

After reporting to his superiors, he is advised by a member of the Ural Soviet Committee that the bodies could be hidden in one of several deep mines located near the Moscow Highway, not far from the original burial place. The mines are filled with water, so Yurovsky decides to weight the bodies with stones before throwing them in. He also conceives of a backup plan to burn the bodies, then pour sulfuric acid on them and bury the remains in a pit.

On the evening of July 17, the bodies are exhumed, loaded onto carts, and transported towards the Moscow Highway mines.

JULY 18, 1918

The carts carrying the bodies break down on the way to the mine. Yurovsky orders a pit to be dug, but halfway through the digging, he is informed that the hole can be seen too easily from the road. Yurovsky abandons the pit and orders trucks to be requisitioned so that the group can continue to the deep mines on the Moscow Highway.

On this day, *Pravda* announces that the Tsar has been executed, but that the Tsarina Alexandra and his son, Alexei, have been spared and moved to a safe location. There is no mention of the Tsar's four daughters or their household staff. The article implies that the executions were carried out on the initiative of the Ekaterinburg guards and not on orders from Moscow.

JULY 19, 1918

In the early hours, the trucks that have been requisitioned as replacements for the broken carts also break down on the rough roads.

Yurovsky orders another pit to be dug. In the meantime he burns the bodies.

The remains are thrown into the pit and acid is poured on top of them. The pit is filled in and railway sleepers—wooden beams set beneath the iron rails—are laid out over the burial site. The trucks are then wheeled back and forth over the sleepers to hide any evidence of burial.

By dawn, the work has been completed. Before departing the burial site, Yurovsky swears the participants to silence.

The bones remain hidden, in spite of an extensive search launched by the White Army when it overruns Ekaterinburg a few days later. The Whites are eventually forced out and control of Ekaterinburg returns to the Red Army.

In the months that follow, stories surface about the survival of the Tsarina and her daughters. Witnesses report seeing them on a train heading for the city of Perm. Another story involves the appearance of a young woman, one of the daughters, who is reported to have lived for a short while with a family in the woods before being handed over to the Cheka, who then killed her. A tailor named Heinrich Kleibenzetl claims to have seen the Princess Anastasia, badly wounded, being treated by his landlady in a house directly opposite the Ipatiev residence immediately after the shootings. An Austrian prisoner of war, Franz Svoboda, claims to have personally rescued Anastasia from the Ipatiev house.

1920

A woman attempts to commit suicide by jumping off a bridge into the Landwehr Canal in Berlin. She is committed to a Dalldorf mental institution, where it is discovered that she has numerous wounds that resemble those made by bullets, and one that appears to have been made by the cruciform blade of a Russian Mosin-Nagant bayonet. The woman appears to be suffering from amnesia and is referred to by the hospital staff as Fräulein Unbekannt ("Jane Doe").

1921

Fräulein Unbekannt confides in one of the Dalldorf nurses, Thea Malinovsky, that she is in fact the Princess Anastasia. She claims to have been rescued from execution by a Russian soldier named Alexander Tschaikovsky. Together, they fled to Bucharest, where Tschaikovsky was killed in a fight.

1922

The woman claiming to be Anastasia is released from the asylum and taken in by Baron von Kleist, who believes her story.

In the years that follow, the woman is visited by numerous friends and relatives of the Romanovs, including the Grand Duchess Olga Alexandrovna, sister of Nicholas II, and Pierre Gilliard, private tutor of the Romanov children, both of whom declare her to be a fraud. Based on a dental mold of her teeth, the dentist of the Romanov family, Dr. Kostrizky, also declares the woman's claim to be false. Not all of those who meet the woman believe her to be lying, though. In Germany, the nephew and niece of the Romanov family physician, Dr. Botkin, vigorously support her claim amid accusations that they are simply after the missing Romanov family fortune, by today's standards said to be worth in excess of $190 million (approximately £90 million).

The legal battle that ensues becomes the longest-running case in German history.

A private detective, Martin Knopf, claims that based on his investigation, the woman is actually a Polish factory worker named Franziska Schanzkowska and that the wounds on her body came from an explosion at the munitions plant where she had been employed.

Schanzkowska's brother, Felix, is brought in to identify the woman. He immediately declares her to be his sister but then mysteriously refuses to sign an affidavit to that effect.

1929

The woman moves to New York, where she resides temporarily with Annie Jennings, a wealthy Manhattan socialite. Shortly afterwards, following several episodes of hysteria, she is once again committed to an asylum, this time the Four Winds Sanatorium.

1932

The woman, now known as Anna Anderson, returns to Germany.

1934

Yurovsky gives a detailed account of the executions and the events leading up to them at a Communist Party conference in Ekaterinburg.

1956

Release of the film *Anastasia,* starring Ingrid Bergman and Yul Brynner.

1968

At the age of seventy, Anna Anderson moves back to the United States and marries John Manahan, who believes her to be the Princess Anastasia. The couple live in Virginia.

1976

The remains of the Romanovs are located exactly where Yurovsky had said they would be, but the information is kept secret and the bodies are not exhumed.

1977

Future Russian president Boris Yeltsin, then Communist Party chief in Sverdlovsk (formerly known as Ekaterinburg), orders the Ipatiev house to be destroyed, noting that it has become a pilgrimage site.

1983

Anna Anderson is once again institutionalized. Within hours of her entering the psychiatric facility, Manahan kidnaps her and the two escape through rural Virginia.

FEBRUARY 12, 1984

Anna Anderson dies of pneumonia.

1991

The skeletons of the Romanovs are exhumed. Through DNA acquired from, among others, the Duke of Edinburgh (whose grandmother was the sister of Tsarina Alexandra), the remains are positively identified as those of Nicholas II, Alexandra, their daughters Olga, Tatiana, and Anastasia, as well as the three household servants and Dr. Botkin. Two bodies, those of Maria and Alexei, are missing.

1992

DNA testing of a tissue sample from Anna Anderson confirms that she is not the Princess Anastasia. The DNA sample is found to match that of Karl Maucher, great-nephew of Franziska Schanzkowska.

AUGUST 27, 2007

Remains believed to be those of Maria and Alexei are located in shallow graves not far from the other burial site.

APRIL 30, 2008

The Russian government announces that DNA testing has confirmed the identities of Alexei and Maria. On the same day, to mark the ninetieth anniversary of the executions, more than 30,000 Russians visit the mine where the Romanovs were buried.

BIBLIOGRAPHY

Bulygin, Paul. *The Murder of the Romanovs.* London: Hutchinson, 1966.

Crawford, Rosemary and Donald. *Michael and Natasha.* New York: Scribner, 1997.

Erickson, Carolly. *Alexandra: The Last Tsarina.* New York: St. Martin's, 2001.

Iroshnikov, Mikhail. *The Sunset of the Romanov Dynasty.* Moscow: Terra, 1992.

Mossolov, Alexander. *At the Court of the Last Tsar.* London: Methuen, 1935.

Steinberg, Mark, and Vladimir Khrustalëv. *The Fall of the Romanovs.* New Haven, Conn.: Yale University Press, 1995.

ABOUT THE AUTHOR

SAM EASTLAND lives in the United States and Great Britain. He is at work on the second Pekkala novel, which Bantam will publish in 2011.

www.inspectorpekkala.com

ABOUT THE TYPE

This book was set in Bembo, a typeface based on an old-style Roman face that was used for Cardinal Bembo's tract *De Aetna* in 1495. Bembo was cut by Francisco Griffo in the early sixteenth century. The Lanston Monotype Company of Philadelphia brought the well-proportioned letterforms of Bembo to the United States in the 1930s.